A HAND BRUSHED HIS CHEEK...

Always a light sleeper, Longarm snapped fully awake. He reached for his revolver under his blankets, then saw that the hand was Maruja's.

"Brazolargo," she whispered, "I am not to sleep so good. Maybe you like to take a leetle walk with me, no?"

"If you mean what I think you mean, Maruja," Longarm replied, his voice as low as hers, "there ain't a thing I'd rather do than take a little 'walk' with you. You're a right nice girl."

"I am not girl," she insisted. "I am woman. Look!"

Maruja shrugged the low-cut blouse off her shoulders. The thin fabric slid down to her waist. She leaned back, inviting him...

*Also in the LONGARM series
from Jove*

LONGARM
LONGARM ON THE BORDER
LONGARM AND THE AVENGING ANGELS
LONGARM AND THE WENDIGO
LONGARM IN THE INDIAN NATION
LONGARM AND THE NESTERS
LONGARM AND THE HATCHET MEN
LONGARM AND THE TEXAS RANGERS
LONGARM IN LINCOLN COUNTY
LONGARM IN LEADVILLE
LONGARM ON THE YELLOWSTONE
LONGARM IN THE FOUR CORNERS
LONGARM AT ROBBER'S ROOST
LONGARM AND THE SHEEPHERDERS
LONGARM AND THE GHOST DANCERS
LONGARM AND THE TOWN TAMER
LONGARM AND THE RAILROADERS
LONGARM ON THE OLD MISSION TRAIL
LONGARM AND THE DRAGON HUNTERS
LONGARM AND THE RURALES
LONGARM ON THE HUMBOLDT
LONGARM ON THE BIG MUDDY
LONGARM SOUTH OF THE GILA
LONGARM IN NORTHFIELD
LONGARM AND THE GOLDEN LADY
LONGARM AND THE LAREDO LOOP
LONGARM AND THE BOOT HILLERS
LONGARM AND THE BLUE NORTHER
LONGARM ON THE SANTA FE
LONGARM AND THE STALKING CORPSE
LONGARM AND THE COMANCHEROS
LONGARM AND THE DEVIL'S RAILROAD
LONGARM IN SILVER CITY
LONGARM ON THE BARBARY COAST
LONGARM AND THE MOONSHINERS
LONGARM IN BOULDER CANYON
LONGARM IN DEADWOOD
LONGARM AND THE GREAT TRAIN ROBBERY
LONGARM AND THE LONE STAR LEGEND
LONGARM IN THE BADLANDS
LONGARM IN THE BIG THICKET
LONGARM AND THE EASTERN DUDES
LONGARM IN THE BIG BEND
LONGARM AND THE SNAKE DANCERS
LONGARM ON THE GREAT DIVIDE
LONGARM AND THE BUCKSKIN ROGUE
LONGARM AND THE CALICO KID
LONGARM AND THE FRENCH ACTRESS

TABOR EVANS

LONGARM
IN YUMA

A JOVE BOOK

LONGARM IN YUMA

A Jove Book / published by arrangement with
the author

PRINTING HISTORY
Jove edition / April 1982
Third printing / May 1983

All rights reserved.
Copyright © 1982 by Jove Publications, Inc.
This book may not be reproduced in whole or in part,
by mimeograph or any other means, without permission.
For information address: The Berkley Publishing Group,
200 Madison Avenue, New York, N.Y. 10016.

ISBN: 0-515-07525-6

Jove books are published by The Berkley Publishing Group,
200 Madison Avenue, New York, N.Y. 10016.
The words "A JOVE BOOK" and the "J" with sunburst
are trademarks belonging to Jove Publications, Inc.

PRINTED IN THE UNITED STATES OF AMERICA

Chapter 1

"If you got any ideas about trying to get away while we're slowed down, Sanger, you might as well forget 'em," Longarm told the man in the seat beside him. "Ever since we pulled out of Durango, you been watching for a place where you can jump."

Sanger had been staring out the window of the coach for the past five minutes, while the train pulled out of Silverton. The little narrow-gauge locomotive hauling the Denver & Rio Grande's short-coupled overnight local was wheezing gustily, starting up the long grade to the eleven-thousand-foot hump of Red Mountain Pass, which lay a dozen miles ahead. Looking past the outlaw's head, Longarm saw the town's lights fade to pinpoints in the clear air of the Colorado Rockies before giving way to darkness.

Sanger pulled his eyes away from the window and looked at Longarm. The renegade was a big man, as tall and broad as Longarm himself. Sanger's shoulders spanned the full width of the backrest and rubbed against Longarm's above the heavy oak arm that divided the green plush day-coach seats the two men occupied.

"Now how much of a chance d'you think I'd have if I dived outa that window, Long?" he demanded. "It's darker'n the gates of hell out there by now, and you've done told me you won't take off these handcuffs."

"Cuffs didn't stop you from getting away before," Longarm pointed out.

"Not mean-mouthing your friend Davis, but he made it too

easy for me," Sanger replied. The wide slash of his lips twisted into what on another man's face would have been a grin, but on Sanger's battered countenance became a leer.

"Davis paid with a bullet in his belly for not watching you close enough while he was taking you to Durango," Longarm said shortly. "Don't look for me to make a fool mistake like that."

"Oh, I wouldn't do that, Marshal," Sanger assured Longarm.

"I wouldn't put anything past you, Sanger," Longarm said, his voice flatly neutral. "But I'll fix it so you won't have a chance to pull any tricks this time."

Sanger watched incuriously as Longarm took the handcuff key from the pocket of his skintight twill britches and unlocked the cuff on Sanger's left wrist. He left the right wrist shackle in place while he brought the other cuff across the outlaw's body and snapped it around the wooden armrest between the two seats. Putting the key back in his pocket, Longarm inspected the new arrangement and nodded with satisfaction.

"You won't be going out the window now, unless you take the seat too," he told Sanger. "And if you try that, I'd just guess it'd take you long enough to break free so's I'd have plenty of time to stop you."

"You can't blame a man for wanting to get a look at the country, can you, Long?" Sanger asked. The pious tone he forced into his rasping voice didn't hide his insincerity. "You know I ain't going to have a chance to see much scenery for a long time, once them gates closes up behind me at the federal pen."

Longarm didn't bother to point out that Sanger was the only one responsible for the fix he was in. The suggestion wouldn't have made any impression on the hardened criminal. He said, "If I was you, I'd get some sleep now. It's going to be a while before this old slowpoke makes a breakfast stop at Gunnison."

Sanger grunted, but made no reply. Ignoring Longarm's suggestion, he turned his head aside and continued staring out into the darkness. Longarm fished a cheroot from his inside coat pocket and clamped it between his strong teeth, flicked a match across a horn-hard thumbnail, and touched its flame to the tip of the long brown cigar.

Through the nimbus of blue smoke raised by the cheroot, he turned his attention to the other occupants of the coach as the train puffed on up the steep grade to the top of Red Mountain Pass, where it would weave its way between the towering peaks of the Uncompahgres for the next three hours before reaching the long slope down into the valley of the Gunnison River.

There were only two others in the coach with Longarm and Sanger. Longarm wasn't greatly concerned about the woman. He'd tagged her when they were boarding the train at Durango as belonging to the company of the footloose women who followed the human vultures that still soared over the slopes of the Rockies.

She could have been a dance-hall girl or one of the high-kicking chorus line in one of the cafe-saloon-gambling halls that were called show houses or theaters in the mining camps. In these establishments, when the chorus girls weren't kicking up their heels on the stage, they hustled drinks from the patrons, and at times offered other services in the curtained private boxes. For that matter, she could have been one of the whores who lived in the red-light houses on the wrong side of the railroad tracks in a score of mining towns like Durango and Silverton, Leadville and Pueblo and Telluride.

Longarm didn't think the woman had crossed the tracks yet, though. She was too young to have made that transition. A number of years lay ahead before the girl's still youthfully unlined face grew haggard, her soft lips hardened, and her firmly rounded breasts sagged. When that happened, the time would have arrived for her to face the prospect of moving into the shacks across the tracks.

With the woman passenger filed into his memory, Longarm made a quick inspection of the man. At the Durango depot, the male passenger hadn't bothered to hide his curiosity at the sight of the handcuffs Sanger wore. Longarm took this as a good sign; if the man had been a confederate of the prisoner, he'd have paid no such obvious interest in the shackled killer.

Still, the gang with which Sanger ran was a large one. Not all of its members had yet been identified by the lawmen who were trying to break it up. Even though the man in the seat at the front of the coach seemed to have lost interest in his shackled prisoner, Longarm didn't count him out as a potential source of trouble.

"Sanger's been running with Whiskers Cleburn and his crew," Billy Vail had warned Longarm. "Cleburn's the one we'd like to get our hands on, of course. So far, that outfit's been able to keep a jump or two ahead of everybody that's been after 'em."

Longarm's bronzed face had grown thoughtful as he'd leaned back in the red morocco-upholstered chair in the chief marshal's office and lighted a fresh cheroot. Stretching his legs out on the Turkey carpet, he crossed the ankles of his stovepipe boots and looked at his chief through the cheroot's smoke.

"If you're giving me a hint, Billy, I'd be right obliged to have you come right out with it. You looking to use me for bait to catch Whiskers Cleburn?"

"No, dammit, I'm not!" Vail exploded. "All I expect you to do is to get up in the morning and take the Denver & Rio Grande day train down to Durango, get Clem Sanger from the sheriff of La Plata County, and bring him back here to Denver. If Sanger hadn't escaped from a federal penitentiary before he got connected with Cleburn, I'd let him stay in Durango to stand trial for shooting Ed Davis when he made his last getaway."

"I don't guess you've heard anything about Cleburn and his bunch of plug-uglies plotting to break Sanger free?"

"Not a thing. If I had—" Stopping short, Vail frowned across his desk at Longarm. "What brought on that question, anyhow, Longarm?"

"Oh, nothing I could name you, Billy. Only it seems like a sort of piddling job for you to call me off my free time to do."

"You know as well as I do that there's no such thing as free time around this office," Vail said severely, glowering beneath his bushy eyebrows. "Sure, the rules the pencil-pushers in Washington send us say there is, but they don't seem to be in the same department we are."

"I ain't complaining, you understand, Billy," Longarm said quickly. "Only even if it is supposed to be nearly summer, I know it's still going to be as cold as a witch's tit up in them Uncompahgres, and you know how I feel about cold weather."

"Wear your winter drawers, then," Vail said unfeelingly. Then he relented and grinned and added in a more sympathetic voice, "If I had anybody else to send after Sanger, I sure wouldn't wish the job off on you. You've got sense enough to know that."

"Sure, I know it, Billy, and I ain't complaining. I'll get

Sanger back here, and if Whiskers and his bunch get in the way, I reckon I can handle things."

"You always have before, I don't expect you to change." The pudgy chief marshal ruffled through the papers that were piled up on his desk. "Get your travel and expense vouchers from the clerk," he told Longarm. "If I don't get started clearing this mess away, I'll be late for supper again tonight."

Longarm stood up. "You did say you just want me to bring Sanger back here, didn't you, Billy? I don't have to ride herd on him all the way to Leavenworth, do I?"

"Just get him back and deliver him to the holdover at the county jail," Vail replied. "We've got a detail of guards coming in from Leavenworth day after tomorrow to transport the four men that were sentenced there at the court term that ended Friday, or I wouldn't bother sending you for Sanger tonight."

"I'll drop in as soon as I get rid of him tomorrow, then. I hope you won't have anything else for me to do right then, though. I'm supposed to set in on my regular poker game at the Windsor Hotel, tomorrow night."

"Well, I sure will try not to let official business interfere with your poker," Vail said, his grin taking the sting out of his mockingly courteous tone. "Now get out of here before I forget what I'm supposed to be doing." He turned the gleaming top of his bald head to Longarm as he dove into the sea of paperwork.

Chuckling silently to himself as he recalled the talk with his chief, Longarm took a quick look at Sanger out of the corner of his eyes. The outlaw had settled down in his seat, his eyes closed now, his face set in an unhappy half-frown.

Taking off the stiff-brimmed Stetson that he wore canted forward on his close-cropped brown hair, Longarm let himself relax, leaning his head on the towel-covered red plush of the seatback. Like the seats of all the day coaches on every railroad he'd ever ridden, the plush released a faint, acrid aroma of long-accumulated coal smoke.

Longarm slid one foot along the floor until he felt it come into contact with Clem Sanger's foot. He left his foot there, pressed close to the outlaw's, sure he'd feel any move Sanger made. Closing his eyes, Longarm let the gasping wheezes of the locomotive and the swaying of the narrow coaches relax him.

He hadn't quite drifted off into a doze when a shot rang out, its sharpness muffled by the closed windows of the coach. The harsh shrieking of suddenly applied brakes sounded from the front of the train, and the coach began bucking.

Sanger jumped to his feet when the first grabbing of the engine's brakes began to slow the train. He began wrestling with the arm of the seat to which the handcuff was attached, trying to wrest the heavy oak arm from its place.

Longarm's hand was snaking his Colt out of its cross-draw holster even before his eyes were fully open. His hand was almost on the butt of the Colt when Sanger twisted his body around and fell back heavily, his weight pinning Longarm's gun hand between the outlaw's back and Longarm's chest.

There was enough play in the short chain between the two ends of the handcuffs to allow the outlaw to keep up his frantic efforts to tear the arm of the seat free. Longarm tried to push Sanger up and away, but he could not get the inch or two of play into his pinned arm that would allow him to flex his muscles to their fullest and use their power to the best advantage.

Shots began breaking the moonless night's silence as the train rasped to a full stop. From the corner of his eye, Longarm saw the streaks of muzzle flashes cut the darkness with bright tongues of orange along the railroad grade.

Bullets began slapping into the double-walled sides of the wooden coach. Longarm had no time to waste worrying about the attackers outside. The seat arm was beginning to give way as Sanger wrestled with it, his frenzy giving him a sudden burst of extra strength.

Longarm realized belatedly that he'd put too much confidence in the anchor point he'd chosen for the cuffs. Sanger's weight was still holding him pinned to the seat. The outlaw's frenzy gave him the extra burst of strength he needed to break the armrest free from the bolts that secured it to the floor, and to tear the seatback loose. He brought the point of his free arm's elbow back, hitting Longarm in the temple. Stunned by the blow, Longarm shook his head, his muscles limp for the moment.

Sanger leaped to his feet. He had the arm of the seat in his hands now, and raised the heavy L-shaped oak piece above his head. Longarm clawed for the butt of his Colt, but Sanger balanced precariously on one foot for the few seconds required to bring up his other foot in a sidewise kick that knocked Longarm's gun hand aside.

Now the outlaw stood towering over Longarm, the crude club poised. Sanger brought down the improvised bludgeon, but Longarm twisted his shoulders and got his head out of the arm's path. The makeshift club hit the back of the seat and gashed the plush, spilling out the thin layer of straw that filled it.

Sanger raised the armrest for a second try, but during the few seconds he took in raising the weapon above his head, Longarm snapped out of the daze that followed the blow Sanger had landed with his elbow, and now his gun hand was moving to the butt of his holstered Colt.

Longarm snapshotted upward at the giant outlaw's chest, and just as his Colt spat angrily, the window behind Sanger shattered. A rifle bullet from the darkness took Sanger in the back at the same time that the heavy .44 slug from the Colt struck his chest.

Sanger's body jerked and spun around, twirled by the impacts of the two bullets hitting him almost simultaneously. Another slug from the darkness outside tore into the outlaw.

Like an oak tree undercut at its base by a woodsman's ax, Sanger toppled slowly forward, his body falling across the seat he'd so recently occupied.

Longarm wasted no time examining Sanger. His experienced eye told him that the outlaw was dead before he crumpled. He looked at the other two passengers in the day coach. They were frozen in their seats, too surprised by the sudden attack to move. Another window shattered with a tinkle that rang thinly above the staccato of gunfire from the right-of-way, and one of the lights that hung from the coach ceiling broke and went dark.

"Get on the floor!" Longarm ordered the man and woman. They stared blankly at him for a moment, their shocked state rendering them unable to move.

Longarm uncoiled from his seat and ran to the back of the coach, bending low, hoping the sides of the car were high enough to shield him from the continuing gunfire. He reached the woman first, dragged her from her seat, and pressed her to the floor.

"Now stay there and lay still!" he snapped, before moving on down the aisle to where the man still sat frozen in place.

Grabbing the slack-jawed man by the ankles, Longarm pulled him to the aisle of the coach. "Just stretch out and don't try to get up till the shooting stops," he said. "Keep your head down and you'll be all right."

Longarm began crawling on hands and knees toward the front of the coach. He stopped below the remaining lamp and risked standing up for the few seconds required to turn the wick down until it flickered and went out. Just as he dropped back to the floor, a bullet whistled angrily through the coach, but the shot had come too late, and it cut through thin air at the spot where he'd been standing.

For a moment Longarm held his position. Outside the coach, the gunfire seemed to be slacking off. He made his way back down the aisle to the end of the car and went through the vestibule door.

A stream of cold night air was sweeping through the open space between the day coach and the baggage car. Longarm shivered when the chilling blast hit him, but the cold sharpened his senses. He saw a spurt of flame as a shot sounded from the right-of-way ditch, and sent a slug from the Colt to the right of the flash before its image faded from his eyes. There was no way for him to tell whether his bullet had found a target, but no more shots came from the place where the red streak had flashed.

Up toward the engine, another of the attackers fired, and Longarm replied to the shot with a bullet from the Colt. He wished for his Winchester, which was a couple of hundred miles away as the crow flies, leaning in the corner of his room in Denver. The job had seemed so short and straightforward that he'd decided at the last minute to leave the rifle behind.

Getting mad ain't going to help now, old son, he told himself under his breath as he swiveled to the opposite side of the vestibule and watched for the telltale spurt of flame that would give him a target.

He held his position, taking advantage of the pause to slip fresh shells into the Colt's chambers to replace those he'd fired. The seconds ticked into minutes, but there was no further shooting.

Ahead, the engine puffed and snorted, and a prolonged blast sounded from the whistle. The cars jerked with a rattle of couplings as the train began to move once more.

Another rifle shot rang out over the noise, but it came from the side opposite the direction Longarm was facing. He knew that no matter how fast he moved, he would not be able to change his position quickly enough to reply to the gunfire, and as he made his decision to stay in place, he saw the shadowy figure of a man on horseback in the cleared space at the bottom of the grade.

This time Longarm had the few seconds required for an aimed shot. The rider got in the first shot with his rifle, but the slug sang harmlessly past Longarm's hatbrim and passed on through the vestibule. Longarm triggered the Colt, sending two quick rounds at the dimly outlined figure. The rider toppled just as the train went by him. Longarm looked back, but the end-lanterns of the day coach had already passed the spot where the man had fallen. Almost total darkness hid the bottom of the grade, and Longarm was unable to see whether or not the downed rider got up.

Certain by now that the scene of the ambush had been left behind, Longarm holstered his revolver. He opened the door that led to the baggage car, and started toward the engine. He was halfway through the car when the door at the front end opened and the conductor came in.

"You mind telling me why that damn fool engineer stopped the train instead of pouring on steam when the shooting commenced back there?" Longarm demanded.

"He stopped because he had a bullet through his shoulder," the conductor replied, his voice as sharp as Longarm's had been. "I don't know how much you know about railroads, Marshal, but the engineer did just what the rule book says he has to."

"I guess he done what he figured was best." Longarm nodded slowly in agreement. "How bad's he hurt?"

"Can't tell yet. The fireman's at the throttle now; he got us rolling as fast as he could. Riley—that's the brakeman—is hurt too. He's laying in the tender with a torn-up leg. I came back here to fix a place where I can tend to them." The conductor shook his head, then asked, "What's it like in the coach?"

"That prisoner I was taking back to Denver got killed, but he's no loss. The other two're all right. Scared, but not hurt. And I think there's a dead man laying at the bottom of the grade, back where they bushwacked us. Unless you got a good reason for us to keep going, I'd like to back up the train and have a look."

"Well—" The conductor hesitated for a moment, then nodded. "I guess it'd be all right, Marshal. We'll lose a little time, but we can make it up. If it'll help you, we'll back up."

"If that gang that shot us up is the one I think it is, and if one of 'em is laying dead back there, the chances are I'll recognize him," Longarm told the trainman.

"We'll back up, then. While we're doing that, maybe you'll give me a hand getting Briscoe and Riley in here?"

"Sure. Let's go after 'em right now."

A new voice spoke from the back of the car. "If I can help, I'll be glad to."

Longarm and the conductor turned to look at the newcomer. It was the passenger from the day coach.

"My name's Clark," the man said. "Drummer. Doctor's goods and medical supplies. I've got a bunch of samples in my valise, bandages and such, that might come in handy."

"They sure as hell will," the conductor replied. "My name's Torgesen, Mr. Clark. The D&RG appreciates you helping out."

"I really didn't have that in mind," Clark said. "After I got over being nervous and surprised, I struck a match and saw there was just me and the woman and a dead man in the coach, so I wanted to find out what was going on."

Longarm and Torgesen stepped out onto the vestibule platform with Clark following them. They stood for a moment on the narrow, bouncing, swaying platform in the cold, biting wind that whipped across the open space. In front of them, separated from the coach by two feet of empty air spanned only by the creaking coupling, the tender towered a foot above even Longarm's head.

Torgesen looked at his companions in the faint flickering light that filtered over the tender's top from the firebox of the locomotive. "I don't know how much time you men have spent crawling over trains, but I'd just as soon not try to move those two men while the train's in motion."

"You were going to back up to where that fellow I brought down is laying," Longarm reminded him. "Can't we do it then?"

Torgesen nodded. "Just what I was about to suggest. I'll go up to the cab and tell Jesse what to do."

Longarm and Clark stood with the icy wind cutting them, while Torgesen shinnied up the narrow iron ladder at the corner of the tender. The train braked to a careful stop a few moments later, and the conductor lowered the brakeman, then the engineer, to where Longarm and Clark could reach the feet of the wounded men and carry them into the baggage car.

Both the engineer and brakeman were conscious, and though their still-taut muscles tensed now and then as they were being moved, the transfers were made without problems. The train creaked and couplings clattered as it slowly started to back up.

"I'll get out on the vestibule and watch for the place where that fellow fell off his horse when I potted him," Longarm said. "Think I can use your lantern, Torgesen?"

"Sure." The conductor handed the lantern to Longarm. "When we get to where you want to stop, lean out and wave it up and down, and Jesse'll put on the brakes."

Longarm located easily the place where he'd swapped shots with the mounted outlaw, because the riderless horse was standing over its fallen master. He swung out and waved the lantern, and the train came to a slow stop.

Swinging off the car step before it stopped moving, Longarm dug his heels into the shifting gravel that covered the right-of-way. Behind him he heard feet grating on the gravel, and looked back to see the conductor following him.

Already feisty from the shooting that had brought down its rider, the horse shied off to one side as Longarm and Torgesen got to the foot of the grade. Longarm held up the lantern to get a clear view of the dead man's face, and grunted when he saw who he'd brought down.

"I guess you recognize him, all right," Torgesen said.

"I sure as hell do. It's One-Eye Carver. His description's on wanted fliers from here to California. He's another bad one, even worse'n the one laying in the day coach."

"You'll want to take him in to Denver with us, I suppose?"

"Sure. No need to worry about the horse, though. I'll get the critter unsaddled and we'll just let it go. It'll wind up at a ranch or a town someplace and find a new boss."

Longarm and the conductor carried the body up the grade and deposited it in the baggage car.

"We've still got another dead one to bring up here," Torgesen reminded him. "The one you shot in the day coach. Might as well move him in here while we're stopped."

"Suppose you and Clark do that while I see to the horse," Longarm suggested. "Then we can be on our way again."

"Which is something I'll be damned glad to do," Torgesen said feelingly. "Thirty years I've been railroading, but I never have made a run as messed up as this one's been."

Within ten minutes the tasks had been completed and the train was moving again. Longarm lighted a cheroot as he looked around the baggage car. The engineer and brakeman were stretched out in the center of the car, with Clark kneeling between them, working at bandaging their wounds. Torgesen was spreading a tarpaulin over the bodies that lay in the dark end of the car. He looked up as the match Longarm struck flared up.

"I'd say we've got things in hand," he said. "I'm going to have to give Jesse some help; he can't handle the throttle and keep the firebox going at the same time, not while we're going through these mountains. If Mr. Clark will stay here and look after Riley and Briscoe, maybe you can try to calm down the lady in the day coach, Marshal. She was right close to being hysterical when we went in to get that outlaw's body."

"I'll see what I can do," Longarm consented.

He went back through the vestibule into the day coach. The woman was bent over in a heap in her seat, her shoulders shaking from the intensity of her sobbing. Longarm cleared his throat to attract her attention, but apparently she did not hear him. He placed a hand on her shoulder and she raised her head, gazing at him with blue eyes filled with tears.

"You don't need to be crying now, ma'am," Longarm told her. "The trouble's all over. There won't be no more shooting to scare you."

"Scare me!" she exclaimed. "Scare me indeed! If you think I'm crying because I'm afraid, you're wrong. Nobody'll tell me anything, and I'm just so damned mad I could chew nails!"

Chapter 2

Longarm was so surprised by the unexpectedly belligerent response that it required a real effort for him to keep himself from laughing. He hid his mouth with his hand by brushing back the bottom edge of his full mustache while he stood looking at the angry young woman.

"Well now, ma'am," he said, when he was sure he could keep any hint of amusement out of his voice, "I guess you'd have to admit there wasn't much time for talking after that bunch of outlaws begun shooting at us."

"No. But there's been plenty of time since the shooting *stopped*," she snapped tartly.

Longarm didn't reply quickly. He was studying the woman, realizing that she wasn't as old as he'd taken her to be when he first saw her in the glaring gaslight of the coach. She stood in front of him, her hands on her hips, elbows cocked pugnaciously at right angles to her sides.

She was not tall, but generously proportioned. Under the tightly buttoned jacket of her dark woolen suit, her breasts swelled out, just a bit too large for her height and stature. Her hips flared out fully from the slim indentation of her waist, and below the hem of her skirt he could see that instead of the high-button shoes most women wore when traveling, she had on low-cut pumps.

At the moment her face was not overly attractive. Her heavy brows were drawn together in a straight line under the brim of her hat, and her blue eyes snapped electrically from their shield of thick, dark lashes. Her cheeks were pulled taut by the straight line into which she'd compressed her lips, and her round chin was thrust pugnaciously outward.

Longarm decided he'd better try to soothe her ruffled feelings. He said carefully, "Nobody's forgot about you, ma'am. It's just that we've all been jumping around too fast to take care of anything that could be put off."

"Meaning that I'm one of those things you men can push aside until it's convenient for you to think about us?"

"Now that ain't what I said," Longarm replied patiently.

For the first time the girl's eyes wavered, and some of the anger seemed to leave her face. She relaxed her mouth, showing full red lips, and said more calmly, "Suppose you tell me a little bit more, then."

"There's some hurt men that had to be looked after," he explained. "And a couple of bodies that had to be put up in the baggage car, and—"

"I know all about the bodies," she broke in. "One of them, at least. That man you killed fell so that his eyes kept staring at me until I nearly went out of my head!"

"That's because—" Longarm began.

She broke in before he could explain further. "Then, when the conductor and that drummer came to carry out the dead man, I tried to get them to explain what had happened, but they just looked through me like I wasn't here and wouldn't say a word!"

"Look here, ma'am—" Longarm began again.

For the second time she interrupted him. "*Miss,*" she said firmly. "*Miss* McGinnis. Blossom McGinnis."

Longarm touched the brim of his hat. "Miss McGinnis. I'm Deputy U.S. Marshal Long, out of the Denver office. Pleased to make your acquaintance."

"I wish I could say the pleasure's mutual, Marshal, but as far as I'm concerned, you're just as bad as all those other men. We've been standing here talking for several minutes, and you still haven't made any effort to tell me what this shooting and killing is all about. I'm getting the idea that you men are trying to hide something."

"Now, that's da—" Longarm quickly changed in midword—"downright silly, Miss McGinnis. I've told you who I am. Why'd I be interested in trying to keep you from knowing anything?"

"I can't imagine why," she snapped. "The question is, are you?"

"Not for a minute, ma'am—Miss McGinnis, I mean," Longarm amended hurriedly. "The plain fact is, all of us have been too busy to do much talking, even amongst ourselves. I got in here just as fast as I could, now that things have settled down, to tell you what's been happening."

Blossom McGinnis seemed to be appeased by his explanation. The angry frown faded from her face and she gave him a fleeting smile. "Well, that's better. It'll certainly relieve my mind to know what all the excitement's been about."

"I guess I better start with why those outlaws jumped the train in the first place," he began. "That man who was in the coach here—you saw he was handcuffed, so I reckon you knew right off that he was a prisoner?"

"It wasn't hard to figure that out, Marshal. I guessed you must be taking him to the prison at Canon City."

"No. He was a federal prisoner, Miss McGinnis, not a state one. I was taking him to Denver, and he'd've gone from there to the big pen at Leavenworth."

"I see. And I suppose the men who attacked the train were from his gang?"

Longarm nodded. "That's about the way of it."

"You don't think they'll ride on ahead of us and try to stop the train again, do you?"

Longarm shook his head. "Not a chance in the world of that happening. What's left of them is way behind us now."

"What's left of them," she repeated, frowning. "Does that mean you shot somebody else, besides the man you killed in the coach here?"

"Only one. But what's held up the train such a long time is that when the gang jumped us, some of the men on the train crew got wounded."

Blossom seemed genuinely concerned as she exclaimed, "Goodness! I hope they weren't badly hurt."

"Well, it ain't ever very comfortable, having a bullet go into your hide anyplace. Anyhow, the engineer and the brakeman was the ones that got wounded. That put the train short of men, so the fireman's running the engine now, and the conductor's up in the locomotive, helping him."

"And what about the man who was back here in the coach

with us? He just ran out of the coach after he'd lighted the light you put out, and I haven't seen him since."

"That'd be Clark. He's a drummer, peddles bandages and medicines and things like that, stuff doctors use."

"Oh, I guessed he was a traveling man the minute I saw him. And I was glad when you got on, even if you did have the mean-looking prisoner with you. I don't have much use for drummers, Marshal. They're generally too pushy with a woman."

"Well, you won't have to worry about Clark tonight. He's in the baggage car, looking after the trainmen who got shot. And the conductor had to go up to the locomotive, like I just told you."

"I'm sorry I was snappish with you a minute ago, Marshal," she said at last. "I hope you're not going to have to leave the car again, at least not for a while."

"I won't unless there's more trouble, which I don't figure's very likely."

"So we'll have the whole car to ourselves tonight?"

"It sure looks that way, at least until we get to Gunnison. That's the next stop, but we won't pull in there until a little bit after daylight."

"Then, if there isn't going to be anyone else in the car, I think I'll take off my hat and this heavy jacket and be a little more comfortable."

"I was thinking we might as well sit down," Longarm said. "Now that you know why things happened the way they did, maybe you'll feel easier in your mind."

Blossom stood up and let the jacket of her dark suit slip off her shoulders. Under the jacket she wore a sheer linen blouse that draped her breasts without concealing their firm but generous contours. She folded the jacket and handed it to Longarm, who laid it on the rack above their seats. While he was placing the jacket, she pulled the long pin out of her narrow-brimmed felt hat and passed it on to him to be stowed away.

Blossom settled down on the window side of the seat beside which they stood. Longarm, after he'd placed her hat in the rack, put his Stetson beside it and sat down in the aisle half of the divided seat.

Blossom was pulling hairpins out of the coil of midnight-black hair that she wore loosely caught up on the crown of her head. When the hairpins were removed, she fluffed the coil, letting her hair drop to spread like a shawl over her shoulders.

When he turned to face Blossom, Longarm received another surprise. He'd assumed from the deep blue of her eyes that she'd be a blonde; the dark hair framing her face in a loose fall softened her features and made her look far younger than she had appeared with the severe line of the drooping hatbrim shadowing her face.

Longarm fished a cheroot out of his pocket and clamped it between his teeth. He had a match out and was getting ready to strike it with his thumbnail before he remembered his manners.

"I hope you won't have any objections to me lighting up my cigar?" he asked.

"None whatever, Marshal. In fact—" Blossom reached in her reticule and took out a small enameled case, from which she extracted a cigarette. "If *you* don't object, I'll join you."

Longarm caught himself in time to keep from showing his surprise. Maintaining a poker face, he flicked into flame the match he'd been holding, held the flame for her to puff her cigarette into life, and then lighted his cigar.

Blossom met his gaze without displaying any false modesty. She smiled and said, "I won't try to put on any airs with you, Marshal. When I saw you sizing me up right after you got on the train, I could tell you guessed what I do."

"Not meaning to offend you, but you work in a show house or a dance hall. I couldn't decide which one, right off."

"Your first guess was better than your second one. Yes, I work in a show house in Durango. But that doesn't make me any less a lady when I'm away from my job."

"Now I never thought for a minute that it did, Miss Blossom," he protested.

"No. You didn't act like most men do. In fact, I think we're going to get along quite well." Blossom gazed thoughtfully at Longarm for a few seconds, then went on, "Look here, Marshal, you've been honest and straightforward with me, and I appreciate it. I feel a need to talk to someone right now, and to my way of thinking, plain talk is the only kind that's worth anything."

"I ain't much of a one for small talk myself," Longarm told her.

"I could tell that," she said, smiling, then went on, "The reason I'm going to Denver is to see my little daughter. She's only four years old, and I've got her in a nursery school there. I don't want her to be around where I'm working, you understand."

"Your a widow lady, then?"

"No." Blossom paused for a moment. When she resumed a tinge of bitterness was apparent in her voice, even though she tried to speak casually. "I'm what people call a deserted wife. My husband just disappeared one day. No hinting that he was unhappy, no goodbye, not even a note explaining why he left."

"So you don't have much use for men, after being treated like that."

"I don't have much use for *some* men." Blossom looked at him and shrugged. "Well, I've told you my story, so why don't you just leave off the 'Miss' and call me Blossom?"

"Why, sure, if you'd rather I did."

"I suppose you've got a first name too?"

"Well, I have, but most folks don't use it. The ones that know me best call me by a sort of nickname I've picked up."

"And what is that?"

"Longarm."

"Of course!" She smiled. "U.S. Marshal Long—the longarm of the law! You don't mind if I call you Longarm, then?"

"Not a bit. I'd be proud for you to."

"Good." Blossom looked at Longarm again, and this time her scrutiny was so searching and prolonged that he began to feel somewhat uncomfortable.

"What's the matter, Blossom? Have I got coal dust on my face, or something like that?"

Blossom didn't reply at once. She took a final puff from her cigarette and leaned forward to drop the stub into the gobboon that stood between the seats. Her move brought her closer to Longarm than she'd been before, and she looked at him closely before settling back into her seat. She let out a long sigh of relief, as though the tension created by the attack was beginning to leave her.

At last she said, a worried frown forming on her face, "No. I was trying to decide what there is about you that makes you so easy for me to talk to. We've only been talking for about ten minutes, but I feel like I've known you forever."

"But don't you—" Longarm had a sudden feeling that he'd been about to say the wrong thing, and stopped abruptly.

Blossom picked up what he'd intended to say. "Don't I talk to men while I'm working, you mean?"

"Something like that, Blossom. Not pointing any fingers at what you do for a living, or running you down, though."

"Oh, I don't have any high-flown ideas about myself or what I do, Longarm. I'm sure you've been around long enough to know what my job is like. I carry drinks to men in the boxes at the theater, but I don't go as far as some of the girls, and let the men in the boxes feel of me, or go out with them later."

"But you still don't feel comfortable in your work?"

"Not always. There's—well, let's not talk about me anymore. Can I ask you a personal question now, Longarm?"

"Why, sure. I haven't got any secrets."

"Are you married?"

"Nope. Never have been. A man that's doing my kind of job don't have a right to get married, the way I figure things. His wife wouldn't sleep good when he was away, wondering if she'd be waking up and find she's a widow."

"But you can go out on a job and not worry about the risks you're taking?"

"Hell—excuse me, Blossom—the risks is what I'm paid to take. They go with the job."

"And you don't get all nerved up and excited while you're—oh, while you're in the kind of fight you were a while ago?"

"Not that I've noticed."

"I don't guess I'd make a very good marshal. I'm still so excited that I'm trembling all over inside. You might not know it, just looking at me, but feel—"

Blossom leaned close to Longarm again and put her hands over his. He could feel the nervous twitches that tightened the muscles in her fingers occasionally—an intermittent, spasmodic twitching over which she seemed to have no control.

"Just sit quiet and try to relax," he told Blossom. "You'll get over feeling nervous after a while."

"I—I'm not sure I want to get over the way I feel," she said, puzzlement in her voice. "I—all of a sudden, I feel like I'm lonesome and need somebody to hold me."

Blossom moved closer to Longarm and leaned against him as best she could with the armrest of the seat between them. He did not move away, nor did he move closer. Blossom shifted her shoulders until the warm softness of her full breasts was pressing on Longarm's biceps.

She asked in a low voice, "Would you mind if I put my head on your shoulder and tried to sleep a little while?"

"Not a bit. Maybe a nap is just what you need."

Blossom cuddled closer to him, reaching an arm around his broad chest to pull herself against him. She closed her eyes, but in a few moments opened them and asked, "Could you turn the light out, Longarm?"

"Sure." Longarm got up and turned the valve through which the acetylene gas flowed from the lamp's generator to its mantle. The car became as dark as the moonless night outside the windows.

"That's better," Blossom murmured, moving back into her former position, with her breasts rubbing against Longarm's upper arm. She wriggled around for a moment, then became quiet.

Longarm leaned his head against the seat's high backrest and closed his eyes. Blossom's breathing settled into a regular rhythm, but he could not be sure she was asleep. He still was not sure when the arm that was across his chest relaxed and slid down to his lap. When he felt Blossom's fingers moving softly over his crotch, feeling and exploring, he was sure at last.

"Are you sure that's what you want, Blossom?" he asked her softly.

Longarm's sudden question startled her. She twitched when he spoke, but did not answer him for a moment. Then she said, "Yes. I knew what I wanted while we were talking, before you turned out the light. There's something about you that just draws me to you, Longarm. Only I was afraid that if I came right out and told you, it'd give you the wrong idea about me."

"I don't see anything wrong with the idea that a woman needs a man, just the same as a man needs a woman, sometimes."

"A lot of men do, though." Blossom's fingers had not stopped their slow, gentle investigations. She began tugging now at the buttons of Longarm's fly, opening them one by one until she could slide her hand inside his trousers. She groped for a moment, seeking the front opening of his balbriggans, then found it, and Longarm felt her warm hand closing around him.

"Oh, my," she whispered, "I didn't know men ever got this big. And you're not even hard yet!"

"I will be soon enough," Longarm assured her.

He rubbed a forefinger along her cheek, down to her chin, and tilted her face to bring her lips to his. For a moment she kept her lips pressed together, then her mouth opened and her hot tongue darted out to seek Longarm's. He began to swell, and her hand closed more firmly around him. She groped for his belt buckle with her free hand, but Longarm's gunbelt kept her from reaching her objective.

"If you're sure you want to go on, let's make a better start," Longarm suggested, breaking their prolonged kiss.

Breathlessly she replied, "I want to go on, Longarm! It's been a long time since I've had a man!"

Standing up, Longarm took off his gunbelt, hanging it over the seat in front of them. Then he turned so that Blossom could reach him, and waited while she finished unbuttoning his tight-fitting trousers and pulled them down from his hips.

"I wish the light was on now, so I could see you," she said. "But I'll be glad enough just to feel you."

Longarm heard a rustle of clothing. In the dimness he could see the white of Blossom's blouse and underclothing as she moved, taking them off and tossing them into the seat across the aisle. Then she was standing in front of him, holding his erection with both hands, rubbing it over the softness of her warm belly.

Finding her breasts with his lips, Longarm swiveled his head from side to side, taking her protruding nipples into his mouth in turn to caress them with his tongue. Blossom gasped and began to quiver.

"Hurry, Longarm!" she gasped. "I'm so hot and trembly inside that I can't wait much longer!"

Longarm fumbled at the side of the coach seat until he found the latch that released its back, and tripped the lever, letting the back down until it was level and formed a long but very narrow bed. Blossom grabbed his hand and pulled him down to her. He felt her soft body wriggling beneath his muscular one as she moved to position herself. Then her hands found his rigid shaft again and guided it to her soft, moist warmth.

"Now," she breathed. "Now, Longarm!"

Blossom gave a soft cry of pain when Longarm first entered her. He stopped, but she writhed beneath him and cried, "Don't stop, please don't stop! It doesn't hurt, really!"

Longarm bore down firmly into her waiting flesh, flesh that

resisted him even as Blossom kept urging him to go deeper. He said, "I'm hurting you, Blossom. We better stop."

"No!" she exclaimed. "It's only because I haven't been with a man for such a long time! Please, Longarm! Go on!"

Longarm felt her hands on his buttocks, pulling him toward her. He let Blossom draw him into her, deeper and still deeper, until she gave a convulsive upward thrust and her body began trembling while high, sharp cries burst from her throat. She kept forcing him into her more deeply, even while she was writhing in a climax.

When Blossom's cries subsided and her frantic wriggling came to an end, Longarm lay quietly, fully within her, his still-rigid member held tightly along its entire length. He felt the pressure ease as Blossom relaxed, and he moved to lift himself away from her, but she wrapped her legs around him and held him in place.

"I'm not going to let you go yet, Longarm," she said, her voice rasping a little from her prolonged sobs. "Even if it hurts me a little bit, it's the best-feeling pain I've ever had. And I didn't do a thing for you, but I will, the next time."

"I can't figure out how you can be so tight if you've had a baby," Longarm said, his voice reflecting the frown she could not see on his face.

"That was four years ago," Blossom said. "And since my husband left me, I haven't let a man touch me. But it's all right, Longarm. You're what I wanted, what I needed." She moved her hips tentatively. "I'm ready for you to start again. Unless you don't—"

"Don't worry, I do," Longarm assured her.

He proved his readiness by raising his hips an inch or two and lowering them with a slow, gentle thrust. Blossom sighed, but this time the sigh was one of pleasure, not of pain. She twisted her breasts against Longarm's ribs, trembling as the mat of brown curls against which she was rubbing them grated softly across their erect tips.

"Go faster, Longarm," she said softly. "Truly, it doesn't hurt anymore. Now I'm enjoying you like I wanted to before."

Longarm did as Blossom wished. He stroked slowly, with long, deep thrusts, while Blossom's body shook with broken sighs that sounded like the purring of a huge cat. Then, as the purring gave way to higher-pitched, ecstatic gasps, he sped up the tempo of his thrusting and no longer took care to be gentle.

Blossom exploded suddenly this time into an orgasm that shook her for minutes in a spasm of tossing arms and flailing legs, accompanied by wild cries that alternated between sobbing and ecstatic laughter. The cries waned and ended, but Longarm did not slow the speed of his movements or hold back the depth of his plunges.

"Come with me this time, Longarm!" Blossom pleaded between her gasping moans. "I want you to feel as good as I do!"

Longarm did not answer. He was reaching the point when he knew his body would take command, and he wanted to delay the moment until Blossom reached her peak once more.

She went into her orgasm with her hips rising to meet his fast downward lunges. Laughter bubbled from her throat, and Longarm held back until he felt her small body shake as though a giant hand were tossing her into the air. Then he let go and pounded deeply with a few final thrusts, while Blossom lay panting beneath him.

Suddenly they were aware of the sounds of the train, which they'd forgotten while they were lost in each other.

Blossom sighed contentedly. "I think you've made me a full woman again, Longarm. But you'll have to help me prove it again, after we've rested a little while."

"I don't need to prove a thing to you, but I'll sure do it," he replied. "And we can rest as long as we want to. The train won't stop till we get to Gunnison, and that's still a lot of miles away."

Chapter 3

"I'm surprised you decided to show up at all," Billy Vail growled at Longarm. "And don't spin me a yarn about the train being slowed down by the snowstorm. I sent my clerk to the depot when you didn't show up at a reasonable time, and the train was exactly an hour and sixteen minutes late. The snow didn't start until after you and that damned train got to Denver."

"Now, Billy, you ought to know by now that I wouldn't lie to you about a piddling thing like being late," Longarm replied calmly. "But I'm right touched to know how concerned you are about where I'm at."

"It's two in the afternoon," Vail went on, pointing at the Regulator banjo clock that hung on his office wall. "That train got in at nine o'clock this morning."

Longarm took his Ingersoll watch from his vest pocket and looked at it. "I think you better have that clock looked at, Billy. I've got four minutes past two."

"Well?" Vail asked. "You want to tell me what kept you from reporting in as soon as you got back, the way regulations require you to?"

"Why, sure, seeing as you're so upset. There was three or four things. One was my stomach, Billy. Doggone it, I hadn't had a bite to eat since supper last night. I had a bath and shave because I knew you wouldn't want me to look dirty and disgrace the U.S. marshal's force. Then I had to put on clean clothes, because I put in part of the night scrambling all over the coal in the tender of the locomotive of that train I rode in. And after all that, I was real tired and needed a nap."

"Don't expect me to believe you stayed awake all night

watching Clem Sanger. Damn it, don't forget I was on the field force a lot longer than you've been. You handcuffed Sanger to the coach seat and slept through the whole trip, like any sensible lawman would've done."

"Now it really wasn't all that easy, Billy—" Longarm began.

Vail cut him short. "Oh, hell, spare me the rest! I guess you did deliver Sanger to the county jail before you ate and had that bath and shave and nap?"

"As a matter of fact, I didn't."

Vail stared across his desk, still piled high with the same unfinished paperwork that Longarm had seen when he'd left to pick up Sanger at Durango. His puffy face getting redder by the minute, Vail demanded, "Now I *do* want an answer to that one! Why the devil didn't you finish your job? I hope you haven't shown up here just to tell me you let the son of a bitch get away!"

"Billy," Longarm said quietly, "if you sent your clerk down to the depot to ask about that D&RG local being late, didn't anybody tell him *why* it was late?"

Instead of answering, and keeping his eyes fixed on Longarm, Vail roared, "Henry!" In a moment the office door opened tentatively, and the pink-cheeked young clerk stuck his pomaded head in the door.

"Yessir, Marshal Vail?"

His voice dangerously calm, Vail asked him, "When you went to the D&RG depot this morning, exactly what did you ask about that local from Durango?"

"Why, I asked just what you told me to—if it had come in on time. They told me just what I reported, sir, that the train was an hour and sixteen minutes late."

"And you didn't ask *why* it was late?"

Henry blinked behind his wire-rimmed spectacles. "No, sir. You didn't tell me you wanted to know anything except whether or not the train was on time."

Vail sighed and nodded. "All right, get on back to work." He waited until Henry had closed the door, then he turned back to Longarm. "Well, go ahead. Tell me what kind of scrape you got into this time."

"Why, sure, Billy. That's why I'm here, to tell you what happened and why I'm so late reporting in. I'll sit down if you don't mind, though. I've still got a few kinks in my legs from all that scrambling around I had to do last night."

Pulling up the red morocco armchair, Longarm eased himself into it, lighted a cheroot, and told Vail the sequence of the night's events. It was against his personal code to lie, but he didn't classify his omission of a few nonessential details as lying, and saw no reason to elaborate on the truth. Longarm ended his narration at the point where the D&RG local left the scene of the attempted bushwacking after picking up the body of One-Eye Carver, and jumped from that point to his arrival in Denver.

"So, since the crew was so shorthanded, I reckon you can see why nobody on that train had much time to sleep," he concluded. "And just like I told you it'd be, it was colder'n blue blazes up in them Uncompahgres. Then, just about the time we pulled into Denver, the snow had begun. I was already half froze, Billy, and I sure didn't need any more cold weather. It took me an hour to warm up, even in a bathtub full of hot water."

Longarm neglected to add that Blossom McGinnis had shared that bathtub with him, and that she'd joined him in the nap that followed the bath, in the room he'd gotten for her at the Bekins House. In fact, he mentioned Blossom only in passing.

Vail nodded slowly when Longarm stopped talking. "It looks to me like you did about all you could be expected to. We're well rid of Clem Sanger; that's just one more convict the government won't have to feed for the next twenty years. I guess this is one time when I can't blame you for not following regulations and reporting in on time."

"Well, thanks, Billy," Longarm said, relighting the cheroot that had gone out while he was telling Vail his story. "But you wouldn't gave got so all-fired upset about me being late unless you had another job waiting for me. I hope it's not someplace as cold as it is here or up in the Uncompahgres."

"It's not. In fact, I've got a hunch that before you finish this case, you're going to wish you were where it snows once in a while."

"Suppose you tell me about it, then," Longarm suggested.

Vail pulled a fat envelope from the stack of papers on his desk and took out a sheaf of folded paper.

"This came in the mail the day you left for Durango," he began. "If you hadn't been on the train already, I'd have sent somebody else to pick up Sanger, but I guess a day or so won't make all that much difference." He laid the thick sheaf of papers on his desk and frowned at Longarm. "You've heard me mention Jim Glass, I'm sure."

"Seems to me I recall he's one of your buddies from the time you was a Texas Ranger. Ain't he a federal marshal now too?"

Vail nodded. "Jim's chief marshal of Arizona Territory now. Headquarters are in Prescott. That's not where your case is, though. You'll be working down at Yuma, and I don't think you'll see much snow, there on the desert."

"I've been down on that Arizona border before," Longarm said. "I know just what it's like. Hot as it is there, it beats freezing up here. But how come your friend Glass had to ask you for help? Ain't he got enough men to cover his territory?"

"I don't think Jim's short of deputies. He can't use one of his own men on this assignment, though. He needs somebody who's not known down in Arizona to work a scheme he's come up with."

Longarm stretched his booted legs out and settled his large frame more deeply in the chair. "It must be some scheme, if you're ready to send me such a long ways to handle it."

"Jim thinks it's the only way he can handle a case of his that's been hanging fire more than three years now," Vail said. "He's being pushed by Washington to get it settled, and you know what that means."

"Sure. His desk must look like yours by now, what with all the mail from headquarters he's got on just that one case. Well, suppose you tell me what I'm running into, Billy."

"I don't know whether you remember hearing about Curley Parker and his gang holding up an army paywagon down in Arizona Territory ten or twelve years ago," Vail began. "That's where this case you're going on got started. The gang killed five men of the escort detail, and left the rest on the desert to die, but not all of them died, of course."

"Billy," Longarm interrupted, "I ain't trying to be a nitpicker, but ain't it the Secret Service's job to handle a case like that? How'd we get into it, anyhow?"

"Mainly because the Secret Service has kept prodding Jim Glass to keep the case alive. To get back to what I was saying, there were only three members of the holdup gang that got away, but they took over fifty thousand in gold with them."

"I can see why the government wants to get it back," Longarm commented dryly. "That's a lot of money, even in Washington."

"It's a lot of money *anywhere*," Vail agreed. "It's hidden somewhere out on the Sonoran Desert right now. Curley Parker's the only one of the gang that's left alive; the other two that came away from the holdup have both died. Parker's doing a life sentence in the territorial prison at Yuma, and he's getting older every day."

"So are you and me," Longarm smiled. "Except we're on the outside and don't know where there's fifty thousand in government gold hid away." Turning suddenly serious, he went on, "You don't have to tell me the rest, Billy. Your pal Glass wants me to go into the prison undercover and worm the place where the loot's hid out of this Parker. Ain't that right?"

"That's about the size of it."

Longarm shook his head. "I wouldn't give you a plugged nickel for your friend's scheme. It won't work."

"What makes you think it won't?"

"I ain't just thinking, Billy. I *know* it won't work. Look here, there's likely to be some convicts in that prison that I've brushed up against at one time or another. Chances are there'd be at least one. Don't you think I'd be spotted in a minute?"

"But if you shave off your mustache and—" Vail began.

Longarm shook his head again, more emphatically this time. "No, Billy. A shave and a haircut won't fool anybody very long, and it's going to take a while for me to get in solid enough with this Curley Parker to get him to talk—*if* I can get him to talk at all. Sometime while I'm still trying to get next to Parker, I'll be recognized, and once that happens, I'll be finished."

"Maybe you wouldn't have to stay in prison as long as you think," Vail suggested. "I had the same thought you did, that it's too dangerous to use somebody like you, somebody that every outlaw and badman for a thousand miles around knows about—"

"I take that as a compliment, Billy, and thanks," Longarm broke in.

Vail acknowledged the interruption with a jerk of his head, and kept talking as though Longarm hadn't spoken. "Now, when Jim first came up with his idea, I decided it was too risky to keep you in the prison very long. Then I thought of a way to change Jim's plan so you'd only be inside a little while."

"Oh? How's that?"

"Suppose the minute you got in, you started organizing a breakout. You could say you've got friends on the outside who'll help, but the break's got to be made fast, before your outside friends drift away—"

"No, Billy. It's a good idea as far as it goes, but it won't work, either. I'd be running the risk that one of those convicts would recognize me right off, the first day or so. How long do you think anybody'd listen to me talking about a breakout if they knew who I was? They'd figure it for a trap right off."

Vail scratched his balding head thoughtfully. "Yes. It'd be a real chancy thing, all right."

"Too damn chancy for a man in his right mind to risk. It ain't that I'm afraid, Billy—"

"I know you're not," Vail said quickly. "And I won't ask any man of mine to commit suicide."

"That's about what it'd amount to," Longarm agreed. "Now if there was just some way—" He stopped and asked, "Billy, how much time has Jim Glass got to find that army gold?"

"Well, Curley Parker's in for life, but he's pushing seventy now, and he's not in real good shape. Jim figures he'll last a little while longer, but can't say how long. That damn prison down in Yuma's not a health resort, you know."

"So I've heard."

"What're you getting at, Longarm?"

"There's bound to be a way a scheme like this one can be pulled off, but it needs to have a new twist put on it. Back in my head there's a little glimmer of an idea, but I can't pull it out yet. Billy, let me sleep on it tonight. If I don't tease at that idea too hard, it might pop up to where I can get at it."

"That's a fair enough deal," Vail agreed. "Go on and take the rest of the day off. There's nothing you can do around here, and from what you told me about your trip back from Durango, I'd say you've got a little time off due you."

From the Federal Building, Longarm walked down Stout Street to 20th, stopped in a saloon to pick up a bottle of Maryland rye, then turned up the street in the direction of the Bekins House. He was smiling.

Chapter 4

He wasn't smiling the next morning as he paced the hallway in front of Billy Vail's office. It was a pisser. No matter how often he told some women that he wasn't the marrying kind, they just didn't seem to listen. His refusal to discuss the subject any further with Blossom had led to a tearful early parting with her last night, and Longarm had wound up in his own digs, alone with his bottle of Maryland rye. And damn it, old Tom Moore just wasn't as good company as Blossom had been.

Henry's mouth dropped open in astonishment at the sight of the tall deputy, who had arrived not merely on time, but actually early for the first time in his memory. "Is—is something the matter, Marshal Long?" he stammered.

"Not so's you'd notice. There's just a few things me and Billy didn't have a chance to finish up yesterday, so I figured I'd get here early for a change."

As he unlocked the door, Henry said over his shoulder, "Well, you won't waste much time waiting. Marshal Vail is always on time. Some mornings he even gets here before I do."

Longarm followed the bespectacled youth into the office. Vail's door was closed. He started across the room, saying, "I'll just wait in Billy's office, then. I wouldn't want to be in your way, hanging around out here."

Before Longarm could reach the door of Vail's office, Henry raced around him and stood in front of the door, his arms stretched out to bar Longarm from entering. He said severely,

"I can't let you in Marshal Vail's office! Why, he has all kinds of confidential papers lying on his desk! I try to help him keep them put away, but there are just so many other things to do that I don't make much headway."

"Now look here, sonny, I'm not interested in that stack of papers on Billy's desk," Longarm said. "All I want is a comfortable chair to set in while I'm waiting, and that red chair in his office is the only one in the place that fits me."

"You'll just have to wait until the marshal gets here before you can go in his office," the clerk insisted. "If I—"

"It's all right," Vail said from the outer door. "I'm here now, so you can relax." He brushed past Longarm and Henry and opened the office door. "Come on in, Long. I don't know what's biting you, but if it's important enough to get you here an hour before you're due to report, I want to hear about it."

Longarm settled back into the red morocco chair while Vail hung his hat on the coat tree in the corner. The chief marshal stood for a moment, staring glumly at the paperwork on his desk, then he shrugged and sat down in his high-backed leather desk chair. He looked at Longarm, a smile twitching the corners of his lips.

"At a guess, it must be a good-sized bee you've got in your bonnet, to get you here at this time of day," Vail said. "Go on and start talking. Maybe we can settle things before the mailman gets here and brings me a fresh load of trouble."

"It's that business we was talking about yesterday, Billy," Longarm began. "Last night, when I went back to my room after my poker game, I got to thinking about it, and maybe I figured out a way that'd make Jim Glass's scheme work."

Vail nodded. "I'm interested. Go ahead."

"You saw what I was getting at yesterday when I said that my trying to go into the Arizona Territorial Prison with some kind of disguise just wouldn't work out, didn't you?" Longarm asked.

"Yes. You're right about there being a better-than-even chance that some of the convicts might recognize you."

"Well, I finally come up with one other way that might make Glass's scheme work. Suppose I was to go into that prison being just exactly who I really am?"

Vail stared at Longarm, a frown growing on his face. After a moment he said thoughtfully, "Let me make sure I understand what you're getting at. The only way you could get into the territorial prison as yourself would be to have a judge sentence you to serve time. Is that what you mean?"

"You follow me right, Billy. I'd have to break some kind of law, pull off some crooked deal that'd get me up before a judge and draw me a term in that pen."

"Dammit, Longarm! Do you realize what you're getting into?" Vail asked soberly.

"I think I do, Billy. But it's the only thing I can come up with that'll make Glass's scheme work."

Vail sat in silence for several minutes. Longarm leaned back in the morocco chair, his face untroubled. At last Vail said, "Your idea's not practical, Long. To carry out a plan like that would mean letting too many people in on the details. The truth would be almost certain to leak out."

"How do you figure that?" Longarm asked.

"Stop and count the number of people, besides Jim and me, who'd have to know what we were doing," Vail told him. "If you're going to commit a crime, there'd have to be a victim who'd testify in court. Then there'd be the officer who arrested you, the judge who'd try you, and his court clerk and stenographer. That's just a start. Include the jailer at a local jail, and the warden and some guards at the territorial prison after you got in it." Vail had been tallying on his fingers while he talked. "That'd be eight or ten people who'd be in on the plan. It's too many, Longarm. Somewhere along the line, somebody would be almost certain to talk out of turn."

"That's what I figured too," Longarm replied coolly. "I wouldn't be worried about you and your friend Glass talking, but you two'd be the only ones I'd feel like I could really trust."

"Well, you see, it wouldn't work out, then."

"Not if all that many was to know what we was up to," Longarm agreed. "I figured that out pretty quick myself. So I decided the only way to handle the setup would be to let just one man besides you and Jim Glass know what was going on."

"Now wait a minute—" Vail started to protest.

Longarm ignored his chief and went on calmly, "You and Glass and the warden at the pen. That's three. We just agreed I wouldn't have to worry about you and Glass. That just leaves one, and I figure that's not bad odds in a deal like this."

32

"Oh, no!" Vail shook his head. "Dammit, Longarm, you're talking about committing a real crime, and a judge sentencing you in court! That means an official record that'd put a black mark against you in your job."

"That's the only way I can see for it to be done right."

"Suppose something went wrong?" Vail asked. "What if Jim and I both died, or got killed before the scheme worked out? You'd be a damned outlaw forever!"

"Now it ain't likely something'd happen to you and Glass at the same time, Billy. That'd really be long odds. And even if you did, I'd guess you could leave some kind of sealed letter or statement that'd put me in the clear."

"It's still too risky," Vail said emphatically. "I couldn't go along with a deal like that. You poked enough holes in the original plan yesterday to convince me Jim's first idea wasn't practical. I don't think the changes you've come up with make it much better."

"Not even if I'm ready to run the risk?"

Vail shook his head emphatically. "No. Maybe if it was a different prison, I'd say the risk's worth taking, but I know a little bit more than you do about what that territorial prison's like. Let's suppose something happened that'd put you in real danger. How'd you get word to the warden?"

"Just like in any other jail, I guess. Tell the guard I had to talk to him."

"What I'm telling you is that the territorial prison's not like any other one you've ever seen, Long. One of its rules is that no convict can talk to the warden. The guards settle all the prisoners' disputes, or the convicts settle things among themselves."

"Well, I guess that kicks my idea into a cocked hat," Longarm said. "Now I'll have to—"

"Wait a minute!" Vail broke in. "The warden's not the only one who could be your safety man inside the prison! It could be another convict, couldn't it? As long as there's somebody who'd be on hand to help you out if something unexpected happened, you'd be all right."

"It sounds to me like you got somebody in mind, Billy."

"Maybe I have. I'd need to send a wire to Washington to see if he'd be available, but I'm sure I could get him detached from his present unit without anybody noticing it."

"Since it's my neck we're sticking out, don't you think I ought to be in on who it is?" Longarm asked.

"Of course. You've heard about the man I've got in mind, but I don't think you've ever met him. He's Tom Boone."

"Boone? The Secret Service agent that's just wound up that counterfeiting case up in Fort Collins?"

"That's the man. He's an old Pinkerton operative, you remember. He did a good job on that case, working his way inside the ring without anybody suspecting him."

"I've heard you mention Boone's name, but I never did get acquainted with him. Wormed his way into that counterfeit ring, the way I recall the case, and got the goods on 'em from inside."

"That's Boone. And one reason I thought about him is that part of that counterfeiting ring worked as far west as Arizona, so Tom would know some outlaws there who'd spread the word he's a genuine crook."

"You know a lot more about Boone than I do, Billy. You think he'd be tough enough to keep quiet if things went wrong?"

"I'm sure he would," Vail said. "And I'm sure I can get him detached on temporary duty to our outfit without anybody in either Arizona or Colorado knowing about it."

"You mean you'd handle it through headquarters in Washington?" Vail nodded and Longarm went on, "From what I seen of him, Boone would be a pretty good man for us, all right. But I'd like to visit with him a while before we settle on him."

"So would I," Vail replied. He sat in thoughtful silence for a moment, then told Longarm, "It's going to take a while to set everything up. You take the day off. I'll get off a wire to Washington and see if I can get Boone detached for a temporary assignment with us. I ought to have an answer by tonight."

"You sound pretty sure you'll get Boone, Billy."

"I am. The Secret Service chief owes me a few favors, and this is a good time to cash one in. Of course, if you and Boone can't get along, we'll have to forget about Jim's idea. Now, the sooner we get this organized, the better. You take the rattler on that new UP spur up to Fort Collins this morning, and talk to Boone. He's still there, closing up that counterfeiting case."

"Fort Collins ain't such a much of a town for size, Billy, but how will I know where to find Boone without giving him away?"

"I'll give you his cover story, and you won't have any trouble finding him. He's still using his cover as a crook, but I understand he's within a day or two of winding his job up, so you won't be doing him any harm. Does that sound all right?"

"Sure. But what happened to that day off you told me to take? It sort of got lost in the shuffle, didn't it?"

"No. Take today off, go up to Fort Collins tomorrow. I'll get a message off right away, and I should have an answer before we close today. Drop in about six, and let's see how things look."

"How in hell did you find me, anyhow?" asked the unshaven, square-jawed man when Longarm identified himself. "I thought I was the only one in Colorado who knew where I'd holed up."

"Billy Vail didn't tell me how he knew where you was," Longarm answered. "All he said was that if I'd come up the alley in back of the Ace-High Saloon and knock on the door of the fourth shanty from the street, I'd likely run into you."

Tom Boone grinned. "I guess I ought to have known I couldn't hide anything from old Billy. Come on inside. I'd just as soon not have any of my former confederates see us talking."

Longarm found the interior of the shanty even less inviting than its shabby, run-down exterior. The one-room structure was more of a shed than a house. It was a shell of a building, bare boards over studding, with no interior finish of any kind. A coal-oil lamp stood on a splintered pine table in the center, and two battered chairs, a single bed, and an oval monkey stove were the only furniture. A frying pan, stewpot, and coffeepot stood on a shelf near the stove; these and a water bucket were the only suggestion of cooking utensils.

In appearance, Boone matched the building. He had on what once had been a suit, but was now a pair of shapeless garments that could be called a suit only by way of courtesy. The sleeves of the coat were frayed and bulging at the elbows, the trousers were baggy and uncuffed, with a fringe of loose threads stringing over shapeless, cracked shoes. Under the coat, Boone wore a collarless shirt with a dingy neckband.

Even Longarm's sharp eyes might not have penetrated Boone's disguise if it had not been for his prior knowledge of the role the Secret Service man was playing. Boone's hair was straggly and uncombed, his beard three or four days old, his face streaked with grime, and his hands grubby. Only his keen eyes and strong, firm jawline gave him away, and these would have gone unnoticed by most people who merely glanced at him.

Tom Boone was giving Longarm the same sort of sizing-up that he was getting. After a moment's inspection, he nodded with satisfaction. "You said your name's Long. You wouldn't be the one they call Longarm, would you?"

"Well, some of my friends got to calling me that quite a while back, and the name sort of stuck."

"It stuck pretty good, I'd say. Since I've been out West working on this counterfeiting case, I've heard Longarm mentioned all the way from Bozeman to Santa Fe and out as far as Salt Lake. You cover hell of a lot of ground, Longarm."

"Well, dammit, Tom, you and me are in the same line of work. You know how a man's name gets throwed around."

"I hope mine doesn't. If anybody knew my real name and threw it around, I'd find myself suddenly dead."

Longarm nodded. "Sure. I know how that is."

"Well, sit down, Longarm," Boone invited, pointing to one of the two rickety chairs the little shack contained.

Longarm balanced himself in the chair, which had one short leg and almost threw him when he first put his weight down. He studied Tom Boone while he took a pair of his long cheroots from his pocket and offered one to his host. Boone shook his head.

"I don't use 'em," he said. "I wish I could offer you a drink, but I haven't got a taste for liquor, either, so I don't keep a bottle on hand."

"I didn't come for a drink, Tom. I come for a talk."

"About my case?"

"No. About a new job Billy wants to send me on."

"What's that got to do with me? I'm not in the marshal's force, you know that. How does the Secret Service come in?"

"Not the whole Secret Service. Just you."

"Why, I don't have any business mixing myself up in cases your department handles, Longarm. Any more than you'd have if you stepped over into one of my cases."

"I know that, of course, but Billy's got an idea—"

"Wait a minute," Boone broke in. "Billy and I have gotten to be pretty good friends since I've been out here in the West, but if he thinks I'm going to give up the seniority I've got in Treasury and join the marshal's force, he'd better think again. Is that why he sent you up here, Longarm? To try to get me to switch over?"

"Not for a minute. He didn't even think about that, Tom. What Billy's got in mind is for you just giving us a hand on a sort of special job the army's after us to do."

"And if I know Billy Vail, he's burning up the telegraph wires between Denver and Washington right this minute, trying to get my chief to assign me to help out on this little special job you're talking about."

"He did say something about sending a wire to Washington," Longarm admitted. "But don't call it a little job, Tom. It's a damn nasty one, and if you don't feel like you want to take it on after I tell you about it, I won't blame you a bit for turning us down flat."

"Now you've got me curious, Longarm. Go on. What's the job, how long will it take, and what would you be doing while I'm doing what your chief wants me to?"

"Maybe it'll be easier if I go back to how the case started and come to your part later on. That suit you?"

"It makes sense," Boone said. "Go ahead."

For the next quarter hour, Longarm talked slowly and carefully, covering all the details of the case as Vail had first explained it to him, and tracing the development of the final plan that he and the chief marshal had evolved. When he reached the end of his explanation and fell silent, it was a silence in which Boone joined for several minutes.

Longarm was the first to speak. "Well, Tom? How does the scheme hit you?"

"Right between the eyes. If it was any penitentiary but that hellhole in Arizona, I'd say it might work. But that one's got a reputation that stinks to high heaven."

"I've heard that too, but I figure it can't be as bad as it's made out to be."

"Don't fool yourself, Longarm. It is. Since I've been on this counterfeiting case, I've talked to a lot of crooks who've handled the Arizona end of the counterfeiting operation. Some of the toughest ones over there took to counterfeiting because they knew if they were caught they'd go to a federal prison instead of the territorial prison in Arizona."

37

"Suppose Billy gets your boss in Washington to assign you to us for this case? Would you kick up a fuss and turn down the job?"

Boone scratched his chin thoughtfully. "No." His voice showed his reluctance. "No, I wouldn't turn it down. I could, you know, according to Secret Service regulations. But I'd look on it as my duty to take the job."

"I guess that's all I need to know," Longarm said. "You reckon the two of us could get along together, if it works out that we go along with Jim Glass's scheme?"

"I was about to ask you that. As far as I'm concerned, I'd rather be working with you on something else, but it's beginning to look like this is the assignment we'll both be stuck with."

"That's about the way I feel," Longarm agreed. He stood up and extended his hand. "Well, Tom, I don't want to stay here any longer than I have to. I know you'd be in a pickle if any of your crooked friends caught you confabbing with a U.S. marshal."

Boone's handshake was firm and warm. "We'll get along all right together, Longarm. If I'm going to prison with you, I've got an idea you'll be pretty good company."

"Even if we act like enemies," Longarm grinned. "Billy or somebody from our outfit will be around as soon as the deal's set up, if it gets set up. If it does, I suppose the next time we'll see each other'll be over in Arizona."

"Good luck, then."

"And I'll wish you the same."

Three slow weeks dragged by before the scheme proposed by Jim Glass could be modified and refined. Coded telegrams between Vail in Denver and Glass in the Arizona territorial capital at Prescott flew like butterflies swarming in the spring. Vail's request to have Tom Boone placed on temporary assignment with the U.S. marshal's force was delayed until Boone wrapped up his case against the counterfeit ring, then was approved by the Attorney General.

Throughout the entire three weeks, the burden of making the arrangements fell on Vail and Longarm. Because Longarm was the only one the chief marshal felt he could trust to man the night telegraph line that connected the Denver office directly to the Justice Department in Washington, Longarm's days were spent in sleep and his nights in the confining cubicle of the telegraph room in the basement of the Denver Federal Building.

"Dammit, Billy," Longarm complained one morning when Vail came in to pick up the latest wires from headquarters, "if I don't get out of here pretty soon, I'm going to think there ain't no such thing as sunshine."

"Don't feel too bad about it," Vail told him unsympathetically. "The weather's been terrible. You've seen as much sunshine as anybody else in Denver. All we've had is one spring storm after another, snow or sleet or cold rain. I'm about ready to go with you to Arizona."

"You think I'll ever get there?"

"It's beginning to look that way. I'll tell you more about it after I've decoded the wires that came in last night. About all that's been holding us up is getting the army to agree to foot the bills for our scheme. The Attorney General was supposed to get final approval from the Secretary of War this week."

"It all comes out of the same pocket, don't it? What difference does it make who pays the bills?"

"It might not make any difference to you or me, but back in Washington they don't do things the way we would." Vail smiled mirthlessly. "Our bosses don't want to spend budget money trying to get back an army payroll. The army's written off the payroll as being lost, so they've got to arrange to find out that what they've said goodbye to on paper might be salvaged after all."

"Politics!" Longarm snorted. "What they need in Washington is somebody to knock a few heads together and try to bang some sense into them damn pencil-pushers! All they do is make work for theirselves to keep their jobs safe, and that makes more work for folks like us who just want to get on with things!"

"Well, it's the system at work, and when you can't buck it, the only thing you can do is learn how to get along with it." Vail looked at the coded messages Longarm had handed him. "I'll get on upstairs and go to work on these. Stop at my office before you go home. Maybe there'll be some good news in these."

An hour later, when Longarm stuck his head into the door

of Vail's office, the chief marshal was smiling. He motioned for Longarm to come in and close the door. Longarm pulled up the red morocco chair and sat down.

"Well, we've got all we need now. We can go ahead with our plan," Vail told him.

"You mean I don't have to be shut up all night in that damn basement anymore? Hell's bells, Billy, a cell in the Arizona pen can't be much worse than that little room downstairs."

"You'll have a chance to compare them pretty soon. And maybe being down there was good training for you. That telegraph room's bigger than the cells at the territorial prison, though, from what I've heard."

"In a snake's ass it was good for me! But that ain't here nor there. I take it them wires was what you been waiting for?"

"They are. All the paperwork's done now. One of those messages was from the Attorney General's office, the other one was from Jim Glass. We're finally ready to move."

"When do I leave?"

"Tonight, if you feel like it. Tomorrow, if you need more time to get ready."

"Dammit, Billy, I been ready to leave for a month!"

"Leave tonight, then. Your papers are all ready. You'll take the D&RG to Trinidad and then the Santa Fe to its new railhead at Flagstaff. By tonight, Jim Glass will have arrested Tom Boone and put him in jail at Prescott for you to pick up and return to Denver."

Longarm nodded. "Just like we worked it out, I see."

"As far as we were able to work it out. After you take custody of Boone, you'll be entirely on your own."

"I been on my own before, Billy. I don't need anybody to tell me what to do after that."

"No, of course you don't. Well, you've been up all night, and I've got other work to look after. We'll take care of anything we've missed when you stop in for your papers this afternoon."

"I thought you said they was all ready?"

"They are. Have been for the past three days."

"Do you figure any more palaver's going to help me any?"

"No." Vail scratched his head. "No, I can't say it would."

"Then, if it's all the same to you, I'll just take my papers now and get the afternoon train out."

"That's up to you." Vail stood up and held out his hand.

Longarm's steel-blue eyes opened wider than usual. It wasn't like Billy Vail to be so formal when he sent a man out on an assignment. He took Vail's hand and shook it quickly. "Good luck," the chief marshal said. "I hope everything works out."

"It likely will, Billy. And if it don't, I'll just have to twist things around until they do work out. I'll see you when the job's done."

Chapter 5

Along the floor of the canyon, a wide, shallow stream tinkled its song through the fast-descending dusk. Longarm sat relaxed in the saddle of the livery horse he'd rented in Flagstaff, and let the animal pick its own way along the rock-studded trail that ran beside the creek. According to his figuring, he had two or three miles yet to go before reaching the flat where he was to meet Jim Glass and Tom Boone.

On either side of him, the walls of the canyon rose in high, broken formations of russet buttes, with serrated yellow ledges running between them. The canyon floor, at the point he'd reached in his leisurely ride from the railhead town, was less than a half-mile across, but the widely spaced trees—oaks and a lesser number of cedars and pines—made it seem broader. The trail was a tricky one, but he'd learned at the outset of his trip that he was better off letting the livery horse choose its own course than trying to guide it with the reins.

Just ahead, the stream dropped from sight as it curved into a fissure in the canyon's floor, and the trail dipped into the same narrow cleft. The horse plodded steadily along as it entered the gorge, whose walls narrowed now to reduce the canyon's visible width to only a few hundred yards. The grade pitched steeply downward, and the little stream that just moments before had flowed placidly and unrippled in its boulder-strewn bed now sang in Longarm's ears as it was squeezed into a narrow white torrent that dashed through a bed of solid rock only a dozen yards wide.

Reining in, Longarm lighted a cheroot and sat looking at

the narrow thread of the trail, which was worn into the soft rock that formed the floor of the cut. He leaned back in the saddle and held himself erect while the horse descended the narrow, precipitous slope. He could see that the trail rose and fell as it followed a natural ledge above the creek. The distant walls of the main canyon were visible now only when the ledge ascended; when it dipped and ran only inches above the surface of the creek, all that was visible was the sky and the stream and the saffron-yellow stone walls that formed the sides of the fissure.

Ahead, the end of the cut was coming into view; its walls had already widened enough to give him a glimpse of the main walls of the canyon curving in the distance. The streambed broadened and the ferns and water-grass that had grown along its edges reappeared. Less than a quarter-mile ahead he saw the lighter green of meadow grass stretching away from the creek. He touched the horse's flank with a boot toe and the animal moved a bit faster.

Abruptly the cut ended. A wide flat stretched in front of Longarm, a grass-grown expanse of meadowland that seemed out of place between the high red-rock walls of the main canyon. This flat supported no pines or cedars, but was studded generously with the towering, dark-barked trunks of the oak trees that had given the creek the name that had come to be applied to the canyon as well. A thin thread of smoke cut a wavy line against the darkening sky, but its source was hidden by the trees.

In all his years of service with Billy Vail, the chief marshal had never before given Longarm such explicit instructions when he was leaving on an assignment, and the rarity of the event had been so surprising that Longarm had followed his chief's directions to the letter. After getting off the Santa Fe train at the Flagstaff railhead, he'd lugged his bedroll and saddlebags along the town's one dusty yellow street until he came to a livery stable, where he rented a horse and saddle gear. From the liveryman he'd gotten directions to the head of the trail that led to Prescott through Oak Creek Canyon.

Delaying his departure only long enough have a swallow of Maryland rye and a generous sample of the free lunch at the best saloon he could find in the little lumbering town, Longarm had swung into the saddle and started out. Somewhere about ten miles along the trail, Vail had told him, he'd see a cabin where Jim Glass and Tom Boone would be waiting for him. With another nudge at the horse's flank, Longarm clucked his tongue to speed the animal up a bit more, and headed toward the thin column of smoke.

He'd almost reached the cabin, a low-walled structure of logs, when a man came around one corner. He saw Longarm and stopped to watch him approach. When Longarm drew closer, he could see that the man wasn't Boone, and decided he must be Glass. He reined in a dozen yards from the cabin and waited for the other man to speak first.

"Are you looking for somebody, friend, or just riding past?" the man called.

"That depends on whether there's another cabin like this one on ahead up the canyon," Longarm replied evasively.

Each of them was openly sizing up the other. Glass was a tall man, but thin, and looked whipcord-tough. He was hatless, and a thick shock of gray hair rose from a wide brow. His eyes were light brown, almost golden in the increasing gloom. He wore a denim range suit—square-cut jacket and narrow-legged jeans tucked into embroidered boots. A long-barreled Smith & Wesson was holstered high on his left side, butt forward.

Glass said, "Now, if you lived hereabouts, you'd know the answer to that. Since you're a stranger, maybe you've lost the trail. You mind telling me who you're looking for?"

"When I asked directions in Flagstaff after I got off the train from Denver, the liveryman told me this was Oak Creek Canyon. Did I take the wrong trail?"

"Not if you know a man in Denver by the name of Vail."

Longarm swung out of the saddle and led the horse toward the stranger. "Thanks. I was hoping you'd give me a hint without me having to be the one to bring up names. You'd be Jim Glass, I reckon?"

"Yes. And you're Long, the deputy that I'm told everybody calls Longarm." Glass stuck out his hand and they shook. He went on, "Lead your horse around the cabin. There's a lean-to there that he can shelter in, with mine and Tom Boone's."

"Tom got here, then?"

"He followed me up from Prescott. I thought we'd better get here early, because the Santa Fe schedule's not real settled yet, and I wanted to be sure we'd be here when you rode in."

"This is a right lonesome place you got here," Longarm commented, looking around the deserted canyon floor.

"I hope I can keep it that way," Glass told him. "This is where I come to be by myself when I've got some private thinking to do. There's not many people know about it."

As Longarm followed Glass around the corner of the cabin, Boone came out the door. For a moment Longarm didn't recognize the Secret Service man. Boone wasn't the shoddily dressed, unshaven semi-derelict he'd appeared to be in Fort Collins. He had on a new pair of twill pants, new boots, and a crisply creased denim shirt. His cheeks and chin were free of stubble, and his hair was combed back neatly.

Boone waved to Longarm and said, "Well, it looks like we managed to get together without anybody noticing us. I hope that's a sign that everything else will run smoothly."

Longarm dropped the horse's reins over a rail of the lean-to and said, "Billy seems to think it's a good scheme."

"So do I," Glass put in. "Of course, I'd be a little bit prejudiced, because it was my idea, even if you and Billy did put a lot of frills on it that ought to make it even better. But let's go inside and have a drink and talk awhile before supper."

Boone waved away the proferred drink. Out of courtesy to Glass, who produced a single bottle of liquor, Longarm sipped indiscriminate bourbon, and quickly lighted a cheroot to mask the sweet taste of the sour-mash whiskey.

"It seems to me that all three of us agree on know how things are supposed to go," Glass said, pulling out a battered pipe and filling it while he talked. "Prescott's not very big, and you men understand how hard it is to keep things quiet in a little place. Why, Billy Vail and I had to use the office code in the wires we sent back and forth. If we hadn't, the telegraph operator would've spread our plans all over town."

"You can trust both Longarm and me to play the cards close to our chests, Jim," Boone said. "But for one last time, let's run over what we'll be doing and when, so we'll have everything straight."

For almost an hour the three men talked quietly. Glass added a few bits of local detail—the geography of Prescott, the character of some of his deputies, an item or two about the way the territorial prison was operated—to what they already knew. Their conference was interrupted only once, when Boone got up to light the lantern that hung from a joist in the center of the cabin. Finally, Glass announced that he was satisfied.

"We've covered everything I can think of," he said. "If we

missed anything, we'd better add it to the plans now, because once we start moving, there's nothing any of us can do to change things."

"I'm satisfied," Longarm announced.

"So am I," Boone agreed. "And I'm also getting hungry."

Glass nodded. "That's it, then. He stood up. "Since it's my cabin, and I know the stove, I'll rustle the grub. I can use some help with the woodpile, if either one of you men is of a mind to."

"I'll take first whack at the ax-work," Boone volunteered. "Longarm can spell me after he gets his horse unsaddled and his gear stowed away."

Boone and Longarm went outside together while Glass rattled the stove lids, getting ready to start the supper fire.

"Well, what d'you think?" Boone asked as they moved away from the door. "Are we in trouble, or home free?"

"I'd be hard put to say," Longarm frowned. "Glass sure took charge and laid out what he wants us to do. Having me stay here three days before I come into Prescott to get you makes good sense. That's about how long it'd take me to come from Denver."

Boone frowned and shook his head. "I don't know. It seems to me that this scheme is too damned elaborate. Too many things can go wrong."

"Well, if things go wrong, all we can do is get 'em going right again," Longarm observed. "I ain't about to lose much sleep over something going wrong, Tom. Glass'll be on the outside, and from the little I seen of him, he's a good man. He knows his own mind and ain't wishy-washy, I'll give him that."

"Yes. And I guess it's as good a plan as we could have. Well, Longarm, when we put on our show in Prescott and the shooting starts, don't forget we're both on the same side. And I'll keep it in mind too, when I'm shooting back."

Longarm reined in at the crest of the bluff; the livery horse was breathing a bit hard after making the zigzag ascent up the road cut into the face of the steep rise. The sun was halfway to the jagged western horizon, but was still high enough to miss blazing into his eyes as he pushed his hat to the back of his head and touched a match to the tip of a cheroot. The blue-gray smoke of the cigar hung in loops around Longarm's face in the motionless air while he studied the little town that huddled compactly around a central square on the high, flat mesa that spread away from the crest where he sat.

From that distance, Prescott looked like a half-dozen other mining towns that Longarm had seen while working on the cases to which he'd been assigned. South and west of the town, the head-towers of mines dotted the rugged hillsides, and the debris of the diggings lay in heaps on the slopes around them. There were lights already showing in some of the shaft-top shacks.

Within the town's limits, which were just short of the diggings, the streets ran in a neat crisscross pattern, paralleling the green patch of the square at their center. Red brick and frame buildings, many of them two and three floors high, lined the streets nearest the square. Within the square itself, in a setting that allowed it to dominate the town, stood a three-story brick building that Longarm took to be the territorial capitol.

Kneeing the horse into motion, Longarm followed the trail that meandered across the flat to the town. At that hour of the hot, sunny afternoon, the blinds at the windows of most of the houses were closed to keep out the sun, and until he'd gotten to the center of town, the streets were deserted. The first real sign of life he saw was a trio of loafers lounging in the shade of an awning in front of a saloon. Longarm reined in.

"Can one of you men tell me where I'd be likely to find a fellow named Jim Glass? I imagine you'll know him," he added. "He's the chief U.S. marshal of the territory."

"You'll find him over to his office," one of them replied. "Can't miss it. Got his name and everything on the door."

"Thanks." Longarm nodded and was about to move on when one of the other loungers spoke.

"Hey, mister!" the man called. "I'll bet you're the deputy marshal from Denver that's come to pick up that crooked counterfeiter Jim brought in the other day."

"That's right," Longarm agreed. "He's going to stand trial over in Colorado, which is why I was sent to take him back."

"That's what Jim said too," another of them volunteered. "I don't know why anybody bothers to try them crooked bastards. A few years ago, we'd've just strung him up to the handiest tree and that would've been the end of it."

"As long as we got laws, they've got to be obeyed," Longarm said. "And that's Marshal Glass's job and mine, to take

47

care of men like this crook he's got in jail. The judge in Denver'll see that he gets what's coming to him."

Longarm rode on around the square to the office that the lounger had indicated. Glass and one of his deputies were waiting inside. Longarm took a quick glance around the bare little office; it had a private office at the back, with Glass's name and title on the door, two desks behind a wooden railing that stretched across the room just inside the front door, and very little else.

"It doesn't look much like what you men have in Denver, does it?" Glass smiled. "We're not as lucky as you are; we don't have a federal building here yet."

"I'd say the government sure don't spoil you with fancy fixings," Longarm agreed.

"This is Ed McGill," Glass said, indicating the deputy. "Ed, shake hands with Deputy Long, from Denver. He's the man we've heard called Longarm so many times."

"Right pleased to meet you, Long," McGill said. "I heard about that fracas you got into up at the Four Corners a while back. Sort of wish I'd been there myself."

"Oh, it wasn't such a much," Longarm said. "There was times I wished I'd had a little help, though. You'd sure have been welcome."

Glass broke into the conversation. "When you plan to take your prisoner back, Long?"

"If I start back to Flagstaff before daylight tomorrow, I can make connections when the Santa Fe train turns around to go back east," Longarm replied for the benefit of Glass's deputy, following the plan they'd agreed on. "I'm in a hurry, because this Thomas fellow's due to be arraigned four days from now, and my chief's promised we'll have him back in Denver by then."

Glass shrugged. "It's up to you. The only reason I asked is because I'm short a man right now, and if you want one of my deputies to go with you—"

"No offense, Marshal Glass," Longarm interrupted, "but I'm only taking one prisoner. I figure I can handle a job like that by myself."

"I imagine so." Glass turned to the deputy. "Ed, you'd better tell the jailer to have Thomas ready to travel by—" He looked inquiringly at Longarm.

"Oh, I figure to leave about four tomorrow morning. That'll

get me to Flagstaff in time to make the train. But I'll need a horse for Thomas. Is there a livery stable where I can rent one and leave it in Flagstaff for somebody else to bring back?"

"I can do better than that for you," Glass replied. "I keep a couple of spare nags for my deputies, and you're welcome to use one. Just leave it at the livery in Flagstaff, and the first time one of the boys goes up there, he can lead it back. Ed, you leave word at the stable for them to let Deputy Long have a horse and saddle."

"Well, that's real nice of you, Marshal Glass. I do thank you." Then, still playing his role according to their plans, Longarm asked Glass, "I don't guess Thomas had anything much on him, when you arrested him?"

"Whatever was in his pockets, a little cash and a penknife. No gun, which surprised me. Oh, yes, he was carrying a valise. I went through it. There wasn't much in it, just some clothes and a pair of boots and a shaving outfit."

"I guess I better have it, let him lug it along. Sure as I don't, he'll bellyache about your men robbing him."

"It's in the storeroom. Ed, you have it ready whenever Deputy Long wants it, will you?"

"Sure thing, Marshal Glass."

"Let's see now," Glass went on, returning his attention to Longarm, "You'll be wanting a place to stay tonight. Try the Hassayampa House, just off the square on Gurley Street. It's clean, and the livery stable's just up the street from it. Now if you need anything else, get hold of Ed or me."

"Thanks, Marshal Glass," Longarm said. "All I need besides a place to sleep is a restaurant where the food won't poison me, and a saloon that might have a bottle of Maryland rye on the shelf. As soon as I get a drink and a bite to eat, I aim to turn in. Tomorrow's going to be a long day."

"You'll find the best place in town to eat right across the street from the hotel," Glass said. "The Silver Bell Café. It's open day and night, the miners change shifts at eleven and five, and a lot of them eat there. The Paydirt Saloon, next door to the Hassayampa House, gets most of the traveling men's trade. They'll have about any kind of drink you fancy."

"That just about sets me up, then," Longarm told Glass. "I don't guess I'll see you again, Marshal Glass, so I'll say thank you now for all your help."

"Don't mention it. I'm glad you got here so fast to take that

Thomas off our hands. He looks like a slick one to me."

"All I know about him is that he's wanted real bad in Colorado. But I'll get him back there without any trouble."

Ed McGill spoke up. "If you feel like waiting just a minute, Longarm, I'll get that prisoner's valise out of the storeroom for you. If you take it over to the Hassayampa House with you, it'll save me bringing it to you later tonight."

"Sure. I'm not in that big of a hurry."

Ed disappeared into the back office and returned in a few moments, carrying a small, badly battered valise. He handed it to Longarm, saying, "I put the inventory Thomas signed in the bag, in case he claims something's missing."

"Thanks, Ed. If you ever get up to Denver, be sure to drop in and we'll have ourselves a night on the town."

"I'd like that, Long. I bet you'd know just where to go for a good time, too."

"We'd offer to show you around Prescott," Glass put in, "but there's not all that much to see. Besides, I'll bet you're more interested in resting than you are in looking around."

"You're right about that, Marshal Glass. I'm heading for that hotel with the funny name right now."

Longarm checked into the Hassayampa House and went next door to the Paydirt Saloon, where he took his time downing two healthy shots of Tom Moore. He left his horse at the livery stable and arranged for it and the horse Glass was lending him to be saddled and ready at four the next morning. Walking across Gurley Street to the Silver Bell, he demolished a gigantic steak, then strolled back to the saloon for a nightcap before returning to the hotel and climbing up to his second-floor room.

In the room, Longarm opened Tom Boone's valise and emptied its contents on the bed. He hefted the small leather bag and nodded with satisfaction; it weighed at least half again as much as an empty bag of its size should. Examining the bottom closely both inside and out, Longarm saw no signs of the false bottom with which he knew it had been fitted, a shallow compartment that the weight of the bag convinced him held three thousand dollars in silver certificates of various denominations, mostly tens and twenties.

"Well, old son," he said to the empty room, "you're here and the bait's ready. Now all you got to do tomorrow morning is act like a poor fish and bite down on it."

Setting his mental alarm clock for three, Longarm shucked out of his clothes. He draped his gunbelt over the head of the bed, with the butt of the .44 Colt readily at hand, laid his Ingersoll watch on a chair beside the bed, and put a cheroot and matches on the chair seat beside the vest. His preparations and precautions completed, he rolled into bed and fell asleep the minute his head touched the pillow.

Longarm's mental alarm did not fail him. He woke, fully alert, and reached for his vest and a match. Blinking in the sudden light, he fished his watch out and checked the time. It still lacked a few minutes of three o'clock. Clamping the cigar in his teeth, he lighted it before the match expired, and lay back and began checking the moves he'd be expected to make in the course of the day that lay ahead.

He lay quietly until he'd smoked the cheroot to a stub, then got up and lighted the lamp on the dresser. With quick efficiency, Longarm went through the familiar routine of dressing and checking his weapons. Then, with a final fingertip-brushing of his sweeping mustache, he picked up Tom Boone's valise and started for the street.

At the jail, Longarm pounded on the outer door and waited until a sleepy-eyed jailer cracked it open.

"You'd be the deputy from Denver that Ed McGill said was here to pick up that federal prisoner?" the man asked after peering through the crack. "Ed said you was as big as a house and had a longhorn mustache, and you sure fit that description."

"That's right. Name's Long." Longarm took out his wallet and flipped it open to show his badge. He looked at the badge himself, and it came home to him suddenly that within the next hour or so, he'd be surrendering it. "I hope you got him ready."

"He's ready, but he ain't very willing." The jailer swung the door open so that Longarm could enter. Longarm stepped through the door and was greeted with the odors of wine and unwashed flesh. The jailer went on, "He's been bellyaching about having to get up at this time of day ever since I roused him up."

"Did you feed him any breakfast?" Longarm asked.

"Why, hell, no, Marshal! Prisoners in here don't eat till seven, and then they all get fed at the same time. We ain't running a damn restaurant. This is a jailhouse!"

"All right," Longarm said. "Get him, and I'll sign him out."

"Sure. You'll find the papers on the table over there. I got everything fixed up the way Ed said to."

While Longarm scribbled his signature on the release form, the jailer disappeared through a barred door; Longarm could see that the door led to a cell-lined corridor. Then he saw Tom Boone coming down the corridor, the jailer behind him. He got out his handcuffs and flipped them open.

"All right, Thomas," Longarm said briskly. "Stick out your hands. They say you're a slick one, so I'm not taking any chances with you."

"Wait a minute!" Boone protested. "You ain't going to put cuffs on me, are you? Why, I ain't had breakfast yet!"

"I'll see you get fed," Longarm replied curtly. "But you're going to wear these until we get to the café. Now put out them hands like I told you to!"

"How about my stuff?" Boone asked, making no move to obey. "I got a valise with my clothes in it someplace."

"It's on the floor, right there. You'll get it when we get on the train to Denver, not before. Now, damn you, put out your arms so I can put these cuffs on!"

Boone extended his arms and Longarm snapped the cuffs on his wrists.

"Let's go," Longarm commanded. "The café's just a little ways from here."

Holding Boone's arm, Longarm led him out of the jail. The jailer stood in the door, watching them leave. As soon as they were out of sight of the jail, Boone said in a low voice, "I hope you don't treat all your prisoners like this, Longarm. Damned if I don't feel guilty, somehow!"

"Cuffs make a man feel that way," Longarm replied. "Now let's see if we can fool whoever's having breakfast. Only don't make your move before we eat. My belly thinks my throat's been cut, and I want at least one decent meal before I go to jail."

"You'd better eat hearty, then," Boone told him. "The menu in this jail here sure leaves a lot to be desired."

Longarm pushed Boone roughly ahead of him to a table near the back of the restaurant. The counter was crowded and about half the tables were occupied by men wearing the rough working clothes and heavy brogans that identified them as miners, eating their breakfasts before reporting for the five-o'clock shift change. They watched as Longarm manhandled Boone to a seat at the table, but none of them moved or spoke.

None of the diners watched them openly, but both men felt curious eyes on them as they moved through the room. No one seemed to be watching them when Boone held his hands out and said loudly, "Well, Marshal, ain't you going to take these off so I can eat?"

"You can eat as good with 'em on as you can with 'em off," Longarm replied gruffly. "Now sit down and shut up!"

Service at the Silver Bell was prompt, and within five minutes after they sat down, Longarm and his companion were served huge platters, each containing a stack of hotcakes, several slices of bacon, and two eggs. A few moments later, the waiter set thick mugs of coffee on the table.

Midway through the meal, they began building to the scene that their plan called for them to stage. Boone leaned across the table and whispered something, and Longarm shook his head angrily. They ate in silence for a moment, then Boone went through the motions of whispering again. This time Longarm's reaction was not as emphatic.

Now Boone gestured to the valise with his manacled hands. Longarm shook his head again, but less emphatically this time. Boone leaned closer to him and appeared to whisper once more, but got the same negative headshake. The miners who'd been eating when Longarm and Boone entered the Silver Bell were finishing their breakfasts now, leaving the café singly and in groups of two or three. Longarm nodded covertly at Boone.

For the next few moments, until they'd emptied their plates, the two ate quietly. Then Boone repeated his whispering, and this time Longarm frowned thoughtfully, but made no gesture of refusal. Boone went on, his mouth close to Longarm's ear, and after appearing to listen, Longarm picked up the valise and motioned to Boone to go outside. He stopped at the cashier's desk long enough to pay their bill, then let Boone precede him through the door.

Outside, at the edge of the board sidewalk, the two men stood close together while Longarm opened the satchel. He took his clasp knife out, slit the bottom lining of the valise, and took out two banded packets of twenty-dollar bills, which he tucked into the breast pocket of his coat.

"Hurry up with the key," Boone whispered. "There's three men coming out right now. It's the perfect time to finish this!"

Longarm passed Boone the handcuff key, making his motions so slow and clumsy that the miners emerging from the restaurant had to notice it. In reaching for the key, Boone let the valise fall to the ground. Longarm bent to pick it up.

Raising his manacled wrists, Boone smashed them down on the back of Longarm's bent head. Longarm collapsed on the sidewalk and lay motionless. Boone grabbed the satchel and ran down the street. Longarm struggled to his knees and drew his Colt. Aiming well above Boone's head, he fired two shots after the fleeing figure of the Secret Service man.

Chapter 6

For a few seconds after Boone smashed Longarm to the ground and ran, the three miners emerging from the restaurant door stood in puzzled silence, peering at Longarm in the dim light that spilled from the door of the cafe.

Still on his knees, Longarm called to them, "Help me catch that fellow! He's a federal prisoner, and he's getting away!"

Two of the miners started running after Boone, a dimly seen figure now, far down the street. As the men ran, they began yelling to Boone to stop. The third man bent over Longarm, helping him to his feet. Longarm took a few wobbly steps in the direction Boone had taken, then staggered and fell. He struggled to his knees again, swaying as though still dazed from the blow Boone had given him with the handcuffs.

Longarm's shots had brought more men out of the café, and across the street still others were shoving through the batwings of the Paydirt Saloon to join those clustering around Longarm, who had not yet gotten to his feet.

Jim Glass appeared from nowhere and pushed through the crowd that had gathered around Longarm. "What's the trouble here?" Glass asked loudly; then, seeing Longarm, he bent over and helped him to his feet. Longarm was still clutching his Colt; Glass took the gun and tucked it into his waistband. Longarm stood swaying, supported by Glass's arm.

Glass asked loudly, "What in hell happened, Long?"

"That damned fellow Thomas!" Longarm replied. "He

caught me off guard and knocked me down. I tried to wing him, but I guess I was too shaky for good shooting, because I missed him."

Glass took a quick look at the crowd clustering around him and snapped, "I'm appointing you men as deputies. You're now a *posse comitatus*. Find that man who got away and bring him back! I'll be here at the Silver Bell, or in my office."

"Wait a minute, Marshal," one of the miners objected. "We got to report on shift in about fifteen minutes."

"Never mind that," Glass said crisply. "I'll square things up with your bosses. Right now you're appointed as temporary federal officers, authorized to capture an escaped prisoner. Now scatter out and look for him! He can't be very far away!"

"We getting paid for this?" one of the men asked.

"You'll be paid," Glass promised. "Now get moving!"

"That fellow we're supposed to chase—he ain't got a gun, has he?" another of the miners asked Glass.

Glass turned to Longarm. "He didn't have a weapon, did he?"

Weakly, as though he had not yet recovered from the blow to his head, Longarm said, "No. He still had the cuffs on, too."

"You heard what Marshal Long said," Glass told the miners. "The man you're after is handcuffed and unarmed. I want you to scatter out. He can't have gotten very far away. Go on—the faster you move, the quicker you'll find him!"

More than a dozen men were in the group that had assembled from the restaurant and the saloon. As they began moving in response to Glass's command, most of them seemed to take their job as a lark, but a few of them muttered unhappily as they started down Gurley Street to look for Boone. Two or three of the latecomers did not join the impromptu posse, but stayed watching Glass and Longarm.

"You feel like telling me what in hell happened, Long?" Glass asked loudly, pitching his voice so the onlookers would be sure to hear him.

"I reckon." Longarm turned to face Glass, swayed, and almost fell before regaining his balance. He said, "I ain't feeling too good, though. Maybe if we went inside the café, where I can sit down—"

With Glass supporting him, Longarm staggered into the Silver Bell and slumped into the nearest chair. The men who'd stayed behind when the posse left followed the pair into the restaurant and stood watching and listening.

Glass called to one of the waiters, "Get this man a cup of hot coffee! He needs something to bring him around!"

A steaming cup of black coffee was immediately set in front of Longarm. He sipped it, swallowed a few mouthfuls, and moved his head gingerly.

"That son of a bitch sure landed on me solid with them handcuffs," he told Glass. "It's my own fool fault he got away, Marshal Glass. I let my guard down when I shouldn't have."

"Yes. I can see that. What did Thomas do to take your attention off him?"

"He—he asked if he could get something out of his valise," Longarm replied hesitantly.

"What was it he wanted?"

"A—well, I guess he asked for a handkerchief, Marshal." Longarm shook his head again. "I ain't trying to duck your question, and I don't aim to lie about anything, but right now I plumb disremember. I guess I'm still sort of groggy."

By now, a crowd had gathered around the table where Glass and Longarm sat. Glass looked at the ring of curious faces, but did not order the men to leave.

"Go on," he told Longarm. "Were you holding Thomas's bag, or was he?"

"I—I guess I was. He had the cuffs on, remember?"

"Yes. Go on, Long. You were carrying the valise, you said. What happened next?"

"Why, I opened it and bent over to get him out a handkerchief. The next thing I recall, I was laying on the sidewalk and Thomas was scooting down the street like a scared jackassrabbit."

"You didn't try to chase him?"

"Now how in hell could I chase him, Glass?" Longarm demanded. "There I was, groggy as a drunk Paiute, and Thomas hightailing it away in the dark." Longarm frowned and added, "I did snapshot at him a time or two. Two, if I recall right." He felt for his Colt, then saw its butt protruding from Glass's waistband. "You can look at my gun and tell. It was full-loaded when I left my room this morning. I always check it before I go out, to make sure."

Glass took Longarm's revolver from his belt, pulled the

57

hammer back to half-cock, and spun the cylinder, inspecting the bases of the shells in each of the gun's chambers. Then he laid the heavy revolver on the table. "Two fired shells, so your memory's right about that, Long."

"Sure he is, Marshal Glass," one of the bystanders volunteered. "I was standing in the door, I seen and heard every bit of what happened."

"Thanks, Cleary," Glass told the man. "I'll talk to you after while." He turned back to Longarm. "A minute ago you told me you opened Thomas's satchel when he asked you for a handkerchief."

"That's right. He said the cold air was starting his nose to running."

"Why didn't you let him get the handkerchief himself?"

"Because he had handcuffs on. Wouldn't you've done the same thing if you'd been me?"

"Don't get upset, Long," Glass said. "I'm just trying to find out why that handkerchief was so important that it took your mind off your job, and let your prisoner escape. You know what my responsibility is in this case. Your chief would be asking the same questions I am, if he was here."

Longarm nodded. "Sure. I guess I'm still a little bit fuzzed up around the edges, Marshal." He took out a cheroot and lighted it. "I ought to've hit the son of a bitch when I let off them two shots, but I reckon I was just too shaky."

"From the reputation you've got, Long, you don't miss very many shots," Glass said. "Even quick shots in bad light."

"Like I said, I hadn't got over that thump on the head."

"That's understandable. Now, I—"

A flurry at the door drew Glass's attention, and he turned to look around. Two men, holding Tom Boone by the arms between them, had pushed into the restaurant. One of the men was carrying Boone's valise. All three were panting, as though they'd been running recently.

"Is this the fellow you're after, Marshal Glass?" one of the newcomers asked. "He didn't have no handcuffs on, but I seen him when he was having breakfast with the deputy there."

"We spotted him when he ducked out from between a couple of houses down on Ninth Street," the second man added. "And he was hanging on to this satchel for dear life. I recall seeing it when him and the deputy was eating."

"That's him, all right. You men did fine," Glass said. "If you'll stop in at my office later today, I'll see that you get the pay you're due as possemen. And if you've got the time, you could help some more by finding the other men who're still out and telling them the search is over. They'll get paid too, of course. Now I'll take charge of the prisoner, and the valise."

Glass stepped over to Boone and took him by the arm. "All right, Thomas" he said sternly. "You've made your try, and you didn't get away with, so I hope you've learned a lesson. Now sit down here and keep quiet while we settle this up."

Glass led Boone to the table where Longarm was sitting, and pushed him into a chair. Taking a pair of handcuffs from his belt, Glass cuffed one of Boone's wrists to a chair leg. He sat down between Longarm and Boone.

Glass looked at Longarm and said, "Now, Long, I know Chief Marshal Vail must want this man in Denver pretty badly, or he wouldn't have sent you all this way to pick him up. But if you can get Vail to release Thomas to me, I can guarantee he'll get five to ten years in the Arizona Territorial Prison for attacking you and trying to escape this morning. What's your opinion?"

"You mean can I talk Marshal Vail into letting Thomas stay here and stand trial for knocking me down and trying to escape?" Longarm shook his head. "I don't know, Marshal Glass. You'd have to find that out from Marshal Vail."

"All I'm trying to do is see that Thomas gets the longest sentence possible," Glass said. "If he testifies at that trial in Denver, he's going to get off with a year or two. If he goes on trial here, he'll get five years, maybe ten."

"If it was left up to me, I'd like to see him tried right here, then," Longarm said angrily. "He owes me a few years for that crack on the head he give me."

Boone broke in angrily, "Don't listen to this sneaky bastard for a minute, Marshal Glass! He's worse than he's trying to make me out to be!"

"Now you shut up, Thomas!" Longarm commanded. "You're heading for real trouble, and you know it!"

"Both of you keep quiet!" Glass snapped. He looked at Boone. "You said Deputy Marshal Long is worse than he's trying to make you look. Suppose you explain just what you meant."

59

"I'm telling you, Thomas, keep quiet!" Longarm threatened.

"Damned if I will, Long!" Tom Boone exploded. He gave the impression of a desperate man, pushed beyond his capacity to endure. Facing Longarm, his voice rising, Boone went on, "You're double-crossing me, Long! Just like you did when we were standing out there in front of the restaurant!"

"Why, you lying bastard!" Longarm snarled.

His hand started for his holster. While his gun hand was still in midair, Longarm acted as though he'd just remembered that the weapon was on the table, and changed the direction of his motion. He was too late to get to the Colt. Glass had clamped his hand over the weapon the instant Longarm made a move toward it.

"Hold it right there, Long!" Glass snapped sharply.

Longarm let his hands fall to the table, and glared at Boone.

Boone said, "He's the one who's lying, Marshal Glass."

"Lying about what?" Glass asked.

"About what happened out there in front of the café."

"Don't let that sly son of a bitch twist you up, Glass!" Longarm said quickly. "You heard what these men said; they told you just what I did about what went on between me and Thomas."

"They told you what they saw, Marshal," Boone broke in. "It wasn't what it looked like! They couldn't hear what Long and me was saying!"

"Suppose you tell me what was said, then," Glass invited.

"Wait a minute!" Longarm said, urgency in his voice. "You can't believe a word Thomas is going to tell you, Glass! Don't listen to him!"

"You're forgetting I'm in charge here, Long," Glass snapped. "This is my territory, you're not in Colorado now."

"Maybe not, but if you're going to believe a damned crook like Thomas, instead of a man on the same force as you are—"

"I didn't say I'd believe Thomas," Glass pointed out. "I'll listen to him, but I'll make up my own mind. Then I'll listen to you, and I'll make up my own mind about what you say too."

By this time the argument between the two lawmen and their prisoner had drawn everyone in the restaurant into a circle around the table where the trio sat.

After he'd quieted Longarm, who sat glaring across the table at him with a sullen frown, Glass went on, "Now, Thomas, go ahead and tell me what you meant when you said Long was double-crossing you. I'm real interested in hearing about that."

Boone stared at Longarm for a moment, then turned to speak to Glass. "What I meant was that Long promised to let me escape from him on the way back to Denver for—"

"He's lying!" Longarm's voice was almost a shout. "I told you he'd lie, Marshal Glass!"

"Keep quiet, Long!" Glass ordered. He nodded for Boone to go on with his story.

"Long said he'd let me get away if I'd give him the money I had in my valise," Boone said quickly.

"I told him that to find out where he had the money hid!" Longarm exclaimed. "We knew he was carrying a lot of loot from that counterfeit ring he worked for. Part of my job was to get it back from him!"

"He didn't know I had a dime till I told him!" Boone said insistently. "When I offered him the money, Long's ears picked up like a coonhound on a scent! He jumped at it!"

"That's another lie! I was just acting that way to lead him on to telling me about the cash!" Longarm told Glass.

"I told you I'd listen to your side of the story later," Glass said. "Now keep your mouth closed until Thomas finishes."

"You don't have to take my word for what went on between me and Long, Marshal," Boone said. "There was two or three men that came out of the café while Long was taking the cash. They saw him open my satchel and take part of the money out and put it in his pocket. He's still got it in there too, I'll bet."

"Sure, I did!" Longarm broke in. "I took it out to hold for evidence. I was going to hand it over to my chief as soon as I got Thomas back to Denver!"

"Then you've still got that cash in your pocket, Long?" Glass asked.

"Of course. Evidence, like I told you." Longarm reached for his breast pocket, but Glass stopped him.

"Leave the money where it is for right now," Glass told him. He turned to Boone. "Thomas, tell me what shape that cash was in. Was it loose bills, or what?"

"It was all in fifties, bundled up like they do in a bank."

"How much was there, in all?"

"There was three thousand dollars in the bottom of that satchel, Marshal Glass. I saw Long put two or three bundles in his pocket, but if you'll add them to what's still in the valise, you'll find out I'm telling you the truth."

Without taking his eyes off Longarm and Boone, Glass tucked Longarm's Colt into his waistband again and took the two steps from the table necessary to reach the satchel. He picked it up and dumped its contents on the tabletop. A tangled pile of clothing fell out, a shirt, a few handkerchiefs and some loose socks, and Boone's boots. Mixed in with the clothing were a couple of banded packets of bills.

A murmuring rose among the spectators when the green of the currency became visible as Glass lifted the wrapped bills from the tangle of clothing and cleared a space in the center of the table for them.

"This doesn't look like any three thousand dollars to me," Glass told Boone. "More like a couple hundred."

"Take another look in the valise," Boone said. "The money was sewed in the bottom, under a false lining. Long didn't rip the stitches far enough, that's why the rest didn't come out."

Glass reversed the valise and peered inside. He reached his hand in and yanked. There was a sharp sound of cloth ripping, and when he upended the valise again, packets of bills showered down on the top of the table. Dropping the satchel to the floor, Glass stacked the currency.

Now a babble of excited conversation broke out among the onlookers. It had started as a whisper when the first packets of bills tumbled out of the satchel, and rose to a crescendo as Glass began to count them and form them into neat piles.

"If those stacks haven't been touched, there's two thousand on the table," he announced. He turned to Longarm. "All right, Long. Hand over what's in your coat pocket."

His face twisted into an ugly scowl, Longarm took from his breast pockets the two packets of bills that he'd tucked away when he opened the satchel outside of the restaurant. Glass put the packets on the others.

"Two packets of twenties, twenty-five bills in each packet. That's a thousand. Added to the rest, that's three thousand even," he said quietly.

While Glass had been adding the three packets from Longarm's coat pocket to the bills already on the table, the crowd had become silent and tense. When the marshal announced the total, the crowd broke into an excited but hushed hubbub once more. They fell quiet when Longarm began talking.

"I told you why I took that money, Marshal Glass," Longarm said, forcing a tone of desperation into his voice. "I knew it'd be needed for evidence."

"Evidence!" Boone snorted. "In a pig's ass you took that for evidence! Damn you, Long, I know what you told me! 'Give me the three thousand,' you said. 'Hand over all the money you've got in there, and I'll let you escape on the trail up to Flagstaff!' Why, hell, you even gave me the handcuff key when I handed you the satchel!"

One of the men in the crowd spoke up. "I seen that, Marshal Glass! Me and Pug Darby and Cliff Ellis was standing right in the door of the café when this fellow"—he pointed at Longarm—"took something outa the valise and handed it to the one that had on the handcuffs."

"Then you men must've seen what happened after that, Lem," Glass suggested.

"Sure we did!" said the man called Lem. "We seen the whole thing from start to finish!"

"Don't forget what happened," Glass cautioned them. "I'll want you and Pug and Cliff to testify for the prosecution when Long goes on trial."

Longarm jumped to his feet. "What d'you mean, when I go on trial?" he asked Glass, his voice just below a shout. "Thomas is the man who's going to stand up in the dock! Not me!"

"You're wrong about that, Long," Glass said, his voice cold and level. "I'm arresting you for obstructing justice by accepting a bribe from a known criminal, with the intent of preventing him from coming to trial."

Now the buzz from the crowd in the restaurant rose again. To the spectators, seeing one United States marshal arrest another was as rare as finding a full beard on a freshly laid egg. The buzz of excited conversation died down when Longarm faced Glass again.

"Now, dammit, Glass!" he shouted, "You can't do that!"

Unruffled, Glass replied, "I just did, Long. You're now officially under arrest. If you've got any weapons on you besides this Colt I'm holding, I order you to surrender them."

"You've got my Colt. You can't see any more guns on me, can you?"

"No. What about your knife?"

"It ain't a sheath knife. It's a clasp knife. But I'll hand it over too." Longarm took his knife from his pocket and passed it on to Glass.

"By God, this does me good!" Boone said gloatingly. "It's not every day that a fellow gets to see one of you stuck-up lawmen get what's coming to you!"

Longarm dived across the table and grasped Boone by the throat. He bore the smaller man to the floor with his weight, carrying with them the chair to which Boone was handcuffed. The two men wrestled on the floor for a moment, Boone gasping and choking.

Glass moved in to break up the fight before Longarm and Boone had time to get really serious. He grabbed Longarm and pulled him off the Secret Service man, thrust him roughly into a chair.

"You stay quiet, Long!" Glass rasped, "Or I'll take those handcuffs off Thomas and put 'em on you!"

Boone was sitting up on the floor rubbing his throat with one hand, the other still cuffed to the chair leg. One of the onlookers helped him up and lifted the chair to its feet. Boone sat down, glaring at Longarm.

"You'd better keep him away from me, Marshal!" he gasped. "He'd like nothing better than to kill me!"

"Don't worry, Thomas," Glass said. "I'll see that you two get put in separate cells."

"Now, what's that mean?" Boone asked plaintively. "I'm your witness against this crooked marshal! You're not going to put me back in jail, are you?"

"I don't know where else you'd expect me to put you," Glass told him coldly. "That's where Long got you, and as far as I'm concerned, it's where you belong. But there'll be a different charge against you this time, if I have anything to say about it. I'm going to do my dead-level best to get custody of you in Arizona, and see that you stand trial for assaulting an officer of the law in the performance of his duties."

"But you just arrested Long for letting me bribe him!" Boone protested.

"Thanks for reminding me," Glass said. "I'll add another charge to the assault charge. You'll also be charged with bribing an officer of the law with intent to obstruct justice."

"Now that's just damned unfair!" Boone said unhappily.

"Maybe." Glass was unmoved. "We'll see what the judge has to say about it, though."

Glass moved around the table and unlocked the cuff that was around the chair leg. He grabbed Longarm's hand and snapped the cuff closed on his wrist.

"Now we're going over to the jail," he told them. "And you two are going to walk together in front of me. There's not going to be any fighting, and there's not going to be any trouble. Is that clear to both of you?"

Both their faces sullen, Longarm and Boone nodded. Glass turned to the spectators and announced, "It's all over, men. I want anybody who saw what went on between these two men in here this morning, or outside on the sidewalk, to leave his name at my office before you go to work. I'll need you as witnesses when these two come to trial."

A few men from the crowd started following as Glass marched Longarm and Boone down Gurley Street toward the square, but they soon saw that there would be no more fireworks and gave up.

As soon as the three were safely out of earshot of the stragglers, Glass said, "Sorry I was so rough with you in the restaurant, but it had to be handled that way. There were too many men watching for me to let up, once the show got started."

"How do you think it went over?" Boone asked.

"Better than a lot of shows I've seen on a stage," Glass replied. "You're both better actors than I thought you'd be."

"We was in the same spot as you," Longarm said. "With all those men watching, we had to make it look real."

He glanced around to be sure they were unobserved; then he reached into his right-hand vest pocket and took out the .44-caliber derringer nestled there. Then, from his left-hand vest pocket he removed his Ingersoll watch, attached by a gold-washed chain to a brass clip on the butt of the derringer. Handing them to Glass, he said, "I'd be obliged if you'd put these in your safe and keep 'em for me. It wouldn't look good if I still had that little whore-pistol when the jailer searches us."

"I'll take good care of them," Glass promised. He looked at the arrangement of watch and gun, and nodded. "Very clever. I'll have to remember that for future use."

"How long do you think it'll take to get the trial set up?" Boone asked.

"A week, maybe ten days. I want to get you two in court as soon as I can, before the witnesses start forgetting things."

"Far as I'm concerned, it can't start too soon," Longarm

said. "The faster we get in that territorial prison, the quicker we'll get our job done and get out."

"I wouldn't be so eager, if I were you," Glass warned Longarm, his voice sober. "From what I've heard, that place at Yuma is a real hell on earth. I just hope that before this is all over, we're not sorry we ever started it."

Chapter 7

Roused but not quite fully awakened by the tiny tickling that irritated his face, Longarm shook his head. The motion hastened the progress of the drops of sweat that were trickling from his brow down to his cheeks, into his four-day beard. Creeping into the beard, the salty sweat had started his face itching again, and Longarm instinctively raised his hand to scratch away the annoying itch.

From the chain that ran between the shackles circling his wrists, another chain drooped between his knees to a third chain that connected the shackles on his ankles. The wrist-chain swung jarringly against his chin and snapped him into the full, quick awakening that was his habit.

In an instant Longarm was completely aware of where he was, and why, and why he felt so strange. He looked down at the thin cotton suit he was wearing, shapeless and wrinkled, a loose jacket and baggy trousers of thin grayish weave. His feet felt strange too, sockless, in oversized laced brogans instead of his trim stovepipe boots. He missed the familiar weight of his Colt in its cross-draw holster, and the shade of his broad-brimmed Stetson.

Tom Boone lay asleep at Longarm's feet. There was barely room for the sleeping Secret Service man to curl up on the narrow bed of the creaking old army ambulance or field wagon used by the Arizona Territorial Prison to transport its new inmates the final twenty miles from the holdover at Yuma to the prison itself. In spite of his cramped position, Boone was sleeping soundly, but the hot bath of sunshine that poured in from the arched opening in the back end of the canvas wagon top was making him sweat profusely.

Longarm remembered Boone having let himself slip to the floor so that he could lie down rather than be forced to balance uncomfortably on one of the narrow plank seats running along each side of the wagon bed.

Longarm opened his mouth to whisper to Boone and wake him, but only a hoarse scratching noise came from his dry throat. He pursed his lips and worked his tongue against his teeth, trying to generate enough saliva to speak, but lips, tongue, and teeth were equally dry and gritty.

Stretching forward, Longarm managed to reach the slit that separated the driver's seat from the bed. He touched the back of one of the blue-coated guards riding in the seat. The slit parted, and the bearded face of one of the guards appeared.

"What d'ya want, greenie?" the man asked.

Longarm tried to articulate the words that would get him water, but only a garbled, unintelligible gasping came from his mouth. Still, the guard understood.

"You're like all the green ones," he said. "Dry up the first few days. Well, you gotta get used to the heat, but I'll help you this time."

Lifting a wicker-covered demijohn from beneath the seat, the guard poured a scant quarter-inch of water into a tin cup and handed it to Longarm. Longarm gulped the few drops in a single swallow. The water was as hot as though it had just been poured from a boiling teakettle, but it was wet. Longarm sat for a moment staring at the empty cup, then held it out to the guard.

"That wasn't enough," he said, his voice grating hoarsely. "How about a real drink?"

"That *was* a real drink out here, greenie," the guard told him, taking the cup and pulling the canvas flap closed as he turned away.

Longarm was suddenly angry. He clubbed his fists and brought them down on the canvas wall. The shortness of the chain made his effort to strike fall short, and his hands barely brushed against the canvas. However, Longarm's movement aroused Boone, who sat up and looked at him with a frown.

"What—what's going on?" Boone grated, his voice as thin and rasping as Longarm's had been.

"I was trying to get the damn guard to give me a drink of water. He give me about as much as you could squeeze out of a fresh-ironed, starched shirt."

Boone struggled erect and lifted himself up to the narrow seat, where he perched precariously. In a hoarse whisper he said, "If this is a sample of what it's going to be like, maybe Glass wasn't so far wrong when he said we might regret taking this job on."

"Whether we do or not, Tom, it's too late to back out now."

"We can always go to the warden and tell him we're through."

"Not a chance. I finish what I start."

"Well, I don't plan to back out, either. We've come this far, and we went to a lot of trouble after setting things up."

With a rustling of canvas, the slit parted and the bearded guard stuck his head through the opening. "Did I hear you two talking back here?"

"What if we was?" Longarm asked.

"You'd better learn the first rule right now. Prisoners don't talk, where you're going. Not until one of us gives 'em permission to."

"You can't expect us to know the rules," Boone protested. "Dammit, we're not even at the prison yet!"

"Like hell you ain't!" The guard's arm came around in a sudden sweep, backhanding Boone and almost knocking him off the narrow seat.

Longarm reacted instinctively. He swung on the guard, but the shortness of the chain between his wrist and ankle shackles stopped the blow short.

Without a word, the guard landed a haymaker on Longarm's jaw. The blow wasn't as effective as it might have been, with the guard sitting down and leaning backward, but it stung.

"Now that'll start you learning rule number two," the guard said with a nasty grin. "Convicts don't hit guards. If we was inside, you'd get ten stripes for that, but seeing as you're green and we ain't quite there yet, I'll let you off easy this time. Just be sure there ain't no next time."

For a moment after the guard pulled his head back through the slit and closed the flaps, Longarm and Boone stared at one another. Then Boone leaned forward and whispered almost soundlessly, "We better keep our ears open and our mouths shut until we learn the rules at that damned place!"

"I got a hunch the rules is what those guards say they are," Longarm observed dourly.

"You're probably right," Boone agreed. "But there hasn't been a prison rule made yet that convicts haven't found a way to break!"

Their throats were so dry that both Longarm and Boone found talking uncomfortable. They fell silent. Longarm stared out the opening in the back and thought of the crowded, hectic days that had just ended.

His own trial had followed Boone's conviction, and the Prescott *Miner* had run banner headlines in each edition, all of the stories predicting the certain conviction of the veteran U.S. marshal who'd disgraced his badge by taking a bribe from an already convicted crook. The outcome, as Glass and Vail and Longarm himself had foreseen, was inevitable. The judge wasted little time, after the jury's verdict, in sentencing Longarm to a five-to-ten-year term in the Arizona Territorial Prison.

And down here they sure don't waste time getting a man to that place after he's been tried, Longarm told himself as he gazed through the arched opening in the canvas at the rear of the jolting wagon.

What he saw was not inspiring; in fact, there was very little to see. The trail over which the wagon was rolling was not rutted, as it might have been in a land where rains fell; it consisted of two bare, shallow scratches across an endless expanse of pale yellow soil, so light that in the sun's glare it appeared almost white.

Aside from some areas where a light fuzz of vegetation covered the otherwise bare ground, the main features of the landscape were rocks and cacti. The rocks looked very similar, despite the differences in their sizes and shapes; some lay on the surface, others were partly buried, and some were mere humps that protruded an inch or so above the surface around them.

There was variety in the cacti. Here and there, the thin, pale stalk of a yucca rose ruler-straight above its base of thin, drooping leaves. There were a few saguaros, their fat, ribbed stems thrusting like erect phalluses into the pale, cloudless sky. Less common were the chollas, which grew in small, forestlike enclaves, their dark, twisted arms looking like the skeletons of some kind of weird and long-extinct animal.

Distantly, he could just make out the ghosts of high mesas and rugged buttes through the roiling heat-haze that shimmered like a translucent curtain over everything farther than a mile or so distant from the trail.

A whip popping over the backs of the mules that pulled the wagon broke Longarm's thoughts. The wagon bed tilted as the team slowed and strained to pull it up a long, steep rise. Longarm craned and twisted his neck, but could see nothing except the vista of bare earth and rocks and cacti, and the veiled shapes of the distant high ground. Then the wagon lurched and creaked to a stop.

Suddenly, sunlight burst dazzlingly into the eyes of Longarm and Boone as the guards stripped back the canvas wagon top. After he'd finally blinked away the blindness brought on by the glare, Longarm got his first look at the prison.

It rose like a fortress from the barren desert. High sandstone walls jutted up from the ground, as though the structure had not been erected by men, but had grown up from the pale yellow earth on which it stood. Buttresses marked the corners of the walls, and each corner was surmounted by a low-roofed tower; in the shade of the roof of each tower, Longarm could make out the dark silhouette of a man holding a rifle.

Directly in front of the wagon was the gate. It was inset between buttresses like those at the corners, and in one of the towers topping the slanting buttresses, Longarm could see the multiple muzzles of a Gatling gun trained on the wagon. The gates began to open, swinging outward, each side of the massive wooden gates pushed by two convicts wearing the same loose, baggy suits that had been given to Longarm and Boone before they left the jail in Yuma City to start for the prison.

Two guards, carrying old-style Burnside carbines, watched the convicts who were opening the gates, and beyond them, breaking the flat stretch of the sunbathed yard of dirt beaten smooth by pacing feet, Longarm saw the outline of the low, circular curb that he was sure enclosed a well.

As the wagon waited for the gates to swing open, Longarm had noticed that the walls in which they were set seemed unusually thick; now he understood why. On the sides and back of the enclosure, the inner walls were lined with rows of small doors, regularly spaced, which Longarm could now see were the doors to cells stood between an inner and an outer wall.

The doors were shaded now by narrow eaves that jutted out from the low-pitched roof.

One of the guards inside motioned for the wagon to enter. Longarm had only a moment or so to sweep the landscape with his eyes. A short distance from the prison walls, on his left, he saw that the land dropped off abruptly. Swiveling his head quickly, following the rim of the dropoff as it sloped gently downward, he got a glimpse behind him of the sunlight glinting on the seething surface of a wide, yellow river.

Then the wagon was inside the walls, and the gates were being closed behind it. Longarm risked whispering to Boone, "Soon as we get our bearings, we'll make a way to talk."

Tight-lipped, Boone nodded imperceptibly. He stopped the movement of his head just in time to avoid being caught by one of the guards, who turned to look back at the prisoners. The man peered at them suspiciously; apparently he'd detected the small hiss of Longarm's whisper. He said nothing, though, and after inspecting them carefully, he turned back to face the prison yard.

Before the wagon had creaked to a halt, two of the guards inside the yard were walking beside it. They had no weapons except billy clubs, which hung by thongs from their belts. The billies were almost two feet long, and tapered from their handles to heads thicker than a man's wrist. As the wagon stopped, one of the guards moved to each of the rear corners and pulled the bolts that held the tailgate in place. The tailgate dropped, and the guards looked impatiently at Longarm and Boone.

"Outa the wagon, greenies," one of the men said curtly, when neither Longarm nor Boone moved. "The warden's gone to his office to sign you in, and you don't keep him waiting."

Shuffling over the packed earth of the yard, one of the guards walking at his side, Longarm looked around the enclosure. The well apparently rose from a natural spring, for it had no pump, and a pipe ran from the top of the well-curb to a sawed-in-half barrel that had been placed at one side to catch the overflow. In addition to the well, the yard had two other features. One was a massive stake, eight feet high and as thick in diameter as a man's waist, which was set in the earth in one corner. The other feature was a large sheet-iron box, almost square, with a low, gabled top. The box stood just past the well, between it and the rear wall of cells.

Longarm quickly tallied the number of cell doors; there were sixteen on each of three sides of the building's inner perimeter. Above the cells, a wooden walkway ran around the entire perimeter, except for the space taken up by the arch of the gate. A waist-high railing enclosed the walkway, and behind the walkway, the outer walls of the prison enclosure rose chest-high. It was clear that the building was designed as a fortress, able to withstand a siege from outside as well as to contain and control the men inside the enclosure.

By the time Longarm finished taking stock of the yard, he and Boone had been led by the guards to the front wall. Here, the pattern of the other three walls had not been followed. The front wall was thicker than those at the sides and back; it was broken by doors and by wide, barred windows opening on the yard. The doors were spaced farther apart, and the windows, although barred, gave the facade the appearance of a house wall rather than that of a prison.

It was indeed a house wall, and an office wall as well, Longarm discovered as the guards herded him and Boone toward a wide door at one side of the main gate. The door led through a short hall, long enough only to accommodate doors leading off to either side, to a third door, which stood ajar. The guard in front rapped gently on the jamb.

"Here's them two new convicts, Warden Crawford," he said. "Ready for you to sign in."

"Bring them in, Freeler," a man's voice replied.

Pushing the door wide open, the guards led Longarm and Boone into a large square office. The room was windowless and had only a single doorway, through which they'd entered, and its gloom was dispelled by an Aladdin lamp hanging by a chain from the low ceiling. A desk and bookcases and filing cabinets lined the office; a plain brown carpet covered its wooden floor. There was only one chair besides that in which the warden sat in front of a high rolltop desk that stood against the rear wall.

Swiveling his chair, Crawford faced the little group. He was a man in his sixties, past his prime, but still sturdy and vigorous, judging from the thick shock of white hair that rose like a crown above Crawford's face, and the healthy tan of his face. The warden had light brown eyes under bushy brows, and wore a full, sweeping mustache similar to Longarm's, but the warden's was snow-white instead of a medium brown.

Crawford did not speak for a moment, but studied the faces of Longarm and Boone. Then he fixed his gaze on Longarm and said, "I suppose you'd be Long, the man who disgraced his badge and oath?"

"That's right, Warden," Longarm said. He jumped as a hard fist nudged his back.

"All you ever say to the warden here is 'yes, sir' or 'no, sir,'" the guard behind him hissed.

"It's all right, Freeler," Crawford told the guard. "Give them a little time to learn." He turned his head toward Boone. "And you're Thomas, then."

Boone had learned his lesson. He said, "Yes, sir."

Crawford picked up two sheets of paper from the desk and held one in each hand while he looked from Longarm to Boone. He said, "Now, as you've just found out, there are some things you two men will have to learn from the guards. The sooner you accept the fact that you're prisoners, and that an escape from here is impossible—no convict has broken out since this prison was first built—the better you'll get along."

He broke off and looked at the two guards, then said, "Freeler, while I finish signing these prisoners in, will you and Jackson do a chore for Mrs. Crawford? There's a wardrobe in the bedroom that she wants moved, and I don't like to take the other guards from their duties. It'll only take a few minutes."

"But how about the prisoners, Warden?" Freeler asked. "We ought not to leave you by yourself with them."

"They'll behave themselves," Crawford said. "And they've still got their cuffs on, so I wouldn't worry about them. You'll just be a few yards away, if I need you. And it'll save time if you do that little chore now, while you're here."

"If you say so, sir," Freeler replied reluctantly. "Come on, Jackson. We'll do the job and get right back."

After the guards had left the office, Crawford said, "You men might as well know that if I'd been consulted about this plan of yours, I'd never have agreed to it. Since it's too late to change it, and in view of the extraordinary letters I've gotten from Chief Marshal Glass and Chief Marshal Vail, I'll do what I can to help you. It isn't much."

"We don't need any help, Warden," Longarm said. "But thanks all the same."

Crawford nodded. "I'm sure you can look out for yourselves. In fact, you'll have to. You understand that I can't lift a finger to help you until you finish your job, unless there's an extreme emergency. If I showed you any favoritism, the mission you've come here to do would probably be destroyed. You'll have to be treated just like all the other prisoners."

"We know that, Warden," Longarm said. "We'll be all right."

"I hope so," the warden told them. "Now I've followed Marshal Glass's instructions and destroyed all the letters that pertain to your plan, so you won't have to worry about anyone else learning why you're here. But I hope you'll do your work as fast as possible, and relieve me from worrying about you. I wish you luck, gentlemen. I'm afraid you'll need a lot of it."

Before Longarm or Boone could reply, the footsteps of the returning guards sounded in the corridor. Crawford swung his chair around and was signing the papers he'd been holding when the guards came in. He looked up and said, "Thank you, Freeler, for the help you gave Mrs. Crawford. You can take the cuffs off these two prisoners now, and get them into cells. I'm through with them."

"All right, you two," Freeler said harshly. "March on out to the yard. Me and Jackson will be right behind you."

Longarm and Boone shuffled out into the yard ahead of the guards. They'd gotten just beyond the well when Freeler's club landed on Longarm's shoulder, sending him staggering. Longarm turned instinctively, ready to fight in spite of the pain, and saw that Boone had been knocked to the ground by Jackson.

Freeler was standing a half-dozen paces away when Longarm turned. The guard's lips were twisted into an ugly grin and he held the billy in front of him, waving it from side to side as though inviting Longarm to attack him. Longarm took a step forward before he remembered his mission and put a checkrein on his temper. He stopped short and froze his face into an expressionless mask that hid the anger seething inside his brain.

"That was just to remind you who you are and who we are," the guard said flatly. "Looks like to me you're beginning to get the idea pretty fast. Now there's a few more things you better find out about right now." Freeler looked at Boone, who was just struggling to his feet. "You listen too, greenie!" he said.

Boone was erect now, holding his fists clenched and his jaw set to keep his temper under control. He and Longarm exchanged looks that promised revenge on the two guards when an opportunity presented itself.

"You'll stay in your cells for the first week," Freeler said, looking from Longarm to Boone. "After that you can go out in the yard. Exercise periods is twice a day, two hours in the morning and two more before supper. You step outa line, you lose the yard time. And it's up to us guards to decide when you're outa line, you understand that?"

Longarm and Boone nodded.

With his billy club, Freeler pointed to the well. "That's where you'll get your water, and you better keep it clean, or the other cons will learn you to. You dip drinking water outa the well and you wash in the barrel." He lifted the billy and pointed to the stake in the corner of the yard. "I don't guess I need to tell you what that's for. You step outa line, it's anywheres from three to ten stripes. I seen one con last up to fifteen stripes, but he never was much of a man afterwards."

Shifting the end of the club, he indicated the sheet-iron contrivance that Longarm had noticed when they'd first arrived. "A lot of cons had rather take a whipping than go in the box," Freeling said. "Once you're in, you get a cup of water a day, and that's all. I seen men come out crazy after they been in the box a week. Some of 'em don't last that long, especially if the other cons don't like 'em, and parade around the box, kicking at it. I never was inside of it, but from what I hear, you'll stay deaf for a week if they give you the kicking treatment."

"You eat twice a day," Jackson said, taking up the lesson where Freeler stopped. "Six in the morning and six in the evening. You wash your plates if you want 'em clean. There's water enough at this time of year so every man gets a bath a month. The other cons will learn you the rest of what you'll have to do if you wanta walk outa here when you've served your time. That's all you need to know to get along."

"Except to keep your mouth shut unless one of us guards asks you a question," Freeler added. "Now I'll take your cuffs off, and you can settle down and make yourselves to home."

He produced a key ring and unlocked the shackles. For a moment Longarm and Boone stretched and rubbed their wrists where the irons had weighed the heaviest; then, in spite of the warning against speaking that Freeler had just finished giving them, Longarm spoke.

"Can we get a drink of water before we go in our cells?" he asked, and added, "That was a hell of a hot ride."

For a moment the burly guard stared at Longarm. He opened his mouth to say something, closed it, thought for a moment, and finally said, "Go ahead. There's some pots by the well."

With the guards standing over them, Longarm and Boone picked up two of the several clay pots that lay outside the well-curb, and dipped them into the water. It was tepid, but seemed clean. They drank twice, then stood up and faced the guards.

"Thanks," Longarm said to Freeler.

Without changing his expression, the guard swung his billy in a sideswipe that would have landed on Longarm's head if he'd been a split second later in bringing up his forearm to catch the blow before it landed.

Still without showing any emotion on his surly face, Freeler said, "I'll let you off easy this time, because you're green. You remember, no talking to us guards means no talking!"

Longarm simply nodded, figuring he'd gotten off light. He turned away from the guards and started moving toward the back wall of cells. He and Boone had no opportunity to exchange as much as a word. Longarm felt no more freedom with his hands and legs relieved of the shackles than he had when he was carrying them.

As they neared the back wall, the guards split, indicating the direction the prisoners were to take by nudging them with their billy clubs. Jackson marched Boone off to the right side of the yard, while Freeler indicated that Longarm was to move to the back of the enclosure. Longarm knew he had no choice. He walked quietly in the direction to which the guard had pointed, keeping a step ahead of Freeler, until he reached the shade of the back wall.

"Move down to number twenty-seven," Freeler ordered.

Longarm looked at the number on the door of the cell in front of which he'd stopped; it was twenty-one. He made a false start, backtracked, and stopped in front of the correct cell. Freeler unlocked the door and swung it open. Rancid human odors—sweat, urine, feces—swept out of the cell in a breath of cool air. A glint of light showed through a small window, less than a foot square, set high in the back wall.

Without waiting for the guard's command, Longarm stepped inside. The door slammed shut behind him, and the key grated in the lock. For a moment Longarm stood without moving in the center of the eight-by-eight-foot cubicle. His eyes grew used to the dimness and he saw that a narrow, shelflike bunk had been built along one wall. He sat down and automatically reached for a cheroot in a vest pocket that did not exist.

Well, old son, he told himself philosophically, *you been trying to quit smoking those damn cigars for a long time. It looks like you're finally getting around to where you're going to be able to do it.*

Chapter 8

It was not in Longarm's nature to devote his time to quiet contemplation. He was too accustomed to days of movement and activity, and he'd had very little of either lately. Being moved to the territorial prison was just a matter of exchanging one cell for another; he'd spent a month in the jail at Prescott while he waited to be tried and while the trial was in progress.

After the cell door slammed behind him, he sat on the hard bunk for a few minutes, recalling other times when he'd been confined. He began tallying up the jails he'd been in: two in Mexico, and at least four others in different places where he'd been assigned to cases involving hostile or crooked lawmen or public officials. There'd also been times when, for brief periods, assorted outlaws and Indians had held him prisoner until he'd managed to free himself.

Those times wasn't exactly the same as this one, though, he told himself, staring through the meager light at the opposite wall of the tiny cell. *None of those places was near as mean and tough as this one is. But there wasn't one of them that couldn't be got out of, if a man put his mind to it, so what you got to do is take it easy. Eat the apple a bite at a time, and pretty soon there won't be nothing left but the core.*

He stood up and began looking around the cell. The walls were made of sandstone blocks, and bore the marks of the drills and wedges that had been used to shape the blocks. In the foot or so of space between the end of the bunk and the back wall, he found a battered tin bucket. He didn't really need to look at the bucket; its smell told him the bucket was his toilet.

On the floor beside the bucket lay a pottery bowl. Longarm picked it up and looked at it. The edges were chipped, and in one place a triangle of clay had been broken out of the rim. A thick film of rancid grease lined the bowl. The corners of his mouth turned down in disgust. He stepped to the vest-pocket-sized window, tossed the bowl through the bars, and heard it shatter on the hard ground when it landed.

Standing on tiptoe to see the ground outside, Longarm could make out the shards from the bowl strewn over the hard soil, but for all anybody knew, they could have been lying there for weeks.

Still poised on the toes of his loose, ill-fitting brogans, Longarm examined the limited vista with interest. A few inches below the window, a dead expanse of dry, colorless earth extended to a dropoff that Longarm supposed was the bed of the Colorado River, and through the swirling of heat-hazed air he could make out the shapes of the bluffs across the stream, reduced by the roiled air to shadows seen through a veil.

Restlessly, Longarm began pacing the cell floor from the window to the door: three paces to the door, three paces back to the window. Each time he reached the door, he paused long enough to peer through the iron grille fixed into its sturdy planks. He could see the whipping post, the iron box, and the well, outlined against the sunlit wall at the opposite end of the yard.

After the first few circuits, sweat began pouring off Longarm's face. It trickled down his neck and mingled with the wetness that was being drawn by the hot air from his shoulders and torso, soaking through the thin fabric of his prison outfit.

By then the routine of three paces each way had become as boring as sitting on the bunk. Longarm stopped at the door and fixed his face to the grill, hoping to see some sign of movement in the yard. He was ready to give up even that hope after standing motionless for several minutes. He turned slowly away from the door, tired of standing, but reluctant to stretch out on the thin, foul-smelling, straw-filled pad that covered the bunk's plank surface. He'd just accepted the idea of lying down when he heard a faint hissing.

Keeping his voice low, Longarm asked, "Somebody there?"

"Yeah, greenie," a whispered reply came. "Conyers. Next

cell to yours. Seen you brought in a while ago, wondered who you might be."

"Name's Long."

"Oh, shit! The marshal that sold out?"

"I guess that fits me as good as anything else. How'd you hear about me in a place like this?"

"Hell, every con here knows what happened up in Prescott. We been looking for you to get here. There ain't no place else you could be sent but here."

"How'd the news travel so fast? The trial's only been over with for a few days."

"Guard detail goes into Yuma City most every day. Guards talk. We hear 'em."

"Makes sense, I guess," Longarm whispered.

"I'm sorry for you, Long. I hate your guts, but I'm sorry for you just the same."

"That don't follow."

"No. I guess not. A lot of us feel that way, though."

Longarm found himself falling into the clipped pattern of speech used by men who must speak covertly and face interruption at any minute. He asked, "Mind saying why?"

"Got no use for turncoats. Got no use for lawmen."

"But you're still sorry for me?"

"Yeah. Everybody's laying for you, didn't you know?"

"I can figure the guards. Not anybody else, though."

"Some of us got friends you put away."

"Any of your friends?"

"No. But you was a lawman."

"That's all the reason you got?"

"It's all I need."

"How about the others?"

"No, Long. I don't peach."

"That's what you call it?"

"Or snitching."

"How'm I going to find out?"

"You will, soon enough."

"I won't push nobody."

Conyers chuckled grimly. "You can't, in here. You're a con. A green one, too."

"That mean something?"

"Sure. Until you learn the ropes."

81

"I pick things up fast."

"Don't be too fast."

"Any reason?"

"Just that I'm sorry for you."

"Thanks, Conyers."

"None needed." The unseen convict paused. "Give you one thing."

"Be glad to have it."

"Watch Feeney."

"Who's Feeney? A guard?"

Conyers snorted. "Worse. Yard boss."

Longarm had heard the term before, but wanted to make sure he understood what his neighbor was getting at. He asked, "What's that mean?"

"About anything Feeney wants it to."

"He's got a deal with the guards?"

"No deal. Just understood."

"Guards look the other way when he moves?" Longarm asked.

"Or go inside."

"Why Feeney? I never heard the name."

"He's heard yours."

"Something personal, then?"

"Not that I know of. Feeney'd feel the same about any lawman."

"And it just happens I'm the one that's in here."

"Comes down to that, I guess."

"Afraid I'll push him?"

For a moment there was no reply, then Conyers said, "No. Feeney's not scared of nothing."

"Don't aim to give me a chance to push him, then?"

"About that. He's done some talking."

"And feels like he's got to back it up, now that I'm here?"

"You're close to right. But I didn't say it."

"I don't peach either, Conyers."

"Good. Maybe you'll get along." There was a long pause, then Conyers added, "If you live long enough."

"I aim to stay alive." There was no reply from the adjoining cell. Longarm waited for a moment, then whispered, "Conyers?" He waited again, but there was only silence.

Longarm stood with his face close to the grille for several minutes longer, but nothing more was said from the next cell.

He gave up then, went back to the bunk, and stretched. He was so accustomed by now to the smell of the cell that the odors coming from the thin mattress didn't bother him as they had at first.

He stretched out on the bunk and stared up at the ceiling, trying to think of a way to make the connection he needed with Curley Parker, and how he could go about getting Parker to reveal the hiding place of the stolen army gold. He hadn't gotten anywhere when he heard voices coming from the yard.

Getting up, he went to the door and looked through the grille again. From the corner of the front wall, two convicts were carrying a huge cauldron between them, followed by a third, who was idly swinging an iron ladle. Behind them, his billy club dangling from one wrist by its leather thong, walked a guard whom Longarm hadn't seen before. The trio crossed the yard to the corner where the cells began, angling as they moved. When they stopped, they were about a third of the way down the first row of cells.

Pulling a massive ring filled with keys off the hook on his belt, the guard unlocked the door of the first cell. A convict came out carrying a bowl and held it for the convict wielding the ladle to fill. The man who filled the plates handed the convict a spoon when he'd emptied the ladle.

By the time the occupant of the first cell was on his way back, the man from the next cell was coming up to be served. When the six or eight prisoners in the cells at the end of the wall had been fed, the trio of convicts moved the cauldron farther along the line to feed the men in the cells at that end.

Longarm had noticed that the convict who filled the bowls gave each man a spoon when the ladle had been emptied, and for a moment he wondered why the spoons weren't simply left in the cells. Then the reason dawned on him.

A spoon could be converted into a dangerous weapon in the hands of a man who had nothing but time ahead of him. Flexing the bowl free at the point where it joined the handle turned the handle into a metal blank from which a fearsome knife could be made. Scraping the edges of the handle across the sandstone walls of a cell would sharpen them and form a point, which could be further honed on a leather boot sole. Long hours of labor would be required, but time would not matter; time was nothing to the man doing the job.

Longarm noticed that there were no conversational exchanges between the prisoners from the cells and those doing the serving. The convicts came from their cells, got their food and spoon, and went back at once to their small, steaming cubicles. No time was wasted; Longarm judged that all the prisoners could be fed in an hour or so.

He shook his head at the feeding operation, recognizing it as a model of cut-and-dried, impersonal efficiency, designed to get the prisoners fed in the shortest possible time, using a minimum of manpower. He watched the convicts being served until the food-bearers got so near the back row of cells that he could no longer see them through the door grating.

Even after he could no longer see the quartet serving the meal, Longarm found that he could judge the progress of the cauldron by the noise of the ladle clanking on the big pot's sides. The clattering was repeated once more; then, after a pause, it was resumed, and sounded even louder.

A little calculation led Longarm to conclude that the group of cells that included his should be served next, and it came to him suddenly that the only bowl intended for his use was the cracked and dirty piece of pottery that he'd tossed away. As hungry as he was getting by now, the memory of the battered, grease-encrusted bowl he'd broken still turned his stomach.

Knotting his jaw muscles pugnaciously, Longarm decided he'd have a new bowl, or know the reason why. He grinned ruefully when he realized that the reason might be to avoid a beating, and began thinking about the best way to get the one and avoid the other. He still hadn't made up his mind what to do when a key grated in the lock of his cell door and the door was flung open. The guard in charge of the feeding detail looked in.

"All right, get on out here with your bowl!" he commanded. "You might be a greenie, but you ain't so dumb that you ain't been watching us. You know what to do."

"I know what to do, but I ain't got a bowl to eat out of."

"What'd you do with the bowl the last man left?"

Using the careful phrasing that had popped into his mind at the last possible moment, Longarm replied, "I sure didn't see nothing I'd call a bowl in here."

With a flick of his pale, cold eyes, the guard looked around the bare little cell. "Maybe it got busted when they carried the last con outa here," he said reluctantly. "You'll have to wait, then. I ain't going to stop my crew for you. I'll send Feeney back with your supper as soon as we've fed the others."

Slamming the door, the guard moved out of Longarm's sight, but not out of his hearing. He heard the door of the next cell being opened and saw its inmate carrying his bowl to the invisible cauldron. It was not until then that the full meaning of what the guard had said hit Longarm.

Now just what the hell did he mean when he said they had to carry out the last man that had this cell? he asked himself. *I ain't no spookier'n the next man, but I'd sure like to know it if I'm going to be sleeping in a dead man's bed!*

Moving up to the grille in the cell door, Longarm watched the progress of the crew carrying the cauldron when it came in sight again, working up the side of the enclosure on his left; he hadn't had a chance to watch the guard who'd taken Tom Boone to a cell on that side of the yard, and he wanted to spot the exact cell the Secret Service man occupied.

Boone came out of a door halfway up the tier. Counting from the front wall, Longarm decided the cell number was in the high thirties, probably thirty-eight or thirty-nine, which was close enough to serve his purpose at the moment. He watched Boone get his bowl filled and walk back to his cell, then the door was closed and the supper crew moved on up the line.

Each time he saw a prisoner come out to get his bowl filled, Longarm's mouth began to water. His breakfast in Yuma City had been less than generous, and he'd eaten it more than twelve hours ago. He went back and sat on the bunk and waited.

A long time seemed to pass before he heard boot soles grating on the packed dirt of the prison yard outside his cell. Stepping up to the door, Longarm looked out and saw the convict who'd been dishing up from the cauldron standing in front of his cell, holding a bowl in his hand.

"I was wondering if I was ever going to get fed," Longarm said. "From what the guard said, I got the idea the last man in this cell starved to death."

"No. He just up and died, nobody knows why."

"You'd be Feeney, I suppose," Longarm said. "The guard told me your name when he said he'd send you back with my supper."

"I'm Feeney, all right," the convict replied. "And I don't

have to ask who you are. You're the damn turncoat marshal named Long, the one they call Longarm."

"That ain't exactly a secret. I'd imagine everybody in here knows about me."

"They do," Feeney said. "But maybe all of 'em ain't as glad to see you as I am."

"I ain't exactly sorry to see you. I been waiting so long, I'd just about give you up."

"Hell, I had to eat my supper first. I wouldn't put off my own meal just to bring some slop out to the likes of you."

"Slop or not, I'll be glad enough to get it."

Longarm could sense the antagonism flowing toward him from the convict, but had no idea what its reason might be. He couldn't remember ever having seen the man before.

He studied Feeney as they talked. The convict boss wasn't tall, but he made up for that in the depth and breadth of his torso. Even under the loose jacket he wore, Longarm could see the bulging of powerful muscles. Feeney's face was not an attractive one. His jaw was squared off under a pair of thick, twisted lips, and his face had a few lumps and scars, bespeaking an active temper that had led him into countless brawls. His brows bulged above puffy eyelids that made his eyes mere slits.

Feeney said, "You'll get fed in time. I've got something to say first."

"I'd be obliged if you'll wait and say it later. Why don't you just pass me my supper so I won't starve to death before we get better acquainted."

"You'll get it when I've had my say," Feeney answered.

"Go ahead and say and get it over with, then."

"Before you went crooked, you put away a hell of a lot of good men, Longarm."

"I guess so. None that didn't deserve to be put away, though." Longarm remembered his undercover role in time to add quickly, "At least that's the way I used to look at it."

"Most of us in here feel like you might still look at it that way, Long."

"I don't see why. I'm a convict now, just like all the rest of you in here."

"Not the way we look at it. You know, none of us got any use for a lawman, and a lawman that switches over's just as apt as not to switch back, so we got even less use for him."

"There ain't much room for me to switch back in, Feeney. By the time that judge up in Prescott finished with me, I was in the soup so deep there's not any way for me to swim out."

"That's as it might be," Feeney said. "But I got a personal score to settle with you, Long. One that's been waiting for quite a while."

"I never brushed up against you in any of the cases I can recall, Feeney."

"Not me, no. But I guess you'd remember a fellow called Long Tom Luke?"

"Oh, sure. He used to steal horses down here in Arizona Territory someplace."

"He did until you tricked him. Suckered him into a showdown and killed him."

"Well, that ain't exactly the way it happened. Long Tom was gunning for me. He finally caught up with me, but I managed to draw faster'n he did."

"So you say. Well, I'll tell you something. Long Tom Luke was the best sidekick I ever rode the owlhoot trail with."

"Funny I never run into you, when I was looking for him to bring him in."

"You was just lucky. If I'd of been there, Long Tom'd still be alive and kicking."

Longarm wanted to avoid the trouble he could smell brewing. Carefully keeping his voice neutral, he told Feeney, "Well, if that's your opinion, I guess you're entitled."

Feeney went on as though Longarm hadn't spoken. "Now I'll tell you something else. I know that nobody could ever take Long Tom in a fair facedown. I say you tricked him."

"You say wrong, Feeney. But that's over and done with. It happened quite a while back, as I recall."

"Not so far back that I've forgot it. But you can't call the shots in here, Longarm. I'm the boss of the yard in this prison, if you hadn't heard."

"Seems I did hear somebody mention it."

"All the cons toe my line, Long. When I say froggie, they hop. The guards let me alone too, they know they can't run this place without me. And that means I've got you where I want you."

"Listen, Feeney, there's not a man in any of these cells, and that includes you and me, who ain't got enough trouble."

"Don't include me in anything you say. I can handle any amount of trouble you try to give me."

"Look here, Feeney, I ain't out to bother nobody. I aim to let everybody alone while I'm in here, and all I want is for them to leave me alone."

"That ain't going to happen, Long. You was on the wrong side of the law too many years."

"Dammit, I'm on the other side now!"

"And we all know how you got there, selling out one of us after you'd took his money to let him go free."

"Now that ain't the way it happened! All that come out at my trial."

"Trial!" Feeney snorted. "That shows you ain't changed a damn bit! Nobody in here's got any use for trials and judges, Long! Shit! Deep down inside, you're still a lawman!"

Longarm saw that nothing he could say was going to convince Feeney. He changed tactics. "All right, Feeney. If you start stirring things up, I'll just have to stir 'em a little bit myself. I guess you know what that'll start."

"Whatever starts, I'll be the one to finish it."

"You're biting off more'n you can chew."

"That's my lookout, Long. I'm going to get you. I'll tell you that now, so it'll be on your mind. I want you to lay awake at night wondering if I'm going to make my move the next day. I don't have to hurry. We're both going to be in here awhile."

From across the yard a man called out, "Feeney! What in hell's keeping you so long? Get back over to the kitchen on the double! Our shift's over and we want to close things up!"

"See there?" Feeney said. "You've already begun getting me in trouble! You just remember what I said, Long. I meant every word of it."

"You've said it, I heard it," Longarm said angrily. He'd given up any hope of reasoning with Feeney. "Now pass me my supper and get the hell away so I can eat it in peace!"

"Sure." Feeney hawked and spat in Longarm's bowl, on top of the stew on which a film of grease was beginning to congeal. He unlocked the cell door and opened it wide enough to slide the bowl in on the floor, then slammed and locked the cell before Longarm could move. "Enjoy your supper, Long!"

For a moment Longarm stood looking at Feeney's back as the convict walked across the yard. Then he bent down and picked up the bowl of stew. He looked at it, disgust battling with hunger. Moving to the window, he took the spoon from the bowl and carefully scraped away the top layer, emptying each spoonful out the window as he removed it. When he'd removed the crust of grease and the blob of spittle deposited by Feeney, Longarm sat down on the side of the bunk and began to eat hungrily.

Chapter 9

Longarm hadn't realized how cramped he'd gotten to feeling in the confinement of his cell, until he was released at the end of the week for the morning exercise period. Even his breakfast had tasted better, though after seven straight mornings he'd come to detest the grits boiled with salt pork that was the standard morning menu. His twice-daily trips to get his food were the only times he'd been out of his cell, and he didn't count them as having been out at all.

Though the morning was still young when the cell doors were opened for the convicts to go into the yard, the little cubicle Longarm occupied was already steaming hot, and he was sweating profusely. He'd been unable to shave for six weeks, and though he could still sweep his mustache into its longhorn curve, his cheeks and chin had sprouted more than a half-inch of crisply curled beard, and the sweat that collected in it was causing his face to itch in a maddening fashion.

He stepped out of the door into the yard, and though the morning air was already beginning to warm up, it was clean and relatively free from odors, and refreshed him like a tonic. He could still smell the miasma of the prison that hung over the yard, but at least it was diluted enough so that the odor wasn't as overpowering as it was in the tiny, almost airless cells.

When Longarm got outside, two guards he didn't recognize were still unlocking doors. The guards patrolling the prison's perimeter on the walkway above the cells were no longer watching the area around the prison. They faced inward now, their rifles moving slowly in arcs that covered the yard.

Only about half the cells had been opened, and he could see that several minutes would pass before they'd reach Tom Boone's cell. The convicts were following a pattern, and Longarm had watched their movements enough through the grille in his cell door to be able to do as the others did.

Immediately on getting out, the inmates carried their toilet buckets to a wheeled trough placed in the center of the yard, emptied them, sloshed the empty buckets in a barrel that stood beside the trough, then carried them back to their cells. After that, the men headed for the latrine that occupied a corner of the enclosure beside the first row of cells, then struck a beeline for the well.

Longarm took his own bucket and dumped it, rinsed it in the already dirty water of the barrel, and took it back to the cell. He visited the latrine, then followed the pattern he'd seen set by other inmates and started for the well, where by now most of the convicts had already gathered. Except for the sentries patrolling along the walkway above the cells, there were no guards in sight. Longarm had already noted, while watching from his cell, that the guards stayed out of the yard as much as possible during exercise periods.

So did Feeney. The self-styled boss of the yard hadn't said much to Longarm after the first night, though he'd been with the supper detail almost every evening. Just the same, Longarm looked around the yard for him. There was no sign of the yard boss, however. Neither was there any sign of Boone, though the door of his cell was now standing open.

Making his way slowly toward the well, Longarm reminded himself that he'd have to work out some way of communicating with Boone. When he and the Secret Service man and Glass had discussed the problem he now faced, they'd agreed that trying to prearrange a method of communicating in the prison would be time wasted, that it could only be done by the two men after they'd seen the layout of the cells they'd occupy.

In the meantime, Longarm did not want to get too close to Boone's cell, or seem to be waiting for him in the yard. The success of the scheme they were trying to bring off depended on keeping up the pretense that they were enemies.

As Longarm got closer to the well, the convicts who'd been grouped around the low stone curbing began drifting away. By the time he reached it, the well was deserted. The men who'd been there drinking had pulled back in the shade, close to the cell doors, and were watching him closely. Convicts coming from their cells on the opposite side of the yard almost invariably headed directly for the well, but those approaching now veered away before reaching it as soon as they saw Longarm standing there.

Longarm needed no one to tell him that Feeney had been at work. The boss of the yard must have spent quite a bit of time spreading the word that the turncoat federal marshal didn't exist as far as the inmates of the Arizona Territorial Prison were concerned. With a mental shrug, Longarm picked up one of the clay pots that was lying beside the curb and dipped it into the water. He drank slowly; the water hadn't yet had time to heat, as it would later, under the beating rays of the desert sun.

Putting down the pot from which he'd drunk, Longarm started toward the wall. As he got closer, the convicts seemed to melt away without appearing to do so. Nor could they seem to see Longarm. He looked from one small group to another, but even those at whom he looked directly refused to meet his gaze. To a man, they acted as though he was invisible. He walked on into the shade cast by the wall and sat down, leaning his back against it. The men who'd been standing close to the spot edged away.

Longarm noticed that as soon as he'd left the well, the normal activity around the low curb had resumed. He saw Tom Boone among the convicts dipping their drinking pots in the water, but made a point of looking at Boone only in passing, as he'd looked at the others. Boone avoided looking directly at Longarm too.

One of the convicts sauntered over from the wall to the well and picked up the pot Longarm had used. He held it to his nose and sniffed noisily. "This damn pot stinks," the man announced loudly. "Smells like some dirty motherfucking turncoat lawman's been using it. It ain't fit for a decent man to drink out of no more."

Whirling around, the convict threw the pot at the wall where Longarm was sitting. Longarm saw the pot sailing toward him and saw that either accidentally or by the thrower's design, it was going to miss his head by a few inches. He sat calmly, and when the pot shattered on the wall only inches from his face, he did not flinch, even though a few chips stung his cheek.

"You ain't very good at aiming," Longarm told the man who'd thrown the pot. "Go on, pick up another one and try again. Maybe you'll do better next time."

For a moment the convict who'd thrown the pot stared at Longarm, his face bewildered. He'd been holding himself tensed, ready to meet the angry rush he'd expected Longarm to make. As his muscles relaxed, the convict deflated so visibly that a few snickers rose from the men near enough to the well to have witnessed the entire incident. The pot-thrower heard the chuckles, turned angrily to face the men who'd uttered them, saw no sympathy in their faces, and stomped away, muttering to himself.

Longarm leaned his head back against the wall and closed his eyes. He'd been sitting in this position for several minutes when he heard a whisper in a voice that was strange to him.

"You handled that pretty smooth, Long. Feeney's going to be fit to be tied when he hears about it."

Longarm did not open his eyes or reply. In a moment the voice reached him again.

"Damn it, I know you're hearing me, Long. I want to have a talk with you. From what Conyers told me, you ain't afraid of Feeney. That makes you the kind of man I'm looking for."

Longarm wasn't sure he could master the convict trick of talking without moving his lips, but he decided to try. Holding his mouth stiff, he made an effort to form the words in his throat and project them in a whisper as he replied, "If I knew why you're looking for men that ain't afraid of Feeney, I might want to talk to you too."

"I know what Feeney's had to say about you," the voice said.

"Conyers tell you that too?"

"Save your breath. I'm asking are you interested."

"Maybe."

"Watch me when I walk over to the box, so you'll know me. We'll talk when we come out this evening."

Without seeming to do so, Longarm slitted his eyes open. A stocky, swarthy convict walked slowly away from the wall to the box and sat down on its edge. He did not face Longarm, but Longarm knew he was watching. He nodded almost imperceptibly. After a few moments the convict got up and walked across the yard to join another group of inmates.

Longarm stayed where he was for a few minutes, then stood up and stretched and, as a number of the other inmates were doing, wandered around the yard with seeming aimlessness, as though he were simply stretching his legs before the exercise period ended. He kept his eyes busy, though, trying to spot Tom Boone in the constantly shifting crowd of convicts, all of whom looked very much alike in the same shapeless clothing.

He saw Boone at last, coming out of the latrine, and changed his direction with the same seeming aimlessness that had marked his stroll thus far. Longarm dropped his head as he walked, to give him an excuse for bumping into Boone. They looked at one another, standing motionless for a split second after they'd bumped together.

"Fight!" Longarm hissed in a whisper.

Boone swung, and Longarm countered the blow, saying as he did so, "Look out for Feeney."

Drawing back and dancing on his toes, his fists jabbing at empty air, Boone replied, "I know. Lucky. Parker's in the cell next to me." He started another swinging blow at Longarm's head.

Longarm let Boone's fist graze his cheek, and dropped to the ground. Boone fell on top of him. "Work detail tomorrow. We'll both be on it. Talk then."

By the time Longarm rolled over, trying to dislodge the Secret Service man, guards were running to stop the fight. Boone was grapped and pulled off Longarm. Longarm sat up, shaking his head as though he were dazed. One of the guards bent over to pull him to his feet; Longarm recognized him as Jackson, the guard who'd been with Freeler the day before.

"All right, Long!" Jackson said sharply. "The fight's over. Why'd you start it, anyhow? You know you get the box for fighting in the yard!"

"I didn't start it!" Longarm retorted, pointing an accusing finger at Boone. "He did."

"I seen it from the beginning," one of the guards patrolling on the walkway called. "The turncoat bastard's telling the truth, the other con swung first."

"Not until he'd cussed me!" Boone said.

"Both of you shut up, now!" the guard holding Boone commanded sharply.

"There's bad blood between these two, Mosk. You know that?" Johnson said to the second guard.

"So I heard. But Fritz up there, he'd know who started it. Hell, I think they both oughta go in the box, though."

Jackson asked, "Can you handle both of 'em while I go see how many days he wants to give 'em?"

Mosk jerked his head toward the guards on the walkway. "I don't look for 'em to give me any trouble. Go ahead."

Jackson went off in the direction of the office and in a few moments came back, shaking his head in bewilderment.

"Warden Crawford must be getting soft," he told Mosk. "He said let 'em both go, as long as there wasn't one of us guards involved. Said they're greenies, don't know the rules yet."

"That ain't like the old man," Mosk said. His bewilderment now matched that shown by Jackson. "Up to now, he's been tougher'n a boot sole on cons for fighting in the yard."

"Well, he's the boss," Jackson shrugged. "If he says let 'em off, I guess we do it." He turned to Longarm and Boone. "It looks like you two are lucky this time. But if either one of you gets into a fight here in the yard again, by God, I'll throw you in the box myself without asking the warden."

Longarm and Boone nodded together. Then Boone faced Longarm and raised his voice as he said, "That's not going to stop me from getting even, you double-crossing son of a bitch!"

"Shut up, Thomas!" Jackson commanded. "And both of you get on back to your cells." He raised his voice and called, "Exercise period's over! Everybody back inside!"

Slowly the convicts began moving back to their cells. Longarm and Boone were escorted to theirs by the two guards, who then began locking the other cells. After the last key had grated in a lock and the guards had left the yard, Longarm lay down on his bunk and stared up at the ceiling.

His thoughts were interrupted by a hiss, and then the whispered call, "Long!" which he recognized at once as coming from Conyers, in the adjoining cell. He got up and went to the door.

"What's on your mind, Conyers?" he asked, pressing his face against the door grating.

"You going to throw in with Recco?"

"Who's Recco?"

"You oughta know, you and him was talking."

"That's his name? Recco?"

"Don't shit me, Long. You know Blade Recco."

"Never saw him before today."

"It don't matter. You in with him now?"

"In on what?"

"Dammit, don't play cagy! Are you in or not?"

"That depends. Are you?"

Conyers did not answer at once. At last he said, "I don't know."

"I'd know more, if you'd tell me what Recco's doing."

"You telling me he didn't say?"

"I swapped maybe ten words with Recco, Conyers," Longarm evaded.

"He didn't tell you, then?"

"Tell me what?"

"How he's trying to push out Feeney."

"That what he's doing?"

"He has been since I don't know how long."

"He got a chance of making it?"

Conyers was silent for a moment, then he said, "Hard to say. Feeney's been awful pushy of late."

"And some of you don't like it?"

"It gets awful old. Like he done you that first night."

Longarm decided it was time he found out more about the source of Feeney's power. He asked Conyers, "How'd Feeney get to be yard boss, anyhow?"

"Killed the one before him."

"Killed him his own self?"

"Maybe. Maybe not. Nobody's sure."

"Recco'd have to do the same thing, then?"

"More'n likely."

"Can he?"

"Recco's tough. Maybe as tough as Feeney."

"He'd have to be tougher, to take over."

"I guess."

Longarm asked, "Where does the warden fit into this yard-boss business?"

"He stands for it. Saves trouble for him."

"And the guards too, I guess."

"Sure. More them than the warden."

"But Feeney does pretty much what he wants to."

"Hell, any yard boss does."

"I might like to be yard boss myself," Longarm said.

"No," Conyers replied quickly.

"Why not? Don't you think I'm tough enough?"

"Oh, you're a hardcase, from what I've heard."

"But that ain't good enough?"

"No."

Conyers didn't explain. Longarm waited a moment, and when he saw that nothing more was going to be said, he told Conyers, "Go on. What else?"

"You ain't regular."

"Because I used to be a lawman?"

"No. You're a double-crosser. And a turncoat."

"But I'm a convict now."

"Not a regular one."

"So you said. How do I get to be regular?"

"Do more time. Five-to-ten ain't nothing."

"It is to me."

"Feeney's a lifer. So is Recco."

"Is that what it takes to be yard boss?"

"Pretty generally."

"That being so, I guess I ain't interested."

"You're in with Recco, then?"

"I never said that."

"Well, you damn sure ain't in with Feeney."

"No," Longarm agreed. "I damn sure ain't."

"It's got to be Recco, then."

"You mean I got to pick one or the other?"

"That's how it is. Let me know when you make up your mind."

As abruptly as he had the night before, Conyers fell silent and Longarm's repeated efforts to get him to respond were futile.

Back on his bunk, Longarm thought, *Things are looking better every minute, old son. All you got to do is stand clear and let Recco and Feeney fight it out. Maybe help Recco a little bit to get him on your side. Looks like the damn yard boss is a better man to have with you than the warden. So play your cards close to your vest, and you'll be out of here a lot faster than you figured, if you got just a little bit of luck, too.*

Soon after the afternoon exercise period began, Longarm located Blade Recco. The swarthy man was sitting on his heels near the doorless entrance of the latrine. He caught Longarm's eye and shook his head, jerking a thumb at the constant stream of inmates entering and leaving. Longarm confined his walking to an area where he was sure Recco could see him, and looked at the waiting man occasionally. Finally, when the latrine traffic had subsided, Recco nodded almost imperceptibly and Longarm entered the latrine.

At the territorial prison, the latrine was nothing more than a slit trench that had to be straddled by those using it. The odor rising from the trench was gaggingly strong, and Longarm stayed as far away from it as he could.

Recco came in at once, and Longarm saw the bulky forms of two convicts move to stand in front of the door.

Recco said, "Don't worry, the cons know I don't bugger." When he saw Longarm's puzzled frown, he explained, "That's the punks' trick. Two of 'em block the door and two more come in for their jollies. It's Feeney's trick too, when some soft greenie comes in and he wants to put it to him."

"But you don't?"

"Nah. I wake up with a hard, I help it along a little myself. I got no use for buggering." He looked Longarm up and down and grinned lopsidedly. "So you're the famous Longarm. And you sold out and got collared. Hell, you just wasn't smart the right way. One of us cons could've pulled it off without no trouble."

"I didn't come in for a lecture, Recco. You said you wanted to talk about Feeney. I'm listening."

"Feeney ain't going to be yard boss much longer."

"I heard you're out after him."

"Where in hell did you hear that?"

"I disremember."

"Damn, you got lines out already, ain't you? Maybe you ain't as big a greenie as I figured."

"Maybe. Go on, Recco. Where do I come in?"

"You're still too green to know how much good a yard boss can do you when you're with him, Long."

"I'm getting a good idea, watching Feeney. I didn't see him in the yard this morning or just now. Where is he?"

"Stuffing his gut in the kitchen, most likely."

"Get down to business, Recco. I ain't got much patience."

"You're a tough rooster, Long. Most of us, we get soft in here. I don't, but most cons do. I can use your muscles."

"What's in it for me?"

"Better grub. No work details. And a chance to get outa here pretty quick."

Longarm stared. He was remembering the Arizona Territorial Prison's reputation as escape-proof. He asked Recco, "You figuring to bust out?"

"Not tomorrow or next week, but soon enough."

Longarm shook his head. "It won't work, Recco."

"With the help I got outside, it'll work."

"Nobody's made it out of here standing up yet."

"Then my bunch will be the first, won't they?"

"*If* you do it. How many you got with you?"

"That's my business."

"How're you going to handle it?"

"Later I might tell you. Not now."

"I'm interested. What do you expect me to do?"

"Nothing now. Maybe a lot, later. You're in, then?"

"I'm in."

"Good. From now on we don't notice each other."

"Fair enough." Out of habit, Longarm extended his hand.

Recco looked at the hand and his lips curled back. "I only shake with friends, Long. Not with you. If I didn't know you're too green to sell me out, I wouldn't be talking to you now. I'll use you, Long, here and outside, after the break. That don't mean I want anything to do with you."

Turning abruptly, Recco walked out of the latrine, pushing aside the men he'd had stationed at the door.

Longarm stood staring after the burly convict. Then he saw the grim humor of his situation, grinned wryly, and followed Recco outside.

During the morning exercise period, the yard had been relatively cool, with a wide line of shade along the east wall. Now the sun was high and its burning rays beat down on almost the entire area; it was very little cooler outdoors than it was in the cells. Most of the inmates were in the corner where the whipping post stood. It was the only place where there was any shade, and the small triangular area into which the broiling sunshine did not reach was crowded.

Longarm started to walk slowly across the yard. The time he'd spent in the almost airless latrine had started his face itching furiously and he stopped at the well and dipped up a pot of water and, after drinking, poured another potful over his head. The drenching washed part of the sweat-salt out of his beard and relieved the itching a little bit, and he felt better as he continued across the yard. Stopping at the edge of the shade, he looked at the prison's inmates.

He'd had little opportunity before to observe them as a group. He saw Tom Boone, squatting on his heels against the wall next to a prisoner with a shock of snow-white hair rising from a head that was half bald. Boone didn't look directly at Longarm, but flicked his eyes at the white-haired man, whom Longarm took to be Curley Parker, the man who held the secret of the gold-laden army pay wagon that was their real objective. Ignoring Boone, Longarm swept the crowded corner with his eyes.

Most of the faces he saw were bearded, like his own, and all of them were still strange. He noticed Feeney, with three or four of his cronies crowding close to him, a little apart from the rest of the men, at the edge of the shaded area. One of the group around Feeney was the man who'd tossed the pot at Longarm during the morning exercise period. Longarm wondered if one of the others might be Conyers, whom he'd never seen. Each time he'd looked at the cell next to his, the door had been closed, or yawning open and the cell empty.

Recco was at the opposite corner and, like Feeney, he had a few men around him. Recco looked directly at Longarm for an instant, but shifted his gaze quickly. The others in the group were the same varied array that Longarm had seen dozens of times before in the towns where his cases had taken him.

Most of the men looked young; aside from Parker, Longarm saw only a half-dozen graybeards among the inmates. Those who were talking spoke prison-style, in voices so low that none of the conversation was audible, though a faint humming, like a hive of bees, rose from the group. When he'd finished scanning the crowd and saw no other familiar faces, he turned away from the triangle and looked out across the deserted yard.

Longarm's fine-honed senses warned him of the danger even before he felt the touch of the knife on his back. The first warning came when the buzzing hum of low-voiced conversation that had filled the air stopped abruptly.

Suddenly aware that something unusual must have caused the sudden silence, Longarm started to swivel on his heel to look for the reason. Before he could turn, he felt his loose prison jacket twitch as though a hand had touched it. Sweeping his own hand back, Longarm caught the wrist of the man who held the knife that had passed through the fabric of the jacket on its way into his back.

A line of pain seared Longarm's side as the point of the knife ran shallowly through his skin for a few inches before the grasp of his strong hand on the knife-wielder's wrist forced the tip of the weapon away. Cloth ripped sibilantly as the knife cut a gash in Longarm's jacket. Then Longarm had completed his turn and was facing the inmate who'd attacked him.

For a moment the two stood side by side, then Longarm's greater strength enabled him to twist the man around and force his arm up high behind his back, between his shoulder blades. The attacker winced as Longarm levered even higher the hand that held the knife. Under the merciless clamping of Longarm's hand around his wrist and the pain of his shoulder, which was on the brink of being dislocated, the attacker opened his hand.

Longarm caught the knife before it fell to the ground, and slid his hand under his jacket to hide the weapon. He could see the face of his assailant now, and a frown swept across his own bronzed countenance. The attacker was young, not yet out of his twenties. He wore a straggly blonde beard and had long, unkempt hair. But Longarm had never seen the man before.

"Who set you on me?" Longarm whispered harshly, his lips no more than an inch from his captive's ear.

"No—nobody," the attacker replied in an equally low voice.

"Was it Feeney?" Longarm asked. The man shook his head. "Thomas?" Longarm demanded. Again the knife-wielder's headshake followed the name. "Who, then?" Longarm pressed.

"Nobody," the stranger repeated. "You put my partner away, up in Brigham City. I'd've got you before now, if I wasn't inside here."

Longarm made a quick judgment. He released the man's wrist and gave him a shove. "Go on back to whoever put you up to this," he said, his voice loud enough to carry to the other inmates. "I'm letting you off easy, but you pass the word that the next man that jumps me ain't going to be able to walk away!"

Chapter 10

"Eat fast," the guard who accompanied the three inmates with the breakfast pot told Longarm. "You and the other greenie got a work detail soon as you've ate."

Longarm was standing outside his cell, waiting for the inmate with the ladle to dish up his morning meal of grits boiled with salt pork. He'd been surprised to see that Feeney wasn't doing the serving, but guessed that the yard boss went around only at the evening meal.

He asked, "Work detail? Doing what?"

"You'll find out quick enough," the guard told him. "Go on, eat up. You better be ready when they come after you."

Longarm was hungry enough to eat every bite of the sandlike grits and glutinous fatback. He was scraping the dish when a key grated in the cell door lock and a guard he hadn't seen before stuck his bearded face in the door.

"All right, turn out," the man ordered. "Work detail."

Putting down the dish, Longarm stood up. His back and side still smarted from the knife cut he'd taken, but he moved easily enough. He'd hidden the knife as best he could in the thin straw mattress of the bunk. It was a prison-made weapon, fashioned from the handle of a spoon, but its point was like a needle and its blade had been honed to razor sharpness. This time Longarm didn't waste his breath asking questions. He went outside, and when the guard jerked a thumb toward the front of the yard, he started walking in that direction, the guard following him.

They'd gone only a few steps when the guard said, "Hold

up, you!" Longarm stopped and turned around. The guard said, suspicion in his voice, "I heard about the fight you and that other greenie had yesterday. You been in another fracas since then?"

Truthfully Longarm replied, "No."

"Then how'd you get all that blood on you?"

Faced with coming up in a hurry with a reason for the bloodstains, Longarm improvised.

"Maybe that old scratch I got on my back opened up again," he replied.

"Pull your jacket up. I want to see that place," the man said.

Longarm lifted the hem of the loose jacket. He'd looked at the knife wound earlier and seen that a scab had formed on it overnight. The guard peered at the shallow gash and snorted.

"Looks fresh to me," he said a bit uncertainly.

"Sure it does. It ain't all that old. You know, that wagon they brought me here in had a lot of snags in it."

"All right, I guess you're telling the truth," the guard said. "Let's get on to the job."

Boone and a second guard were waiting at the entrance to the latrine. A dirt-sled, with wide planks for runners and a box for a body, stood a few feet away. Studiously, Boone and Longarm ignored each other.

"Which one of you's going to shovel?" Boone's guard asked, looking from Boone to Longarm. When neither of them answered, he said, "I guess it don't matter. You"—he pointed to Longarm—"you got the longest arms. Strip off and grab the shovel. The other one can pull the sled."

It took Longarm only an instant to decide that he wanted to know badly enough to risk asking a question. "You mind telling me why I got to strip? That damn place in there's full of flies, and if I ain't got any clothes on, they'll drive me crazy."

"You don't have to if you don't feel like fighting flies," the guard replied. "But you'll be smeared with shit from top to bottom before you're finished. You won't be able to stand yourself until you get a clean suit, which'll be three weeks."

"Just thought I'd ask," Longarm nodded. He'd given up his long balbriggans on leaving Prescott, knowing the reputation the territorial prison had for being only slightly cooler than hell's hinges. Undressing was a matter of taking off his jacket and unbuttoning the baggy trousers, letting them drop to his feet. Bending, he untied the loose brogans and stepped out of them and the trousers at the same time.

"Jesus!" the guard gasped, Looking at Longarm's scarred torso. "You ain't hardly old enough to've been in the War."

"I made the army by a whisker a little spell before Appomattox."

"You got all them while you was just a lawman?"

"Every last one."

"Then you must've been in one hell of a lot of fights!"

"Enough to last me," Longarm said shortly, reaching for the long-handled scoop that leaned against the wall. "I'm ready to start when you say so."

Boone pulled the dirt-sled into the latrine, and Longarm planted his feet on either side of the slit trench and began shoveling. He soon discovered that the guard had been right. No matter how careful he was with the shovel, he could not keep from spattering himself with the semiliquid excrement as he brought the loaded shovel out of the pit and emptied it in the body of the sled.

Boone could stand far enough away to avoid the mess, and the guards stood in the doorway until he'd hauled the first two loads away and dumped them in a ravine a hundred yards distant from the prison walls. When Longarm began shoveling to fill the dirt-sled for the third time, the stench in the latrine had become so nauseating that the guards retreated, leaving Longarm and Boone alone for the first time.

As soon as he decided that he and Boone could talk safely, Longarm dropped his voice and, without interrupting the regular rhythm of his shoveling, asked the Secret Service man, "I guess that was Curley Parker setting by you yesterday evening?"

Boone nodded. "I haven't mentioned anything about the army gold yet, though. It's too early."

"Sure it is. But cut your time as short as you can. There's a bust-out in the making."

Boone's eyes widened. "The hell you say! Who's behind it?"

"Blade Recco, if you know who he is."

"I wouldn't know him if I saw him, but Parker's mentioned him. Recco and Feeney have a feud going on, you know."

"Looks like me and Feeney's got one going too. The fellow

that tried to knife me was likely Feeney's man."

"He didn't hurt you badly, did he?"

Longarm turned to show Boone the scabbed cut. "Nothing I can't get along with."

"What'd you do to rile Feeney?"

"He says I put one of his sidekicks away a while back. He's out to get me, all right."

Boone frowned thoughtfully. "There's no such thing as a secret in this damned place. I've heard about prison grapevines, but I didn't understand how good they are."

"That means we got to be careful is all, Tom. You're better off than I am. They figure you're one of them. Me, I'm still a lawman to most of 'em, and a turncoat one, at that."

"You'll have to be careful, then. You're still a target."

"I been one before. I'm able to handle it." Longarm dumped a final shovelful into the dirt-sled. "You better haul. If we take too long getting a load out, the guards are going to come in to find out why."

Boone hauled the dirt-sled away, and Longarm stepped to the door for a breath of fresh air. One of the guards had gone to escort Boone to the ravine where the dirt-sled was being emptied. It was a short haul, and the gate had been left open until they returned. The guard who'd remained behind was leaning against the wall, puffing on a cigar. He stood a good ten feet away, and Longarm's first thought was how easy it would be for him to get to the gate before the guard could catch him, armed as he was with only a billy club.

There'd still be a few obstacles, such as the guards on the walkway and the Gatling gun in the gate tower, but Longarm felt sure he could find a way to overcome them, once he was outside the gate. Then the guard spoke, and Longarm decided that he must have been reading his mind.

Without any preamble, the guard said quietly, "Don't get no ideas, greenie. You ain't got a chance of getting out. Them men up on the walk'd fill you full of lead before you got halfway to the gate."

"What give you the idea I was thinking anything like that?" Longarm asked, frowning.

"Hell, I know what you greenies think before you do. You might know crooks from the time when you was a lawman, but I know convicts. Your mule's just coming in the gate. Get back in there and start shoveling shit again."

Turning away, Longarm went back into the stinking latrine and waited impatiently for Boone to come in with the dirt-sled.

"One thing we got to do, Tom," he said as he attacked the mass in the slit trench again. "We got to figure out a way to let each other know when we got something important to pass on."

"That's been on my mind too," Boone replied. "Have you got any ideas?"

"About all I can come up with is some sort of signal we can make through the bars on the cell doors. I can just about make out your door when I squint off of one side of that hole in mine, so I guess you can see my door out of yours."

"I can, if I get over to one side of the door and look sideways. Why?"

"Well, if I got something to tell you, right after breakfast I'll poke my finger out between the bars and wiggle it. You do the same if you got something to pass on to me."

"Sounds all right. Then we'll say whatever we need to while we're going by each other in the yard."

"Something like that. We'll just have to do the best we can when we're around anybody else, like you did when you jumped me."

"We'll try it, then. I sure haven't got a better idea. We can't signal in the yard, we're not supposed to be on speaking terms."

"Good enough." Longarm paused in his shoveling long enough to wipe the sweat off his forehead with the back of his forearm. "About two more loads'll see this stinking job done. By the time I wash off, it'll be about time for us to have our spell in the yard. We'll try it out right after that."

Two more dirt-sled loads did finish the dunging-out of the pit, and as soon as Boone had left to drag the final load to the ravine, Longarm went outside.

"I guess I get to take me a bath, don't I?" he asked. "You was right about me not wearing clothes in there, but I sure can't put 'em on until I wash this shit off of me."

"A bath goes with the job," the guard told him. "Come on. Since there hasn't been any doctor here, we've been using the infirmary for a place where you cons can wash. But you'll have to haul your own water."

Standing in a washtub in the unused infirmary, Longarm was rinsing off the last thin lather of the yellow laundry soap he'd bathed with when Warden Crawford came into the room.

The warden was pale and walked unsteadily. He saw Longarm and stopped.

"I—I didn't expect to find anybody in here," he said. He frowned. "What are you doing here, Long? This isn't bath day."

"Don't let me bother you, Warden," Longarm said. "I just got finished cleaning the latrine, so the guard let me have a bath, even if I wasn't due one."

"I'm glad you're here." The warden paused, looked around the room and through the door opposite the one through which he'd entered, and finally peered out the window. "Good. There's nobody close enough to eavesdrop. How are you and your partner getting along? Are you making any progress?"

"Not much. Of course, our week in solitary ain't been over but a little while. Now that we can mix in with the convicts, maybe we can get someplace."

"I hope so. This—" Crawford gasped and grasped his stomach, clamping his hands around his midsection.

"You sick, warden?" Longarm asked.

"I—I don't feel very well. Haven't been feeling good all day. And Mrs. Crawford's gone into Yuma City and won't be back until late this evening."

"What about the doctor? Where's he?"

"We don't have a doctor on duty right now. The one we had quit to go to California, and they haven't found anyone to take his place yet." Crawford's face contorted in pain and he began to tremble. A chair stood near the door, and he stumbled over to it and sat down, saying, "I—I thought I might find some kind of medicine here that would help me."

"Give me about half a minute to get the rest of this soap off of me, and I'll see what I can do to help you," Longarm volunteered. He splashed water hurriedly over himself and, without waiting to dry off, stepped into his baggy pants.

One look at the warden told Longarm that Crawford needed more help than he could give him. He said, "You sit quiet, Warden. I'll go get one of the guards. Maybe they know more about sick folks than I do."

Both of the guards who'd been in charge of the work detail were standing outside the infirmary door. They came running when they saw Longarm come out, water streaming from his bare torso, and when he explained to them what was wrong, both hurried into the building.

107

Warden Crawford was still sitting in the chair, but now his face was ashen and his eyes had rolled up in his head. A foul smell filled the air, and under the chair a small pool of watery, greenish-yellow fecal discharge had collected.

"Hell, he's got the cholera!" one of the guards exclaimed. "I seen plenty of it, when I was down South during the War. If there's one thing I know, it's the cholera."

"What's good for treating it?" the other asked.

"Not much of anything," Longarm said, forgetting the rule that forbade prisoners speaking first to the guards. "You might see if there's some laudanum in the medicine chest, if this damn place had got a medicine chest. That'll sort of ease him, but it ain't going to cure him. He's either going to live or die."

Warden Crawford died shortly after midnight. By that time, four guards were writhing in the stomach-twisting paroxysms of the fast-acting illness, and a dozen of the inmates had also been stricken.

By noon of the next day, five of the fifteen guards had been laid low, and two of the four who'd been the first victims had died. Eighteen of the prisoners were ill in their cells, with other prisoners attending them, and four of the first twelve inmates to be stricken had succumbed.

Over the entire prison area the miasma of disease hung heavily, and while the guards who had escaped the illness kept the inmates in their cells, the precaution was not really necessary. Most of the inmates who were not sick were too shaken by the mass panic to think of trying to escape.

Shortly before noon of the fifth day, a detachment of mounted infantry from Fort Yuma arrived to take charge. With the soldiers came a military doctor and two hospital corpsmen, as well as the medicines necessary to treat the sick. The doctor at once set his corpsmen to work, banned the use of water taken from the well, and started the soldiers boiling all the water that was used for drinking or cooking.

Longarm found himself pressed into service first by the prison guards, then by the army. He did what he was told, and by the time the army arrived to take over, the enmity that had been general on the part of both guards and inmates had largely subsided.

Feeney was the exception. The yard boss used the influence he'd acquired by establishing himself as a middleman between the guards and inmates to secure himself a job as a mess orderly, and stayed close to the kitchen, which the army cook had taken over. With the army in control, Feeney lost his assumed authority, however. The worst he could do was to taunt Longarm, to repeat the threats he'd already made, and to promise that as soon as the army detachment left, he'd find a way to take the revenge he'd threatened.

By the end of the third week of army control of the prison, the epidemic had run its course. Those who'd been the sickest were still in bed, but those who had escaped the worst ravages of the cholera were able to move around again. Eight guards, nearly half of the total force, had died. Seventeen inmates were dead, and ten more were still bedridden.

When a new warden was appointed by the governor and arrived to take charge, the spirits of the prisoners began to perk up. Most of them resented the constant cell confinement the army had imposed, and were chafing to get back to the daily exercise periods in the yard.

"How much longer you think the damn army's going to stay?" Conyers asked in one of the whispered nighttime conversations he and Longarm had been having fairly frequently under the relaxed supervision that had been given the yard since the cholera hit.

"Soon as the new warden gets enough guards to keep the place running, I'd imagine."

"Sure, but when's that gonna be? He's been here near a week now, and I don't see he's doing much."

"You ought to be glad he ain't, Conyers."

"What in hell you mean by that?"

"Ain't you never heard about a new broom sweeping clean? Old Warden Crawford, now he knew the ropes, didn't have to prove it. This new man, he's going to have to show everybody what he can do. Chances are he'll be tougher'n nails, till he feels like he's setting firm in the saddle."

"Just the same, I wish we had him in charge instead of the damn army."

"Well, I reckon you'll get your wish pretty soon, and I sure hope you ain't sorry."

Conyers got his wish sooner than he'd expected. Four days later the inmates woke to find the mounted infantry company making preparations to ride out. By noon the army was gone, and at the time that had always been devoted to the exercise period, the prison guards began making their rounds, opening the cell doors and ordering the convicts out into the yard.

The exercise period was almost over before the new warden appeared. He was a small man, with a small mustache that he waxed into needle points that stuck out a full inch beyond his cheeks. Because of his small stature, he could not see the men well, so he climbed up onto an overturned barrel in order to speak to them after the guards had herded their charges to the center of the yard.

"You inmates don't know me," he began. "Few of you even know my name. I am Clinton Dade, your new warden, and you will call me Warden Dade if you should have occasion to address me. I see no reason for your having to address me. You will remember that you are here to be punished, and rigid discipline is part of your punishment." Dade had a rather thin voice, which tended to get lost in the open air. He went on, "You will continue to obey the same rules that have been in effect here. I will expect you to obey them, and will see that any violation of rules, no matter how slight, is suitably punished. Discipline has become lax during the recent misfortune. It will be enforced fully from this moment on."

Dade surveyed the inmates for a moment, his face expressionless. Then he stepped off the barrel and, without looking to the right or left, disappeared into the doorway leading to his office.

Longarm's face was expressionless too, as he stood watching the new warden leave. In the air of crisis that had engulfed the prison for the past month or more, he'd given very little thought to his mission. Now it had just come home to him that with Warden Crawford dead, he and Tom Boone faced a major problem. There was no one now, except Marshal Jim Glass and Billy Vail, who knew that they were in the prison on a case. As far as the new warden was concerned, they were simply two more inmates.

Well, old son, Longarm told himself, *you really are in a pretty pickle right now, and a real sour one too. That Dade don't act like he'd be a very understanding man to talk to, and he sure made it clear he didn't want no convicts bothering him. But he's the only man in here that can help me get this sour pickle sweetened up, so I got to try my luck.*

Longarm started for the warden's office and had almost reached the door before a guard stopped him. It was one of the new guards who'd come with Dade, replacing those who'd died during the cholera epidemic.

"You!" the guard called. "Where in hell you heading?"

"I got to talk to the warden right away," Longarm answered.

"By God, you must be a real soft-head! Didn't you just hear Warden Dade say he didn't wanta talk to none of you cons?"

"Oh, I heard him, all right. But I figure he'd want to talk to me, especially after he hears what I got to tell him."

"Suppose you tell me, and let me tell him."

Longarm shook his head. "I can't do that. What I got to tell the warden's real private."

"Sure. It always is. You're outa line and outa luck. The only way you'll get in to see the warden is to knock me down, and you know what happens to a con that hits one of us guards."

"Now, you know I ain't about to hit you, nor nobody—"

Longarm focused his eyes on the doorway behind the guard and opened them wide, as though we were seeing something that had frozen him into terror. When he saw Longarm's expression change, the guard swiveled around to look for himself. Longarm took a step forward, and before the guard knew what had happened, one of Longarm's big hands was clamped solidly over his mouth, and he had his free arm around the man and was lifting him off his feet.

He pushed through the door into the hallway, as the guard squirmed and kicked. Some of the kicks went home, but Longarm ignored them. He stopped in front of the door to the warden's office and whispered in his most grating voice, "Now knock on that door, damn it!" The guard knocked.

Dade called, "Come in."

Longarm commanded the guard, "Open the door, if you know what's good for you."

Dade glanced up from the papers on his desk, his mind still on whatever he was reading, saw the guard's uniform, and turned back to his reading for a moment. Then he realized what he'd really seen and swiveled his chair around to face Longarm and the guard.

"What the devil kind of game are you playing, Flaherty?" he asked the guard. "Having a convict carry you in—"

Longarm broke in on Dade's question. "He didn't have me carry him in, Warden Dade. Don't blame him. I sort of tricked him. It was the only way I could figure to get in to see you."

Flaherty had stopped struggling for a moment; but now he began squirming again, and muffled noises came from his throat as he tried to speak.

Dade said, "What's your name, prisoner? I'll see that you get flogged fro this!"

"My name's Long, Warden. Custis Long. Former deputy U.S. marshal, working out of the Denver office."

"Oh, yes!" Dade said, recognition in his voice. "The one they call Longarm. I recall your case well. It was reported very completely in the newspapers." He paused and went on, a thoughtful frown growing on his face, "I'm sure you know the prison rules. You know the punishment for striking a guard."

"I didn't strike Flaherty, Warden Dade. I just picked him up to help him into your office with me."

"Hmf," Dade grunted. "A hair-splitting lawyer too, I see. Well, you can put Flaherty down now. I'll think about your punishment later, but I'll listen to you for two minutes before I decide what to do with you."

Longarm released Flaherty. The guard drew his billy club as he spun around, but a sharp word from Dade stopped him from using it to bash Longarm's head.

Dade said to Longarm, "All right, go ahead."

"No, sir. What I got to say is just for you to hear, and nobody else. If you don't mind asking Flaherty to leave—"

"Long, are you insane?" Dade demanded.

"No, sir. Leastwise, not any crazier than anybody else. I know what I'm about, even if it might not look that way."

For a moment the warden seemed undecided, then he nodded to the guard. "Step outside, Flaherty. I'll listen to him alone." When the guard had closed the door behind him, Dade nodded to Longarm. "Go ahead. You have two minutes."

"Warden Dade, I ain't a real prisoner in here. I got sent up on a case that I'm working on. Warden Crawford knew about it, but he was the only one. Now I—"

"You don't have to go any further, Long," Dade broke in. "It's obvious you've cooked up some fancy lie that you think will deceive me and get you special privileges, or even a release, if I were fool enough to listen to you."

"No, sir! I'm telling gospel truth! It's a federal case that's real secret and damned important."

"You're trying my patience, Long," Dade snapped. "If you were in here on an assignment or a case, there'd be a record of it in Warden Crawford's files. There isn't. I've just finished going through them, and your name's not mentioned."

"It wasn't supposed to be! I told you, it's a secret! But if you want to find out, you can wire Marshal Glass in Prescott or Marshal Vail in Denver. They'll back me up!"

"You seem to be determined to underrate my intelligence, Long. Why, I'd look like a jackass if I sent the kind of message you're suggesting! I'd be the laughingstock of the territory!"

"Warden Dade," Longarm began desperately, "you've got to—"

"I don't have to do anything!" Dade retorted. "You're just another prisoner, Long! And if you bother me with your cock-and-bull yarns again, I'll have you on the whipping post!" He raised his voice. "Flaherty! Come get this prisoner! And if you ever let him get near me again, you'll be looking for a new job!"

Chapter 11

For the next two nights, Longarm slept with frustration. He thought about talking over the problem with Boone, but there was no way he could find for them to have a private discussion long enough to cover the entire subject. It was, Longarm concluded, something he'd have to work out by himself. For his part, Boone showed no inclination to talk to Longarm. He was devoting his attention to Curley Parker, and while Longarm hoped he was making progress in softening up the old bandit, he also worried that Boone might complete his job before the problem of getting out of the prison had been solved.

Around him, the prison and its guards and inmates were settling back to normal. Feeney resumed his regular rounds with the work detail that served supper, but he ignored Longarm. When the cauldron stopped to serve the group of cells that included Longarm's, and Longarm came out with his bowl, Feeney filled it without commenting or looking up. Longarm began to wonder why. Feeney didn't impress him as the sort who'd back down on a brag. Recco, too, seemed determined to keep his distance from Longarm. They passed each other in the yard occasionally, but neither showed any signs of recognition.

Another day slid past, then another, and nothing changed. Longarm's worry increased, and he forced his problems out of his mind now and then, hoping he'd unconsciously come up with a solution, as he'd done before on more than one occasion.

Longarm walked out of his cell when the guard unlocked the door for the morning exercise period. The heat of the day still lay ahead. Most of the inmates were on the east side of the yard, in the narrow strip of shade cast by the wall. They stood or hunkered down in small groups, three here, four there, a pair, occasionally a loner, with most of them in the area between the well and the door to the latrine. Except for the sentries who paced endlessly back and forth along the overhead walkway and those in the tower, there were no guards visible in the yard.

Longarm took his time, inspecting the groupings as he walked without seeming to show any interest in them. Blade Recco and two of his adherents were nearest to Longarm's path, but he angled away from them. Feeney was not among the inmates; he seemed to spend most of his time somewhere else during the yard periods, Longarm thought, and wondered where it could be.

Near the center of the wall, a half-dozen of the convicts had formed a rough circle and were playing an ancient children's finger game; Longarm remembered it from his own curtailed schooldays back in his West Virginia boyhood. It was a simple guessing game, played with nothing more than hands. Each player held out a fist, and at a count of three extended either an open hand or two fingers, or held his fist closed. Paper, scissors, rock.

To himself, Longarm murmured the ritual words that went with the game: "Paper covers rock, scissors cut paper, rock blunts scissors."

His memory of the game aroused Longarm's interest. He stopped near the men and stood watching.

Only four players remained when Longarm finally stopped, and they were playing with the kind of concentration they would have shown if cash had been at stake. For several rounds, all four put out fists. On the next round, three gambled on scissors, one on paper, and the bad guesser had to drop out. A three-way split followed: "paper," "scissors," and "rock." The game was a tie, since all three would have been eliminated and there'd have been no winner. The climax came when two of them guessed the third would show "rock" and thrust out open hands. The third man displayed two fingers.

With a triumphant grin, the winner doubled up his fist and the losers braced themselves with biceps flexed against their ribs. The winner pounded the five losers with solid swings that set them rubbing their arms ruefully.

For a moment the group laughingly replayed the game, as though it had been a major sporting event. One of the players looked at Longarm, who hadn't bothered to hide his interest while he was watching. He said, "You act like you know how t'play this fool game, greenie."

"I used to, a long time ago," Longarm replied.

"Well"—the convict hesitated, then turned to the other players—"well, I don't guess we'd mind, if you want to play."

One or two of the others shrugged, the rest nodded with varying degrees of indifference. It was Longarm's turn to hesitate now, but he did not waste time making up his mind. He'd been so isolated for such a long period that he felt unusually gregarious.

"I don't mind if I do," he told the man.

There were no formalities, such as introductions. The six convicts who'd been playing knew who Longarm was, and assumed he knew them as well. They formed a circle, and the man who'd won the last game chanted, "One...two... *three.*" At the count of three, all seven of the players thrust out a hand. None of them had any fingers extended. They pulled their hands back and waited for the count. At "three" the hands came out again. This time there were five fists, including Longarm's, and two pairs of fingers.

Without commenting, the two who'd shown "scissors" stepped out of the circle. The other five men closed the gaps in the circle and waited for the count. Two sets of paired fingers, two fists, and a single open hand were extended at the count of three. No winner was possible, so the five pulled back their hands. In the next round, was one of the three players who showed a fist; the remaining two displayed "scissors," and dropped out.

Now there were only three players remaining. They showed "rock," "scissors," and "paper," another tie. At the next count, Longarm and one of the other players thrust out fists, and the third man showed two fingers and stepped back. For the next five minutes, Longarm and his opponent played neck and neck, each of them trying to outguess the other.

Rapidly the number of games mounted to ten, then eleven, and on the twelfth game, Longarm showed an open hand while his opponent held out a fist. A murmur ran through the players who'd been beaten earlier and who'd formed a circle around the two as the tied games went on and on.

"Damned if the greenie didn't whup you, Clegg," one of the beaten players said, and added quickly, "Not that you didn't give him a good run."

None of the men spoke to Longarm. He started to move away, but the man named Clegg called him back, saying, "Hold on there. You got licks on all of us. Come on and take 'em."

For a moment Longarm thought of refusing, but decided that he'd create more resentment by being magnanimous than he would by administering the arm-thwacks to which his win entitled him. He came back and stepped into the little circle the six men had formed.

Clegg said, "I was the last loser, so I'll take the first lick." He flexed his left arm and braced his feet.

Longarm decided to go easy on the man. He took a short swing and landed a solid but not all-out blow that was far short of the blistering jolt of which he was capable. He was turning away from Clegg to deal with the next man when, from the corner of his eye, he saw Clegg start to swing on him.

He jerked his head out of the way, his fast reflexes saving him from a really damaging blow that could have floored him, but even his lightning reaction was not quick enough to let him completely escape the convict's flying fist. Clegg's blow caught Longarm at a sharp angle, missing his chin, but scraping along his jaw and sending him reeling into one of the other men.

Suddenly he realized he was fighting for his life. As though they'd been poised and waiting, the other inmates closed in on him.

There was too little room for them to use their fists with the greatest effectiveness, but he took several sharp jabs in his stomach, which drove the wind out of him, and although his opponents crowded in so closely that none of them had the room to launch a really effective blow, Longarm was equally hampered in using his own fists effectively.

He struggled to stay on his feet as his assailants tried to pull him down. Longarm had no illusions about the sort of brawl in which he found himself involved. Once he was on the ground, the others would use their feet, and he knew they'd have two prime targets, his belly and his hands.

A rifle cracked from the walkway, and for a moment the men hesitated. He did not stop, though. He found an opening and dropped one of the convicts with a buttonhook left, while kicking at the shins of a second brawler. He was dimly aware of shouts rising from the other inmates in the yard, but did not hear the thumping feet of the guards who'd been alerted by the shot and who now came racing across the yard to break up the fracas.

As quickly as it had erupted, the fight ended. Longarm's first intimation that the guards had arrived came when a billy club caught him a glancing blow on the head, dazing him. Clubs were flailing everywhere, and the weaponless convicts were quickly reduced to a line of seven men, two of them with bloodied noses, the rest with angry red marks on their faces where fists had landed. The yard had fallen whisper-quiet, the prisoners backing into compact knots along the building wall.

Longarm took stock of the guards. There were three, and two were familiar faces: Jackson and Flaherty. Jackson seemed to be in charge.

"What in hell's this all about?" he asked angrily, looking along the line of red-welted faces. None of them spoke. Jackson looked at Longarm again and said, "You got one bad mark for fighting already. You want to tell me what set this off?"

Longarm stared straight ahead, as though he hadn't heard the guard's question.

Jackson shrugged and he turned to Flaherty and said, "We'd better see what the warden says, there's so many of 'em. Can't put all of 'em in the box at the same time. He'll have to decide how to handle it."

Warden Dade, when he followed Flaherty back to the yard, stared at the inmates just as Jackson had. He said, "I know it's against what you call your 'code' to talk, but I'll ask you the question anyhow. Who struck the blow that started this fight?"

None of the inmates spoke, but none of them needed to. As one man, they stared at Longarm. Then, as though they'd momentarily forgotten that an accusing look can be as damaging as a spoken word, they quickly turned their eyes to the front again. Longarm thought the show was too pat; it stunk of prearrangement. He had a hunch he'd been set up, but he too kept silent.

"I don't think any of you need to say anything," Warden Dade said briskly. "All of you know that any man starting a fight is put in the box. It's not big enough to hold all of you, but I'll promise that all of you will damned well be punished." He fixed his eyes on Longarm and went on, "You don't have to say a word, Long. The look these men gave you is all I need. And when I was checking the records, I noticed you've got another fight on yours. Have you anything to say?"

Longarm tightened his lips involuntarily, but stared straight ahead, his face expressionless.

"Jackson, put this man in the box for twenty-four hours," the warden said, indicating Longarm. "Give the others forty-eight hours' cell confinement on bread and water, and no latrine visits."

Without looking at any of the inmates, Dade wheeled and marched back to his office. Longarm still kept his face expressionless, staring into space.

"You men heard the warden," Jackson said. He told the other guards, "Flaherty, you and Bailey take these six to their cells. I'll handle the one that's going in the box."

Longarm still stared ahead at nothing while the guards marched the other convicts away. Jackson came and stood in front of him, but Longarm avoided the guard's eyes.

"You might think you're tough, Long," Jackson said quietly, "But I've seen other men who thought the same thing. Now, you get to fill up with water before you go in, and if you take my advice, you'll take your time and drink all you can hold. Once you get in the box, it won't be opened until time for you to come out. Now go get your water and take off your shoes, and I'll put you in."

There was no more point in arguing with Johnson, or even speaking to him, than there was in telling the sun or the moon to stop, Longarm had decided. He walked quietly to the well, conscious of the eyes of the men still in the yard. He drank all the tepid water he could hold, filling his stomach until he was uncomfortable. As he drank slowly, he watched what the guard was doing.

Instead of escorting Longarm to the well, as he might have been expected to do, Jackson had gone to the sheet-iron box and raised its lid. As Longarm came up to where the guard was standing, he saw the reason for the gable in the center; the box was divided down its center into two halves.

Jackson was holding up the lid of one side. He pointed to Longarm's feet, and Longarm untied the heavy brogans and stepped out of them.

"You take those off because an inmate strangled himself with his shoelaces a few years ago, after he'd been in the box twenty-four hours," Jackson remarked unemotionally, as though commenting on the weather.

Longarm did not wait for a command. He stepped into the

119

box. The metal bottom was uncomfortably warm on his bare feet even now, and he was ready to lie down when Johnson nodded. The box was barely wide enough to accommodate his broad shoulders, and his head scraped one end while his toes touched the other.

Johnson's eyes met Longarm's for a moment, then the guard lowered the lid with a metallic clang, and Longarm entered a world of total darkness and constant heat.

For the first few minutes after the door closed, Longarm did not feel warm. Then the heat began to make itself felt, but it still stopped short of being intolerable. Longarm reminded himself that the box hadn't yet had time really to warm up, and that in a little while, as the sun climbed higher, it would be miserably hot in the enclosed metal box.

He started exploring the interior, feeling along the seams. He was lying on his back, the top of the box only an inch or so from his face, but by shifting his body toward the side where the box was divided and the top rose in a low gable, he found that he could bring one arm along the side wall and explore the inner surface and part of the bottom with his fingertips. That kept him busy for only a few minutes; there was nothing to feel but the same galvanized metal surface wherever his fingers moved.

By bracing his elbows on the floor, he found that he could slide his bare feet over the bottom end, but this told him nothing except that his feet were in contact with a sheet of warm metal. He tried to turn over, but there was not enough height to accommodate the breadth of his shoulders, no matter how hard he tried to pull them together. He shifted back to the center of the box and lay quietly for a few moments.

Closing his eyes, Longarm went to sleep.

When he awoke, it was not in the same world he'd left for his nap. He had not been aware of the progressive buildup of the heat inside the box; he was suddenly engulfed in a hell of flames that beat on his skin from crown to toe, that pushed searing needlepoints into his eyeballs and sent a stream of burning coals pouring down his throat.

Longarm's entire body tensed. The darkness as well as the heat became his enemy. He blinked, filming his eyeballs with moisture that brimmed and overflowed and ran in slow trickles down his temples. His brain was churning with sensations he thought he'd trained himself to ignore, and for a few seconds he felt closer to panic than he had since he was a child.

After he had reached maturity, Longarm had always felt in command of any situation in which he found himself. Even when facing overwhelming odds, or when staring down the barrel of an enemy's gun, he'd always been certain that he was in control. He called on that control now, and the momentary confusion that had seized him ebbed away. Calmness returned.

As suddenly as it had struck him, the heat seemed to abate. His taut muscles relaxed and he felt loose and free instead of confined. Then he touched the metal that enclosed him, but his fingertips were seared each time he pressed them against the box.

He said aloud, "Good Godamighty, old son! You must've died while you was asleep and the devil dragged you down to hell, coffin and all!"

When the thought of a coffin flashed through Longarm's mind, he knew only that he had to fight his way out at once. He tried to raise his hands, to close them into fists and beat on the lid of the box, but the space above him was so scanty that there was not enough room to allow him to bend his elbows. He turned on one side, shifting clumsily, and his upper arm and shoulder came into contact with the top of the box. It was like laying living flesh in a frying pan. Longarm pulled away and settled down into the position he'd been in before, on his back.

For a moment he lay limp, and bit by bit the alien sensations that had been sweeping through him faded away. He was once more aware of where he was, and how he'd gotten there. The box was not a coffin any longer, but a sheet-iron case in the yard of the Arizona Territorial Prison.

He understood that even if he could raise his arms and flail them about, there was no way he could break out of the box, and he knew he must accept that as a fact and put aside any idea of fighting free. He inhaled deeply, and gasped. Even though he knew now that he was inhaling air instead of live coals, he was barely able to endure the fierce heat that passed over his lips and tongue.

Armed with the awareness that he'd regained control of his body and that he was not in danger of imminent cremation, Longarm became himself again. He forced his taut muscles to relax, and after the tension had left them he began to think of the hours that lay ahead, and to prepare himself for them.

Twenty-four hours, the warden said, he told himself. *That ain't such a long time, old son. You've stood a lot of misery for a lot longer than that. All you got to do is keep cool—if there's any way to do that when the sun gets up toward noon and starts beating on all this damn sheet iron—and before you know what's happening, you'll be out of here. Now the best thing you can do to make that time go by faster is to go back to sleep a while. Even if you ain't sleepy this soon again, it's nice and dark in here, so just lay back and think it's nighttime, and the first thing you know they'll be lifting up the lid and you'll be back outside where you belong.*

Letting himself become totally limp, Longarm closed his eyes and tried to go to sleep. In the early years of his adventurous life, he'd learned to sleep whenever sleep was possible, in a variety of places and positions. He'd learned the trick of dropping off for a refreshing nap when there was no immediate threat of danger, just as he'd learned to stay alert and awake for long periods of time whenever wakefulness was necessary. The habit of years deserted him now. He could not go to sleep.

Suddenly he became aware of silence. It was as though he'd been stricken with deafness. He strained his ears, listening with all the concentration he could muster. There was no sound. He tapped the bottom of the box, and managed to produce a muffled reverberation, almost inaudible, but enough to assure him that his ears hadn't stopped working. He exhaled a sigh of relief and, for a few moments, relaxed again.

Until now, the heat had been unpleasant at best, maddening at worst, but now Longarm began to be affected by the staleness of the superheated air around him. Before, he'd managed to ignore it, if not to forget it, during those minutes when he had brought his mind and body back under his control after the sudden flooding of uncharacteristic uncertainty. He was in full awareness of his situation, and knew now that what he felt was not something from his imagination, but a tangible physical fact.

Darkness had bothered him when he first woke up, but now he discovered that in one or two places along the rim of the box, where the lid and sides came together, there were small areas where the two fitted imperfectly. A faint, crepuscular light seeped through the cracks. None of them was longer than a finger or much wider than the diameter of a hair, but they were there, invisible until now, when Longarm's pupils had dilated enough to allow him to see them.

Although they were visible, the cracks did not let in enough of a glow to allow him to see anything in the box. He raised his hand until his fingers encountered the lid, pulled them back as soon as they touched the scorching metal, then held them as high as possible without coming into contact with the lid, and tried to arch his neck to look at them. His forehead bumped on the top of the box, and in spite of the heat that flowed into his brow, he held his head up while he strained his eyes. His fingers remained invisible.

The heat seemed even worse now. Reason told Longarm that the heat was increasing in the box because the sun was high in the sky and beating down on it with its fierce glow unabated. That he could deduce the reason gave him little comfort.

He'd been sweating since he woke up, but it had been only a filming of his entire body with moisture, and its effect had been to make him feel cooler. Now the film became drops and the drops increased to trickles, the trickles to streams. The thin cloth of Longarm's jacket and pants drank up the wetness for a short while, but they quickly grew sodden and clung to him uncomfortably. Despite the heat, the clinging of his clothing made him feel clammy, not a cool clamminess, but a warm, soupy wetness that gave him the sensation of having fallen fully clothed into a bathtub filled with hot water.

For a short while, Longarm managed to close his mind to his discomfort and to lie without moving. He grew aware of the smell of his sweat, sour and rancid. His bladder was growing uncomfortable by now. He considered the situation for a moment and then allowed the urine to flow. It ran down his thighs and along his buttocks and back, and for a moment he felt cool, until the moisture evaporated and only the acrid odor remained.

His anger and outrage, suppressed until now, overtook him as the intensity of the smell increased. He kicked out against the end of the box, but his bare feet made no sound as they struck the hot metal. Longarm discovered another reason why he'd been ordered to remove his shoes. The heavy prison brogans would have clanked loudly and set the box to reverberating, reminding not only the other inmates, but the warden and guards, of the punishment some poor devil in the box was enduring.

Slight as they had been, his kicks and squirms of protest had exhausted him. He lay back limply, his arms and legs trembling and his entire body twitching nervously. Then, in spite of the heat, he started to shudder, and the shivering drained his strength still further. He fell into a daze, and began to hallucinate.

He was jolting along in a stagecoach with beautiful blonde Emma Frye sitting beside him, being chased along the banks of the Yellowstone by a band of screaming Bannocks, in bed with the seductive Silverheels in Leadville, cramped in the primitive cell of a *rurales'* jail in Old Mexico, sloshing through a swampy tangle near the mouth of the Trinity River in Texas, embracing the enchanting Jessibee Vann in a shack in the Indian Nation. Then he was striding parched across the sands of Goblin Valley in Utah Territory, and the circle came complete as Longarm realized for a few moments that he was in the iron box in the prison yard, and that he'd stay there until he shriveled away.

There were more visions after that before the blackness came, and after the blackness there was sanity again. Longarm's sense of time had deserted him by now. He could have been in the box for an hour, a day, or a week. He was sure of only one thing: he was lying confined in a metal container and getting increasingly hot. Everything else was a dream.

Forgetting for a moment that he could not turn over, he moved instinctively to lie on his side, as his back began to ache from having been pressed flat against the metal bottom. The cloth of his jacket sizzled when it touched the top of the box, and then the heat passed through the thin, dry cloth to scorch his shoulder. He squirmed quickly to lie on his back again before the darkness returned.

Blinding light flooded his face, and Longarm squeezed his eyes closed to shut out the painful glare. The glare passed through his closed lids, and by instinct he brought up his forearm to shield his eyes better. He realized with surprise that he could raise his arm without bumping it against hot metal. He tried to sit up, and was even more surprised when he succeeded.

"All right, come on out," a vaguely familiar voice said gruffly. "You done your twenty-four hours. Maybe it learned you a lesson, maybe not. Get on your feet now. I ain't going to stand here and hold up the lid of this damn box all day."

Longarm tried to open his eyes again, and this time he found that he could keep them open. Jackson was standing at the foot of the box, holding up its lid. The lid shielded Longarm from the direct rays of the sun, which bathed the prison yard in light. He struggled to his feet, shaky, but still able to hold himself erect by gripping the box's lid. Looking around, he saw the inmates clumped in groups in the shade of the building, just as they had been when the box closed on him.

"Dammit, if you don't feel like you've been in there long enough, lay down and I'll close the box again!" Jackson snapped impatiently.

Longarm finally overcame his surprise enough to move. He stepped out of the box, feeling the ground hot and rough on his bare feet. The well caught his eye, and he moved toward it, his first steps uncertain and staggering. Some hidden reserve of strength came to him and allowed him to reach the well.

Sitting down on the narrow curb, Longarm picked up one of the pots lying handy and dipped it in the water. He knew the danger of drinking too much too fast, and forced himself to sip slowly until the pot was half emptied. Then he held the vessel up and poured the rest of the water on his head. It trickled down his face and neck and felt so good that he emptied a second pot over himself before drinking again.

Still somewhat shaky, Longarm stood up and slowly made his way along the wall to his cell. None of the convicts offered to help him, though all of them watched curiously as he moved with careful steps down to his cell. The door was standing open. He went in and fell on the bunk, the thin, straw-filled mattress feeling to him like a feather bed. He was asleep within a minute.

Chapter 12

Hunger pangs rumbling in his stomach woke Longarm a few minutes before the inmates with the cauldron arrived on their supper round. Feeney was ladling out the food this time. Longarm tried to ignore him, but the yard boss fiddled with the ladle long enough to whisper in a tone pitched too low for the guard to hear, "I ain't done with you yet, turncoat! You've played in luck so far, but your string's bound to run out. When it does, I'll get you!"

Longarm ignored Feeney and his threat. He took his filled bowl and walked back to his cell without speaking. Just as he was about to enter the little cubicle, he saw a finger wiggling frantically from the door grille of Tom Boone's cell. With the guard waiting to lock him in again, he could not respond until the supper round had been completed. He ate, watching the light that trickled in through the grille and the tiny window fade from gold to pink. Then he stood up and, looking out through the grille, saw Boone's finger still signalling him.

Pushing a finger through the grille of his own door, he waggled it in reply to Boone's signal. Boone's finger withdrew. Longarm stood looking at the deserted yard for a moment longer; he had started to turn away and return to his bunk when Conyers hissed from the adjoining cell. Longarm hissed back.

"You come outa the box real good," Conyers said. "Ain't many does."

"Maybe I looked better'n I felt."

"Pretty bad in the box, I guess."

"Bad enough. A man can stand it, though."

"I ain't ever been in it."

"You ain't missed no treat."

"Recco was looking for you this evening, in the yard."

"I slept through the break."

"He said to tell you he's ready to talk again."

"If he wants to talk, all he's got to do is open his mouth."

"You going along with him?"

"That'll depend on what he's got to say. He ain't putting on no tea party. Busting out of here's going to be a real job."

"He told me he's got connections outside that'll help him."

"I'd say the same, was I trying to get help on a bust-out."

Conyers was silent for a moment, then he said, "I reckon so."

"Recco say anything else?" Longarm asked.

"No. That was all."

"I'll go back to bed, then."

Longarm was more interested in finding out what progress Tom Boone had been making with Curley Parker than he was in Blade Recco's plans. Unless the Secret Service man could persuade the old lifer to join the breakout effort, neither of them could leave the prison. Stretched out on his bunk, forgetting its hard surface in the luxury of being in the fresh air and daylight, Longarm weighed the situation.

Recco ain't likely to be interested in Parker. He's so old he wouldn't be much help fighting out of here. But likely Recco'd take Parker, if he knew about the army gold. Trouble is, if Blade Recco got in on a deal like that, Parker'd be the only one he'd take, and me and Tom'd be left sucking a dry hind tit. It's going to take some real fancy figuring to come out of this one with a whole skin and the gold.

Longarm cudgeled his brain trying to come up with a plan, but he was still tired from the ordeal in the box. In the midst of his thinking, he fell asleep.

Recco walked past Longarm in the yard at the beginning of the morning exercise period the next day. Without meeting Longarm's eyes or giving any indication that he was even noticing him as they passed, the swarthy plotter indicated a vacant portion of the building wall with a quick jerk of his thumb. Longarm did not respond, but gradually changed his direction to reach the spot to which Recco had motioned. He sat down, leaned his head back against the wall, and closed his eyes to slits.

Several minutes passed before Recco came up. He paid no attention to Longarm, but stopped several feet away and hunkered down with his back to the wall. One of his cronies came up and squatted beside him.

After a moment, without turning to face Longarm, Recco said in a low but carrying whisper, "Last chance, Long. You with us or not?"

"I'll tell you that when I know your play," Longarm replied through stiff lips, without opening his eyes.

"Day after tomorrow."

"Pretty sudden, ain't it?"

"Best time's now. Green guards, new warden."

"You got a point," Longarm said slowly. Then he said, "Tell me all of it."

"Evening. The middle of yard time. Friends outside dynamite gate. Gun cache by wall. Horses down by river. We get across to Mexico. That's it."

"Not all of it. How about the Gatling gun?"

"Ammunition switched. It'll jam before we're hurt."

"You sure?"

"I'll be outside too, Long. I'm sure. Now, you in?"

Longarm took his time replying while he juggled geography in his head. He didn't know the exact distance from the prison to the river, but judged it to be a bit more than two miles. He guessed that Recco was counting on the guards' being busy with the inmates while the escape was taking place. With weapons to hold off any pursuit, and horses waiting at the Colorado, the plan might succeed.

Finally he asked Recco, "How many going?"

"Seven, counting you."

Recco didn't offer names, but Longarm hadn't expected him to. He didn't ask. Instead he said, "Don't count me in till I hear the rest."

"Go on. Ask."

"They're bound to have horses here. We can't outrun 'em."

"All the horses is a wagon horse and the warden's buggy horse. Neither one's saddle-broke."

"Where'll we hole up across the river?"

"Safe place. Not far."

"What's the payoff to your friends?"

"We do a job for them. Not here—in Mexico."

"Holdup?"

"Just call it a job for now."

"Anything in it for us?"

"Plenty. It'll be a big one."

"Then we split up?"

"If we feel like it." Recco waited for another question, but when Longarm said nothing, he asked his own. "Satisfied?"

Longarm took his time answering. Nodding almost imperceptibly, he said, "I'm in. Don't sound like I can lose."

"You can't. Be ready, then."

"Whenever you say."

For a few moments longer, Recco stayed where he was, then he and the man who'd come to sit beside him got up and wandered off across the yard. The entire conversation between Longarm and Recco had lasted less than five minutes, and neither man had looked at the other while it was going on.

When he'd waited long enough to keep his moves from being connected with Recco's, Longarm stood up and started a leisurely tour of the prison yard. He spotted Tom Boone almost at once. The Secret Service operative was at the well, just dipping a pot into the water. Longarm waited until he was sure Boone had seen him, then moved toward the well. As he approached, Boone turned his back so that Longarm would pass behind him.

"Latrine," Longarm said, not looking at Boone, and pitching his voice to make sure that the men in the shade of the wall did not hear him. He went on to the latrine, entered, and squatted over the trench.

Boone came in, turned his back to Longarm, and straddled the trench several feet distant from him.

"Get Parker ready to go out day after tomorrow," Longarm said.

"What!" Boone's voice betrayed his surprise.

"We're going with Recco, Tom."

"Can you trust him?"

"No. But we'll worry about that when we're outside."

"Where outside?"

Longarm shrugged, realized Boone couldn't see him, and said, "Damned if I know. It's his breakout, not mine."

"How'd you talk him into taking me and Parker?"

"I didn't."

"You mean he doesn't know about us?"

"No. When he does, it'll be too late for him to say no."

"That's crazy!" Boone objected. "It won't work!"

"Maybe not. We'll try, though."

"Dammit, I haven't even talked to Parker about breaking out! I'm not sure he'd agree."

"He ain't all that big or heavy," Longarm said curtly. "If he balks, we'll carry him out."

"You've got a reason for the hurry, I guess?"

"Dade's the big reason. We're on our own now, Tom. Dade don't know a thing about us, or why we're here. Even if he did, I wouldn't feel comfortable with him."

"I've thought about Dade," Boone said slowly. "Thought of getting a letter out too, but Parker says it can't be done."

"So I've been told. Don't leave us much choice, does it?"

For a moment Boone didn't answer. Then, in a discouraged voice, he said, "No. I'll do what I can with Curley Parker."

"Just have him ready to go, that's all."

Leaving Boone in the latrine, Longarm returned to the yard. He wasn't at all sure he'd done the right thing, with Parker such a question mark, but the chance to use Recco's already-formed breakout plans was too good to pass by. Poker had taught Longarm one thing: If you had good cards, it was better to play them and risk losing than to fold and let a bluffer take a big pot with a pair of deuces.

During the remainder of the exercise period, Longarm made himself as inconspicuous as possible. He went over the scanty information he'd gotten from Recco, wondering all the time how much of it he could believe. He understood Recco's unwillingness to spell out every detail of the scheme; if the warden or one of the guards got wind of it, even a whisper overheard by a stool pigeon, the plan would certainly end in disaster.

Finally he decided that if Recco wasn't reasonably sure the breakout would succeed, he wouldn't be trying it. After that, he dismissed his worries and began thinking of his own role in the escape attempt, and how he was going to work Boone and Curley Parker into it.

After breakfast the next morning, Longarm used the finger signals he and Boone had worked out to inform the Secret Service man that they needed to meet. He didn't think it wise to use the latrine again; anyone who might have noticed both him and Boone going in at the same time on the previous day might suspect that something unusual was going on and come to investigate. During the short time Longarm had been in the territorial prison, he'd discovered that very few things happened that somebody didn't observe.

When Longarm left his cell for the morning exercise period, he carried his left arm stiffly. Clamped in his armpit, under his jacket, was the knife he'd taken from the inmate who'd tried to stab him. Walking toward the well to wash, he saw Boone; the Secret Service man had already taken up a spot against the wall where Longarm would pass him soon after leaving his cell. Without stopping and without looking at Boone as he passed, Longarm spoke quickly through stiff lips.

"Knife," he said. "In overflow barrel. Get it. Threaten Parker if he balks."

Out of a corner of his eye, Longarm saw the surprised look that flashed across Boone's face and hoped his message had been understood. He went on to the well and waited until all the inmates who'd been lined up to wash their faces had finished.

Taking his time, Longarm went up to the half-barrel that caught the overflow and bent over it while he sloshed water over his head and face. When he dipped his hand in the second time, he let the thin blade slide down his sleeve into the barrel. He stood beside the barrel, rubbing his hair dry, until he saw Boone coming up; then he stepped away, giving Boone an angry look as they passed one another.

Going back to the wall, Longarm sat down and watched Boone as he stepped up to the barrel. He didn't see Boone get the knife, but as Boone was rubbing his face with his left hand when he finally walked away from the barrel, Longarm guessed that he was carrying the blade up his sleeve. He made no effort during the rest of the morning exercise period to get near Boone, for the Secret Service man went from the well to sit beside Curley Parker, and stayed with the old lifer until the period ended.

Meanwhile, Longarm turned his attention to Recco, who'd been wandering around the yard in a seemingly aimless fashion. Longarm deduced quickly that he was passing the final word about plans for breakout, and decided to stay put, knowing Recco would get around to him eventually.

Before the exercise period was over, Recco did. He passed by the spot where Longarm was lounging and stopped, scanning the yard as though he were looking for someone. Out of the side of his mouth he said, "Tomorrow. About this time. Get close to the gate and watch me." Then, without waiting for a reply, he moved on, still looking from one end of the yard to the other.

Boone made no effort to get near Longarm before the convicts were locked in their cells. He waited until the afternoon yard period, and it was almost over before he walked past Longarm and whispered, convict-style, "Parker's going. When?"

Longarm had no time to give Boone any details. Before the Secret Service man got out of earshot, he replied, "Watch me." Boone signaled his understanding with a brief jerk of his head.

When Longarm went out for his morning dish of grits and salt pork, he was surprised to find Recco handling the ladle. The guard had gone to unlock the cell next to Longarm's, and Longarm risked asking, "Everything all right?"

"Just be ready." Recco said, filling Longarm's bowl. "If it's changed, you'll know."

To all appearances, everything was normal in the yard when the prisoners were released for the morning exercise period. The inmates milled about in their usual fashion, first the line into the latrine, then the stop at the well to wash and drink, and finally to the shady side of the wall to lounge or stroll back and forth until it was time to be locked up again.

On the walkway above the cells, the guards paced back and forth, and in the gate tower Longarm could see the silhouettes of the Gatling gun and the guard who stood beside it. The guard stood gazing out across the desert; the oversized barrel of the rapid-fire gun was a more menacing outline, relieved only by the glow of the burnished brass on its right side and the ammunition hopper on top of the breech.

He located Boone quickly. The Secret Service man was at the well, drinking, and Curley Parker stood beside him. Parker also held a pot in his hand. They did not notice Longarm, for they were engaged in a conversation that, judging by their expressions, must have been serious. Longarm turned his head away and moved to one side, trying to lose himself behind a half-dozen inmates who were lounging in the shade of the wall.

As the midway point of the exercise period drew close,

Longarm noticed that several of the men who'd been lounging toward the rear of the yard now began to edge up in the direction of the tower. They did not move as a group; first one, then another, would stroll forward a few paces, stop to look around, then, with no obvious destination in view, continue toward the front of the yard. Recco was not among the men moving toward the gate. He was nowhere in sight, Longarm determined after an unobtrusive survey of the yard.

Longarm got as close to the gate as he thought wise, then turned back to look at the yard. Everything still seemed normal, with the usual groups of inmates and the few solitaries lounging in the shade. The sentries on the walkway moved at their customary deliberate pace, dividing their attention between the yard and the terrain outside the prison walls.

When the explosion shook the ground and a cloud of yellowish smoke erupted around the gate and tower, all the men in the yard froze momentarily except Recco's group. Longarm waited to make sure Boone and Parker were heading for the gate before he started forward to join the half-dozen men who were already sprinting for the front wall. Shouts began rising from the two guards who were on duty watching the yard. Billy clubs raised, they were running across the yard to where the inmates had begun milling around.

Recco appeared as if from nowhere, already at the gate, holding a knife to the throat of the convict whose job it was to swing open one of the massive portals. Another convict joined Recco and slid back the massive iron bolt that kept the gate from swinging. By this time others of Recco's group were arriving and the gate was swung open a crack.

When the blast had gone off and the sentries on the walkway got over their initial surprise, they had concentrated their attention on the outside perimeter of the prison. Belatedly, they swiveled to cover the yard with their weapons. Shots were fired and bullets raised puffs of dust in the area between the mass of the convicts in the yard and the bare area just inside the gate.

Longarm ran toward Boone and Parker. He'd almost caught up with them when he saw Feeney coming toward him. Longarm didn't think about swerving, and he didn't think Feeney was close enough to him to try to stop him. Feeney put on a surprising burst of speed for a man of his bulk and thrust a foot out, tripping Longarm.

As Longarm stumbled and started to fall, a bullet from one of the sentries on the walkway clipped the sleeve of his jacket and then punched into Feeney's heart. The little slits of the yard boss's eyes opened wider than Longarm had ever seen them. Feeney's mouth opened, but what he was about to say was drowned in a gush of scarlet blood as he crumpled to the ground.

Longarm didn't stop. He caught up with Boone and Parker and found that the old lifer was already panting, trying to keep up. Longarm grabbed Parker by one arm and Boone took hold of the other. A chunk of hot lead sang past Longarm's head and instinctively he ducked. Half lifting, half dragging, they got the old man outside before the sentries could concentrate their fire on them.

When Longarm and Boone got Parker through the gate, Recco and the other five escaping convicts were already a hundred yards or so away, trotting west toward the river. They had rifles in their hands now, and stopped every few minutes to return the fire of the sentries on the walkways, who were now peppering the escaping convicts.

One of Recco's men dropped and lay still. The others began running again, leaving the downed man behind. In the tower, the man with the Gatling gun had first swiveled the muzzle to cover the yard. He swung the rapid-fire gun around now, and explosions of dust rose from the dry soil in a line just behind Longarm's group.

Longarm jerked on Parker's arm to start the trio zigzagging, but at that moment the sharp, threatening staccato of the Gatling gun stopped abruptly. Glancing back, Longarm could see that the gunner had swung the magazine away from the loading port and was working to clear the jam that had stopped the gun. Longarm knew that Gathings were usually sighted for their extreme range of eight hundred paces. He measured the distance back to the prison walls with his eyes; his guess told him that they still had two or three hundred yards to run before they'd be out of certain range of the rapid-fire weapon.

A rifle bullet sang past, and Longarm swung the trio around to run at a different angle. He knew the Burnside carbines used by the sentries had an effective range of only five or six hundred yards, and that now any slugs reaching them would be lucky shots. He looked ahead. Recco and the others were able to run faster than him and Boone, hampered as they were by having to slow their pace to match Parker's.

They'd reached the spot where the fallen convict lay, and Longarm let Boone handle Parker for the few moments it took him to run to where the downed man was lying. The convict was dead. Longarm recognized his face, but had never learned his name. He picked up the gun that lay by the corpse; it was a Spencer carbine, and he could tell by its feel that its magazine was still almost full.

"At least I got five or six good arguments if Recco gives us any trouble about Parker," he muttered as a shot from the prison walls kicked up dust a yard away from his brogans.

Rejoining Boone and Parker, Longarm started them moving again. He looked back at the prison, but no pursuit had been started. Recco had apparently been successful in immobilizing the few horses that were kept there, Longarm thought, and turned his full attention to what lay ahead.

Recco's group was far in advance of them now, starting down the steep bluff that led to the Colorado River. The trail descended in serpentine fashion along the face of the bluff, which was not sheer, but was steep and precipitous enough to be troublesome for someone like Parker to navigate.

At the foot of the bluff, the river flowed wide and greenish brown, its placid surface indicating a fairly rapid current. Between the bottom of the bluff and the stream there was a narrow sandspit on which Longarm saw several saddled horses and three or four men waiting.

"You and Parker take your time getting down," he told Boone. "I'll go on ahead and make sure Recco waits up for us."

Running, leaping occasionally to cut the corner off a sharp curve in the trail, Longarm caught up with Recco's band two-thirds of the way down the bluff. Recco saw him coming, and stopped to wait. As Longarm closed the gap between them, Recco came back a few paces to meet him. He was carrying the twin of the Spencer in Longarm's hand, and his face was twisted into an angry scowl.

Looking at him, Longarm realized that this was the first time he'd actually seen Recco face to face at close range. He'd never known that Recco's lips were blubber-thick and his eyes an opaque, obsidian black, or his face so totally merciless. Recco looked at the carbine Longarm held and hesitated, but his anger was too big to contain.

"What in hell was the idea of bringing them two along without saying you was going to?" he demanded.

"I had my reasons," Longarm replied levelly. He'd already decided, after gauging Recco's anger, that he'd have to tell him about the wagonload of gold.

"Damn you, Long, this is my deal! You've fucked it up for me! Now, you can take your two friends and haul ass! I don't want any more of you!"

"You might change your mind, Recco."

"Like hell I will! You'll get no more help from me! If you want to swim the river, that's up to you, but it won't be on one of them horses down there!"

"You don't even want to listen to what I got to say?" Longarm asked quietly.

"I—" Recco's curiosity overcame his anger. "Damn you, I'll listen, Long, but don't think I'll believe any kind of yarn you spin me!"

"You know who the old fellow is, I reckon?"

"Parker? Sure. They say he—" Recco stopped short. "You mean he really pulled off that big job he's supposed to've done a long time ago? A wagonload of gold?"

"He pulled it, all right. And hid it. And he's the only one alive that knows where it's at."

"I always figured that was just talk, Long. You sure about him being the one? You sure that wagonload of gold is real?"

"I'm sure. And Thomas has just about talked him around to where he's ready to tell where it's hid."

"Why'd Thomas take you in on it? I thought you and him was ready to kill each other."

"Gold's got a way of making men forget they're mad."

Recco grinned lopsidedly, but the smile didn't reach his eyes. "Yeah," he said. "Like me, right now."

"There's enough for everybody, Recco. The gold, and that big job you've got waiting, hell, we can be rich!" He waited a moment to let that sink in, then said,

"Well? Do we go with you?"

"Sure. We can get along all right. And I'd like to have you on my job too. The gold can wait till we've finished it."

"It's a deal, then. You go on and get the horses ready. I'll help Thomas bring Parker on down to the river."

Less than an hour later, with the help of the horses that Recco's friends provided, Longarm and Boone swung off their mounts. Recco was several yards away, talking to the men who'd been waiting at the river.

Boone looked back across the greenish, swirling current and said, "I didn't think we'd make it for a while there."

"Oh, it wasn't all that bad, Tom."

"I guess not. And at least we're out of that damn prison and safe."

"Yeah," Longarm said unsmilingly. "For a little while, we are."

Chapter 13

Longarm lay in his blankets in the cool predawn air and watched the day growing brighter. The jagged wall of the little canyon to which Recco's friends had led them in the early darkness loomed in silhouette above his head against the pale, cloudless sky. The huddled, blanket-swathed forms of the others in the party were dotted around the ashes of last night's supper fire. Longarm counted them and frowned when he came up short. The men who'd helped them escape had vanished sometime during the night.

Then, at the back of the canyon he saw what he'd missed the night before: a cluster of huts made from branches and canvas. He realized then that Recco's "outside friends" must live in the canyon, were probably fugitives from either Mexican law or U.S. justice. The small *jacales* in which the semipermanent residents of the canyon lived were still quiet. Behind the huts, a horse stamped the ground and winnied, and Longarm saw that at the narrowest end of the canyon there way a rope corral with horses and a few mules penned inside it.

He brought his hand up to his face and felt the month-old growth on it, a full beard now, and an image flashed through his mind of himself sitting in a barber's chair, a glass of Maryland rye in one hand and a cheroot in the other, while his whiskers were shaved off. He sighed and popped back to reality when, somewhere behind the *jacales,* a rooster crowed.

Longarm slid out of his bedroll and stepped behind a waist-high clump of prickly pear a few paces away, where he relieved himself before walking the short distance to the trickling, spring-fed stream to wash. He was hunkered down, splashing his beard with the cool water and rubbing it vigorously to get the grime and the salt rime of dried sweat out of it, when he heard the soft swishing of footsteps behind him and turned to look.

A young woman of the mixed Spanish-Indian bloodstreams that Mexicans called *tipo Benito Juarez* was making her way to the brooklet. She was wearing a thin, low-cut blouse that dipped well below the point at which her firm young breasts began to swell. At least two skirts billowed from her waist to her ankles, and on her otherwise bare feet were a pair of loose *huaraches*.

She stopped when she saw Longarm. *"Dispensame, señor,"* she said, pointing to the water, then rubbing her face. *"No conozco que algún sera aquí. Vengo para llavar."*

Longarm hadn't made use of his scanty Spanish since his trip down to the Llano Estacado quite some time back, but he got the meaning of the girl's words. Since he'd learned that to pretend ignorance of a language often gave him an edge at a crucial moment when others used the language to discuss matters they did not want him to understand, he replied in English.

"I guess that means you come to wash your face," he said. He gestured to the stream. "Come on, then. There's plenty of room for both of us."

"Excuse, please," the girl said. Her English was about on a par with Longarm's Spanish. "I am speak Eenglis a leetle bit. You are not to care that I wash by you?"

"Go right ahead."

She knelt on the bank and began washing. Between splashes of the morning-cool water on her face and bare arms, she said, "Ees queek now *la desayuna*. You have hungry, no?"

"I have hungry, *sí,*" Longarm smiled. "You got a name I can call you by?"

"Ah, sí. Maruja."

"And my name's Long. Most folks call me Longarm, though."

Frowning, she said, *"Brazolargo?"*

"I think that's how it is in Spanish."

"So I am call you thees, no?"

"Sure. Now what's that you was saying about me being hungry?"

"Ah, sí. Adelita ees get up when I do, she is cook now the tortillas, and so soon they feex ees *huevos con frijoles refritos."*

"Whatever it is, it sounds good, and I'm ready to eat. Come on, we'll walk on back together."

With the exception of Curley Parker, who was still in his bedroll, the camp was awake and stirring when they got back. Maruja excused herself with a smile and went to help the two older women who were squatting beside the rekindled fire, where, on a square of sheet-iron, thin tortillas were cooking and a pile of the griddle beans left from last night's hasty supper were being reheated. Recco came over to Longarm.

"Better than that stinking place we got away from, ain't it?" he asked. Recco was not quite the same man that Longarm had met in the territorial prison. He no longer spoke convict-style, short sentences and clipped words. Now his face was not fixed in the sullen half-scowl he'd shown when in prison, though his dark eyes were still unreadable. He glanced around the canyon, now bright with the light of the rising sun reflecting off its western wall. "I told you we'd make it without too much trouble."

"You was right, Recco," Longarm agreed. "I guess you had a little bit of help someplace, to pull off fixing that Gatling gun and all the rest of it, but I got to admit it was smooth."

"It'll be smooth from now on," Recco assured him. "We'll take care of the job my friends got us out to do, and then we'll go dig up that gold the old man hid. After that, we'll all have so much money we can scatter and go wherever we feel like going."

"When'll we start your friends' job?"

"That depends. Pretty quick, I guess. Blás ought to be here today to tell us more about it."

"You mean you don't know yet what the job is?"

"I know what it is, but I don't know all the little stuff like where and when. Even if I did, it's Blás's job to tell us that."

"Who's Blás?" Longarm asked, frowning.

Recco hesitated for a moment, then shrugged and said, "You wouldn't know about him. Blás Mentutes. He's a real big wheel along the border here, sort of a middleman between men like us and the politicians that think they run things."

"I know the kind of man you mean." Longarm didn't add that he had little use for them. "He'll be showing up pretty soon?"

"More than likely today sometime. The word I got from

him while we was still inside was that he wanted us out of prison as soon as we could make it, so I guess the job's getting ripe."

"Your friend Mentutes fixed up this hideout here, I guess?"

"It's a place he uses pretty regular. He needs a place he can keep people who're on the run."

"And the women? Sort of like the ones they call *lavanderas* in the Mexican army?"

"One or two of the old ones are. They service the men that stop over here. The young one you was talking to, she's kin to Mentutes, cousin I guess. Her folks got crosswise with Díaz, and they're in jail down in Jalisco someplace. They're lucky, though. Maruja's husband got stood up in front of a firing squad. Blás is hiding her here till he can straighten out the mess."

A tall drink of water of a man walked up and, after nodding to Longarm, said to Recco, "When are them friends of yours going to get here, Recco? I'll feel better when I find out what we're supposed to do. So will Gotch and Pete."

Longarm recognized the voice at once, but he waited for Recco to answer. Recco said, "I was just telling Long, we'll know by tonight. Maybe sooner."

"It can't be too soon for me."

Longarm said, "You're Conyers. I'd know that voice anyplace I heard it, even if I never got to see you."

"Well, Recco didn't think it'd be smart for the guards to notice us talking too much in the yard. They might've changed one of us to a different cell."

"Well, I'm obliged to you for telling me things I didn't know about. Saved me a lot of grief."

"Recco wanted me to. Especially to warn you about Feeney."

"Feeney's dead," Longarm told them. "He was trying to keep me from getting out of the gate, and one of the guards had the same idea. Feeney took the slug I should've got."

"He deserved it," Recco said curtly. "Sorry I didn't get to finish him off myself." He glanced at the fire, where a stack of tortillas had grown on the griddle beside the beans, and where a half-dozen eggs were now sizzling invitingly. "Let's eat. I'll be damn glad to have something besides grits and fatback for breakfast, and I imagine you two feel about the same way."

Blás Mentutes arrived in a high-wheeled box buggy as they

were finishing breakfast. He was an immensely fat man, with three chins spilling down the front of his ruffled satin shirt, a paunch that swelled out a foot in front of his shoulders, and bulging arms and legs to match. His eyes were a crystalline topaz hue, as clear and cold as the gem itself, and he did not try to conceal the close scrutiny he gave to each of the men.

He and Recco went off to one side and, for a half hour or more, stood out of earshot while they talked in low tones. From time to time Mentutes would fix his eyes on one or another of the men while still keeping up his conversation with Recco. At one point Mentutes took a map or chart from his pocket and unfolded it, then he and Recco spent several minutes tracing over it with their fingertips. Finally Mentutes nodded with satisfaction and handed the map over to Recco. He started for the buggy, Recco walking beside him, and before Mentutes got into the buggy, Recco lifted a large sack out of its bed.

Longarm wondered where Mentutes had come from. During the hurried trip from the river to the hideout, there'd been no way for him or any of those with the escapees to get an idea of where they were going. Occasionally he'd seen lights, which might have been small villages or large ranches, but Recco and his helpers had been careful to steer the group around these inhabited areas. But Mentutes must, Longarm thought, have his own headquarters somewhere fairly nearby, in order to keep an eye on the hideout and those who used it.

After Mentutes had started back down the twin tracks that led out of the canyon, Recco came over to the fire where the men were sitting. He lowered the bag to the ground and said, "Blás brought some guns and ammunition. You men decide which ones you want."

Longarm asked, "Did he tell you about the job?"

"Yes. I'll go over it with you later on. I got to study things out myself, first."

"I hope you ain't counting on me doing nothing," Curley Parker said. A plaintive note crept into his voice as he added, "I got to admit, I ain't the man I uster be."

"We'll manage without you," Recco assured him.

Conyers had opened the mouth of the bag and was reaching inside. Longarm and Gotch and Pete hurried to join him. Longarm saw the unmistakable butt of a Colt in the miscellaneous mixture of revolvers in the sack and closed his hand around it an instant before Gotch reached for it. He looked at the weapon; it was chambered for a .41-caliber cartridge, but the weight and heft almost exactly matched his own .44, which now rested in Glass's safe in Prescott. He rummaged through the assortment of holsters that was included in the sack and found one that, with a little work, would fit the pistol.

"This'll do me just fine," Longarm said.

He looked at the guns the others had chosen. Recco held a late-model Smith & Wesson .38, and Tom Boone had managed to come up with an old .44 Colt. Conyers had chosen a French-made Le Mat .41, Pete a forward-breaking Garland-Somerville .44, and Gotch an old-model .41 Smith & Wesson. All of them were trying to match the guns they'd chosen with holsters.

Longarm went back to rummaging in the sack and found that the bottom was awash with cartridges of all calibers. He went through the ammunition and picked out a double handful of .41 shells, as well as a supply of .50-caliber shells for the Spencer carbine. He decided he could get by until the chance came to get a heavier-caliber revolver and a holster that fit it exactly.

"All right, we got the guns," Longarm told Recco. "Now we need some decent duds. Damn it, I feel like I'm walking around half naked in this damn prison suit!"

"Blás is sending out a bunch of pants and shirts from town," Recco said. "Boots and hats too. They'll be here sometime this evening. They better be, because we'll have to ride out by noon tomorrow to get where we're going in time to pull our job. We'll talk about that in a little while, after I do some thinking."

There was dismissal in Recco's tone. Longarm left the other men sorting out ammunition, and wandered back to the fire. The women had vanished, to the *jacales* he supposed. Curley Parker had gone back to his bedroll after eating, and Longarm stepped over and hunkered down beside him.

"You feeling all right, Curley?" he asked.

"Good as I got a right to, I reckon. All that damn running around and riding and suchlike yesterday sorta brought a misery to my back. I ain't scooted around that much since I was on the owlhoot trail, and that's been more'n fifteen years ago."

"That's when you used to run with the Scovill gang?" Longarm asked. "Before you struck out with your own bunch? Because you didn't get very far away from Arizona Territory after the Scovill brothers got killed."

"You know a hell of a lot about me, don't you?" the old outlaw asked. "And that Thomas fellow does too. If I didn't know what you two done outside, I'd suspicion you was in cahoots."

Longarm smiled. "Hell, you're famous, Curley. Everybody knows about what you done, it don't matter which side of the law they're on." He stood up. "Well, you go ahead and rest. I'm going to mosey around a little bit and get the lay of the land."

Longarm walked down to the brook, where he bent down and drank from his cupped hand. The water was cool and fair enough to the taste, but still carried a trace of strange elements brought with it from the underground depths from which it flowed. He looked around idly, noting the scanty foliage, the rock formations that might serve as shelter or as landmarks. An almost invisible trail met his eye. Longarm had nothing better to do, so he set out to follow it.

For a hundred yards or so, the faint trace ran beside the little stream. It crossed where a boulder in the middle of the brook served as a steppingstone and, shortly after that, veered to run at a gentle slant up the wall of the canyon. Longarm strolled casually up the path, which had become less and less visible.

Only an occasional pebble dislodged from its place, a smooth spot in the dust where a foot had been planted, now marked the path. The trail seemed to end ahead in a vertical wedge of stone that rose almost to the rim of the canyon. Longarm walked on to the upthrust and peered around it. A shallow cave ran back from the canyon wall, a ledge in front of it. Maruja sat on the ledge, looking down into the canyon.

She sensed Longarm's presence and looked around, giving a small exclamation of surprise when she saw him. Then the smile became a frown and she asked, "You are follow me here, no?"

"No. I seen the tracks down by the crick and followed 'em, all right, but I didn't know it was you that made 'em."

Maruja looked at Longarm searchingly for a moment, then bobbed her head slowly, seriously. "I am believe you, Brazolargo. Ees not your kind of man that follow women. Is women follow you, no?"

"Well, I wouldn't exactly say that. But I didn't aim to bust into your private place, Maruja. I'll leave you alone." He turned to go, but Maruja stopped him.

"No, Brazolargo. Ees good for me I do not be only weeth myself too much. Come and seet by me. We weel talk, no?"

"If you're sure you don't want me to leave."

"I am sure. Come. Seet down." She patted the packed soil that covered the ledge. "You weel tell me theengs of what you are do, why you—" She stopped short and covered her mouth with her hand. "Oh, no! Blás is say thees theeng I must not ask of men who are come here."

Longarm swung around the vertical stone column and sat beside Maruja. Close to her, he caught the faint woman-smell of her body. He asked her, "Does your cousin bring many men here, Maruja? Or maybe I ought not ask you about that."

"Hee ees never to tell me I should not say what I see. Ees not many men, no. Are men who run from *los rurales*. Like deed *mi madre y padre, y mi esposo*. Only Blás ees not soon enough to get them away. Now he ees say I must go where I weel be safe, to your country, Brazolargo."

"You'll get along all right there. A pretty girl like you always gets along wherever she goes, Maruja."

She shook her head. "I am not girl. Am woman."

"Girl or woman, you're real pretty."

"You are not say thees like joke?"

"No. I'm not joking."

"I theenk I like you, Brazolargo. You do not reach to touch me, like do some men who are come here. *Son como los brutos!*"

Longarm had been without a woman since he'd left Denver. He was very conscious of the warmth of Maruja's young body, the swell of her breasts, the faintly musky aroma of a woman's skin without the artifice of perfume. He felt himself beginning to stiffen, suddenly remembered that he wore nothing under his flimsy prison suit, and shifted his position to hide the bulge that was beginning to show.

Maruja said quickly, "Ees not you I am mean, Brazolargo. Do not move away from me, I do not have fear from you."

"I wasn't trying to move away. I was just making myself more comfortable."

"*No soy disparatado*, Brazolargo. I am have husband two years. You theenk I do not know of men?"

"I think you're a real nice young lady, Maruja. I'd like—"

Out of the corner of his eye, Longarm saw Recco moving around the canyon floor, saw Tom Boone and Conyers and the other men, including those who'd helped with the escape the day before, gathering around the firepit. His interest in Maruja diminished and his beginning erection faded.

He said quickly, "I'd a lot rather stay here and visit with you, but I got to get back down there right now. Recco's getting all of us together, and I need to be there too."

"We weel talk more later, no?" Maruja asked as Longarm stood up and started hurrying toward the trail.

"Sure. Maybe later today."

Hurrying down the trail, Longarm got to the canyon floor just as Recco was asking the others where he'd gone.

"I was just out taking a walk," Longarm said quickly. "It's been a while since I could do that, remember."

"All right, all right!" Recco snapped impatiently. "I've been going over Blás's map, and it looks like we ought to be able to handle this job without any of us getting hurt or caught."

Boone spoke up, "Maybe it'd help if you start out by telling us what the job is."

"I'm just getting to that," Recco replied curtly. "And it sounds like a lot bigger job than I've had it figured to be."

"Well, go on!" Conyers urged. "Just exactly what is it?"

Recco looked along the faces of the men in front of him. "A real good one. We're going to steal a boxcar load of solid silver bars from the Mexican government!"

Longarm and Boone looked at each other involuntarily, then quickly faced Recco again.

"Now hold on!" Longarm objected. "How far are we going to have to travel to do this job? The way you put it to me, it's something that we was to pull off right close by."

"It is," Recco replied. "Just about fifteen or twenty miles from here. The Mexico City mint's broke down and can't be back in business for a year, so the Mexican government's shipping a boxcar full of silver bars to the U.S. Mint in San Francisco to be coined into pesos."

Longarm nodded. "That's different." Then, his tone implying that stealing a boxcar full of silver was not much more of a job than walking down to the corner saloon for a drink, he asked, "When do we do it? And where?"

Recco took out the map he'd been given by Mentutes, unfolded it, and spread it out on the ground. The men gathered around to look at it. It was a simple sketch map, and Longarm could see at a glance that it was not drawn to scale. Recco put his finger on a spot marked with a dot, just off the center of the map.

"Here's where we are," he said. He moved the finger an inch or so. "Here's the railroad junction at Rujito, where the silver train is switched to the spur that goes to the border and connects with the Southern Pacific. We take the car about ten miles north of Rujito."

"Wait a minute," Longarm interrupted. "Is this a day job or a night job?"

"Night. Mentutes pulled enough strings to fix that."

"How're we supposed to steal a whole damn freight car full of silver?" Conyers asked. "Won't the Mexican government send a lot of soldiers with a shipment like that?"

"There'll be some soldiers, sure," Recco replied.

"And what're we supposed to do? Kill all of them?" Conyers went on.

"No," Recco snapped. "The train's just got three cars: a car with soldiers behind the engine, the car with the silver in it, and another carful of soldiers behind that one." He moved his finger a fraction of an inch. "Between Rujitos and the border, we pull the coupling pin and cut the last car loose. A little further on, we cut the silver car loose. Then we pull the silver car to a spur that ends in a deserted mine about two miles off the main track, and hide it. That's what the job amounts to."

"I guess you and Mentutes have got all of it figured out," Longarm said. "But it sure sounds loose as a goose to me."

"How?" Recco asked.

"What's them two carloads of soldiers going to be doing while we're monkeying around with their train?"

"Hell, I just told you it'll be nighttime. The ones in the back car won't know they've been cut off until the engine's gone two or three miles. The ones in the front car won't know the silver car's gone. Anyhow, one of you is going to be in the engine, holding a gun on the engineer to make sure he don't do anything like stopping the train."

"Where do we get an engine to haul the silver car to that mine you're talking about?" Boone asked.

"We don't," Recco replied. "We use horses. It's a level grade along there. Three horses can pull that boxcar damn near as fast as an engine can."

Conyers shook his head mournfully. "And when whoever's holding a gun on the engineer hops off, the engineer backs up

147

the car with the soldiers to the spur the silver car's on, and they chase us down."

"Not likely," Recco retorted. "We'll dynamite the tracks between the silver and the rest of the train."

"You know, Recco," Longarm said thoughtfully, "it seems to me that a boxcar's a mighty big thing to hide. How in hell do we do that?"

"There's a spur running right into the main shaft of that old mine," Recco replied quickly. "We just run the car in it."

"I don't know, Recco," Gotch said slowly. "It sounds to me like a whole shitpile of work. I don't like it."

"You'll like the money you'll get for doing it, Gotch."

"How much?"

"Thirty thousand."

"Shit, that ain't such a hell of a lot!" Pete objected. "It only splits up to about five thousand each for the six of us."

"Thirty thousand *apiece*, Pete," Recco said swiftly.

"Oh," Pete said. "Well, I guess for a wad like that, a man can afford to do some hard work."

"You've worked on a lot of train jobs, Long," Recco said. "That's one reason I wanted you on this one. You was on the other side then, but that don't matter. How does it look to you?"

"You'll have to let me think about it awhile," Longarm replied. "How much time we got to figure out the fine points?"

"We'll leave here about noon tomorrow," Recco answered. "So I guess that's how much time we've got."

"Then let's take our time thinking," Longarm suggested. "I might come up with something if I got tonight to sleep on it."

"There ain't a hell of a lot we can do till we get the new clothes Blás is sending us," Recco said. "We'll talk about it with him when he comes back out in the morning."

Most of the afternoon was spent trying on clothes from the assortment that arrived soon after lunch. Few of the men could wear the garments they wanted, but all of them were so tired of the shapeless flapping prison suits that they didn't complain. Longarm wound up wearing a bright cerise satin shirt, *charro* trousers, and a pair of needle-toed, high-heeled boots.

He felt uncomfortably conspicuous in his finery until he saw how the others looked in their selections. By suppertime they'd all stopped feeling self-conscious, though most of them swore

148

at the stiffness of their clothing when they struggled out of it at bedtime.

Always a light sleeper, Longarm snapped fully awake when a hand brushed lightly across his cheek sometime during the night. His hand was on the revolver under his blankets before he saw that the hand that had awakened him was Maruja's.

"Brazolargo," she whispered, "I am not to sleep so good. Maybe you like to take a little walk with me, no?"

"If you mean what I think you mean, Maruja," Longarm replied, his voice as low as hers, "there ain't a thing I'd rather do than take a little walk with you. And it don't matter much to me where we walk to."

Chapter 14

Silently Longarm followed Maruja as she picked her way between the blanket-covered forms of the sleeping men and started toward the brook. The *jacales* were dark, the horses silent. A sliver of moon cast a ghostly glow on the bare canyon walls as they crossed the little stream and picked their way up the now-invisible trail that led to Maruja's private retreat.

Following the girl up the winding trail along the canyon wall, his eyes adjusted now to the dim light, Longarm saw that she was wearing the same outfit she'd had on that morning. Longarm himself had stripped off his stiff new clothes before crawling into his blankets, and rolled up the prison suit to use for a pillow. When Maruja had awakened him, he'd slipped into the loose-fitting prison suit because it was both handy and easy to put on. He was wearing the brogans instead of the tight new needle-nosed boots for the same reason.

They reached the vertical pillar and Maruja slipped around it, Longarm behind her, and they stood on the ledge. At its rear, the arched mouth of the shallow cave was a black crescent in the mottled canyon wall.

Longarm said, "You sort of like this place up here, don't you, Maruja?"

"*Sí*, Ees place I can be not bother. I sleep up here some nights when ees make too much noice Catarina and *su hombre*."

"If you want to be by yourself, how come you asked me to come along?"

Maruja turned to face Longarm. "You are theenk I am *puta*

for to ask you to come weeth me here, no?" she asked, her voice low and a bit troubled.

"I don't think anything of the kind, Maruja. What I think is that you're a real woman. I've found that women have mostly got the same feelings men do, only a lot of them ain't brave enough to admit it."

"I am not brave, Brazolargo. But I am not *puta*. All I am want from you ees only to be weeth me for a while."

"Sure. I know that."

Longarm put a hand on Maruja's bare shoulder. Her flesh was warm, and as he passed his hand over the satiny skin of her shoulder and up to her chin, he felt her flinch and draw away.

"I ain't aiming to hurt you none, girl," he said. "If all you want to do is set up here and talk awhile, why, that's what we'll do."

"You are want to seet? Wait, I feex the place."

Maruja fumbled at her waist and bent forward to step out of her full-cut outer skirt. She stood for a moment in her thin underskirt, then waved the garment she'd taken off to straighten it out before spreading it on the ledge. Unfolded, the skirt was large enough for both of them to sit on.

"Sientese, Brazolargo," she invited, settling down and stretching her legs in front of her.

Longarm sat down by her, jackknifing his legs and folding them under him. He looked at her for a moment in the dim light. She was watching him, a frown on her face.

"Do I say sometheeng to make you angry, when you are leave me so queek this morning?" she asked him.

"Of course not. Why?"

"You are seet so far from me now. I theenk maybe you do not like what I say, or that I come wake you up now."

"I'm real glad you woke me up, Maruja. And this morning I just seen Recco looking for me and had to go talk to him."

"I am theenk when you go, maybe you are not to like me."

"Why, that ain't so, Maruja. You're a right nice girl."

"I am not girl," she insisted. "I am woman. Look!"

Maruja shrugged the low-cut blouse off her shoulders. The thin fabric slid down to her waist, and in the dim light Longarm saw the dark rounds of her breasts. She leaned back, her nipples thrust forward, inviting him. Longarm bent to caress them with his lips and tongue, and Maruja pulled his head down hard to bury his bearded face in the soft, resilient mounds. She arched her back, her shoulders moving from side to side, rubbing the pebbled tips against the soft abrasion of his beard.

Longarm ran the tip of his moist tongue up Maruja's chest and found the soft hollow of her throat. He lingered there for a moment, caressing her breasts with his fingers, until Maruja took his head between her hands and brought it up level with hers. She leaned forward until their lips met. Her tongue darted into his mouth and probed deeply.

From the moment he'd first touched Maruja's resilient flesh, Longarm's erection had been growing; the time he'd spent in prison had whetted the urgency of his desire. Maruja's hands were wandering over his chest, her fingers slipping beneath the loose jacket and clawing gently at the crisp curls on his chest. She ran her hands lower, to his groin, until she found the firm bulge that had risen under the thin cloth of his trousers, and closed her hand around it.

Longarm was impatient, but held himself back. He lifted Maruja's underskirt and ran his palms over the taut and quivering muscles of her rounded stomach and for a moment stroked the wiry curls of her pubic hair. Maruja parted her thighs to let Longarm's fingers slip into the warm and pulsing wetness of the lips that nestled between them. She had freed his erection now, and held it firmly in her hands.

"*Ay, qué grande!*" she said, her voice a soft sigh. "*Ponele por dentro, Brazolargo!*"

By now Longarm was more than ready. He lifted himself above Maruja and she spread her thighs wider, brought her hips up, and guided him into her. Longarm felt himself enclosed in wet, throbbing heat, and plunged. Maruja gasped as he went in, burying himself in that first swift drive. She clamped her legs high, around Longarm's waist, pulled herself up, and held him to her, her hips rocking gently and her breast heaving against the firm muscles of his chest.

"*Es magnifico, Brazolargo!*" she breathed, her cheek pressed firmly against the curls of Longarm's beard, her warm breath fanning his ear. "*Soy colmado! Colmado completamente!*"

Longarm did not answer Maruja. He was too surprised at himself to speak. The moment he'd completed that first long, deep thrust he'd found himself coming, draining but unsatisfied, his urgent desire unslaked, but only able now to hold himself inside her until his spasm had ended.

"*Se pase algo?*" Maruja asked. "*Ha ya terminado?*"

"It's all right, Maruja," Longarm assured her. "There ain't a thing wrong that a little waiting won't cure."

"*Ay, qué mal suerte!*" she breathed. "*Soy quemadura, Brazolargo! Dame que pobrezo!*"

Maruja was writhing beneath Longarm, her breath gusting. Her hips were thrusting up against him in her eagerness to go on to completion. Longarm looked down at her face, her eyes wide and questioning, her mouth twisting with the urgency of her desire.

He covered her lips with his and drove his tongue in to meet hers. As their kiss was prolonged, he felt himself beginning to swell again, but even though Maruja's writhing grew more and more urgent, Longarm did not move until his erection was full again.

Maruja's hips were still thrusting upward against him when he began to stroke once more. This time Longarm had his body firmly under control. He plunged into her with deliberate slow lunges, unhurried, while Maruja gasped as she felt the strength and depth of each prolonged penetration.

"*Ay! Es mejor!*" she breathed into his ear. "*Dame todo de esto nabo silvestre rigido, Brazolargo! Más que ahora!*"

Longarm could feel Maruja's body responding to the vigor of his thrusts as he continued to sink into her with long, leisurely strokes. The tempo of her gusty breathing increased, and Longarm matched it with the speed of his deep lunges.

Her mouth was open now, her head drawn back, her hips rotating in the beginning of her frenzy. Longarm thrust faster. Maruja began trembling, her eyes closed, and her head rolled from side to side. She moaned as ecstasy took her, and her moans swelled to small, quick shrieks as she responded to Longarm's quick, hard stroking.

"*Más! Más! Adelante!*" she groaned. "*No arrendese, Brazolargo! Adelante! De prisa, de prisa!*"

Longarm was building fast. He let himself go, wanting to prolong their embrace, but wanting more to join Maruja. She was tossing like a wild thing now, her hips bouncing, her muscles trembling. Longarm felt her orgasm beginning, and drove with a frenzy matching her own to bring himself to his own peak.

An animal-like scream escaped Maruja's throat. Her body

became rigid for an instant, then her hips heaved up and she held herself pressed against Longarm's groin, trembling and tossing in diminishing spasms while Longarm reached his peak and pushed down to hold himself against her firmly, spurting and throbbing until he lay spent on Maruja's soft, relaxed form.

"Ay, qué maravilloso!" she sighed at last, after a long period of silence. *"No es verdad, Brazolargo?"*

"If you feel as good as I do, it was."

Instead of replying, Maruja turned her head and found Longarm's lips with hers. They lay motionless for several moments, mouth pressed to mouth. Maruja stirred and Longarm moved as though to leave her, but she clasped her arms and legs around him and held him in place.

"No. I like you thees way, Brazolargo. Not more better as before, but for now ees nice."

"It'll be nicer in a little while, after we've rested for a spell," Longarm promised. "We don't have to think about anybody but ourselves till daybreak, and that's still a long time away."

Recco came up to Longarm after breakfast. "We'll have to start getting ready to ride out pretty soon. You get any ideas last night that we need to talk about?"

"Nothing special. You and Mentutes, or whoever it was put the job together, done pretty good. Except there's one thing that sort of bothers me."

"What's that?"

"You didn't say a word yesterday about what happens after we get that carload of silver to the old mine where we're supposed to hide it. Ain't you got any plans for a getaway?"

"We don't need any, dammit!" Recco snorted. "Once we get the silver car hid, we just come on back here and wait."

"Wait for what?"

"Why, for Blás to come pay us off."

"And when's that supposed to be?"

"Soon as he checks up on the silver. He ain't going to pay until he's sure we did the job."

Longarm nodded. "Can't blame him for that, I guess."

"Well?" Recco asked. "You satisfied now?"

"I reckon. There's one other thing on my mind, but that's your business, and I got no right to mix into it."

"Go ahead, as long as it's about the job."

"I been wondering who's going to do what when we take

that train. It ain't that I don't trust you and the three men that's going with us, but I don't know 'em as good as I'd like to."

"I've told everybody but you what they're supposed to do," Recco replied. "They all know where they're supposed to be and what they've got to handle."

"Maybe you better tell me my job," Longarm suggested. "I don't want to be the one that messes things up."

"I'm not worried about you," Recco said quickly. "I'll get to your part in a minute. First of all, Gotch and Conyers is pulling the couplers on the last car. Then Thomas uncouples the silver car. I'll have one of my men tending his horse, because we don't know right exactly where Thomas is going to jump off. I'll take care of the car once it's rolling free. Mentutes's men will be waiting with the extra horses, and I'll see they handle their part right. Pete's the one that'll blow the tracks. You don't know Pete, but he's as good a dynamite man as you'll find anyplace."

Recco paused, and Longarm looked at him inquiringly. "That takes care of everybody but me."

"I think you're maybe the smartest man I got, Long, so I saved you for the toughest jobs."

"Jobs? You mean more 'n one?"

"That's right. Your main job is to get in the engine cab and hold a gun on the engineer and fireman, so they don't pull no smart tricks like stopping the train."

"That don't sound too hard. What's the other one?"

"Making sure the other men do what they're supposed to. If Thomas or Conyers gets hurt or misses their jump, you take on their jobs too."

"I ain't sure I can move all that fast, Recco."

"You can handle it. And if anything happens to either one of 'em, you get their payoff on top of your own."

Longarm thought for a minute. "All right, I'll do the best I can. Now, then. You said we all meet at the old mine after the job's done, for the payoff?"

"That's how I set it up. If the soldiers get too close to us, we'll need every man we got to fight 'em off."

"I can see that," Longarm agreed. He nodded. "It's a good plan, Recco. Now all we got to do is make it work."

Preparations for the ride to the holdup scene were completed almost casually. Recco produced a stack of fresh bandannas and said, "I figure you men are smart enough to see to your own guns and ammunition, but I ain't sure you'd remember you'll need a big bandanna to cover your face, so everybody better take one. All of you know what you're supposed to do, and I promise you I'll see that anybody who fucks things up won't live long enough to be sorry. Now let's get our asses outa here and go to work."

When Longarm got his first look at the spot where the silver train was to be attacked, the rapidly setting sun was beating on his back.

It was rough, broken country, in which a hundred men could have concealed themselves behind separate rocks or in individual shallow gullies and remained invisible to any but the most attentive observer. The tracks of the railroad spur connecting the *Ferrocarriles Nacional de Mexico* with the Southern Pacific ran on a roadbed whose cuts had been gouged out of a myriad of hills and rises and ridges, and wound like a lazily stretching snake over humps and into hollows.

Looking at the sinuous rise and fall of the rails, Longarm told himself, *This might not be such a tough job after all, old son. There ain't no engineer in his right mind's going to push a train faster'n a sleepy snail can crawl over a right-of-way like this one, not even a bobtail like that silver train's supposed to be. Why, a man can walk faster'n that train's going to have to crawl along a track like this one.*

Consulting his map, Recco spotted the men where they were supposed to be to carry out their jobs. Since they'd reached the tracks above the actual spot where the action would take place, the *peon* who was to hold Longarm's horse was the first to be detached from the band.

"You'll have to leave your nag here and ride double with Gotch or Conyers," Recco told Longarm. "It ain't far to where you'll wait to hop the engine, so I guess you can stand it."

Longarm dismounted and handed the reins to the *peon,* and swung up to the rump of Conyers's mount.

Pete, whose last name Longarm had never learned, was the next to be left behind, at a wooden trestle that spanned a wide, deep gully. He was already getting his dynamite out of his saddlebags when the remainder of the group rode on.

The next to drop out was Boone, along with the *peon* who would hold Boone's horse while he was on the train and lead the animal along the tracks for Boone to mount after he'd pulled the coupling pin on the silver car. Boone caught Longarm's eye in the light that had begun to fade as the sun's rim was cut off by the western hills. He raised an eyebrow and shrugged. Longarm had no chance to acknowledge the gesture, for Recco was already moving the last of the bunch along the tracks.

They reached the spur to the abandoned silver mine, a set of rusty rails on decaying ties that angled off the main line and dipped almost at once into a canyon. Recco reined in and let out a shrill, piercing whistle. Within a few moments a horseman came out of the canyon and loped beside the spur until he reached the diminished group.

"*Adonde 'stan los caballos?*" Recco called.

"*Ahí,*" the man replied, motioning toward the gash into which the tracks disappeared.

"*Cuántos hay?*" Recco asked.

"*Ocho.*"

"*Y mozos?*"

"*Cinco.*"

"*Bueno.*" Recco nodded. "*Volvio pronto. Ayudate.*"

A half-mile farther on, at the brow of a long, steep slope, Recco halted them for the last time.

"You won't have no trouble hopping on," he told Longarm and Conyers. "That damn train won't be moving faster'n a duck-waddle by the time it gets up here." He waggled a finger at Conyers and added, "Just be damn sure you cut loose that car full of soldiers while it's still on the downslope. Long," he went on, "if the engineer balks or tries to back up, kill the bastard. By God, you better shoot him anyhow, just before you jump. That way it'll take 'em longer time to get to the junction and report what's happened."

Longarm shrugged. "Whatever you say, Recco."

Recco flicked the reins to turn his horse, then remembered something and swiveled in the saddle to call, "Don't forget where you are, either. That damn train's supposed to be right about here inside of the next hour, but if it ain't, wait for it! I never did see a Mexican train that run on time!"

Longarm slid off Conyers's horse and Conyers dismounted, as did Gotch. They watched Recco until he disappeared in the darkening dusk. Conyers said, "Well, we're sure to hear the train before it gets here. I'm going to find me the softest place I can on this damn hard ground and grab me forty winks."

"That's the best idea you've had in a long time," Longarm

told the lanky man. He hadn't been looking forward to swapping talk for an hour or two with Conyers. The convict was both long-winded and quick-witted, and if they talked he'd have to be on guard to avoid making a conversational slip. "Guess I'll do the same."

Gotch said, "Hell, if you're gonna sleep, that don't leave much else for me to do, I guess."

After Gotch and Conyers had tethered their horses, all three of them stretched out on the smoothest piece of ground they could locate. Longarm didn't bother watching his companions. He'd had no sleep at all the night before, and knew he needed to be alert every instant after he'd boarded the train. He made a pillow of his hat and in a few moments was asleep.

Conyers's hand shaking his shoulder roused Longarm. The thin man said, "I heard something that sounded like a train a few minutes ago, but I ain't seen a headlight yet."

"In this place you might not see a headlight till the train gets ten feet from us," Longarm grunted, sitting up. He put the crease back into the hat and downed it before getting to his feet. Looking down the track, he thought he could see a faint glow still several miles distant. He said to Conyers, "Your ears are pretty good. I'd swear that's a steam engine headlight yonder."

"Sure looks like it to me too," Conyers agreed.

"If it's the train," Gotch put in, "I guess we better start getting ready."

"I been ready ever since we got here," Longarm told him. "But that's the train, all right, and it's going to be on us before too much longer. If I was you, Gotch, I'd get the horses back from the right-of-way, where the headlight won't pick 'em up. Me and Conyers are going to have to lay down close to the tracks and try to look like rocks."

Gotch started leading the horses away from the tracks. Conyers asked Longarm, "What d'you think, Long, had I better jump first, or had you?"

"It don't make that much difference, the way I see it. Why don't we just figure on jumping when the car we're supposed to get on comes by us?"

"What happens if we miss our jump?"

"If anybody misses, Recco told me to cover their jobs too. Of course, it wouldn't hurt anything if you was to handle what I'm supposed to do, should I miss out on jumping."

Conyers chuckled grimly. "The best thing to do is for us not to miss."

"Oh, sure. But just in case—"

"Yeah. I'll cover you."

"We better stretch out about now," Longarm suggested. "I can hear that engine's pistons working."

They stopped to listen. The train's headlight had grown steadily brighter while they'd been waiting, and as Longarm had remarked, the slapping hiss of the locomotive's pistons was now audible. Conyers walked a dozen yards down the slope, to be sure he'd get the coupling pin out while the last car was still going up the grade. He was soon out of sight in the darkness.

Longarm walked slowly to the head of the slope. The noise of the engine had grown much louder, and now the headlight was swinging around the curve at the foot of the grade. Longarm found a boulder by the right-of-way and crouched down behind it. The locomotive began puffing more laboriously as it chuffed up the slope. The ground around Longarm's hiding place was drenched in the yellow glow of the headlight.

Shielded from the headlight's glare by the boulder, Longarm folded his bandanna into a triangle and tied it in place. The train was close enough now for him to see along the ground the streaks of light made by the lamps in the two coaches. He saw Conyers jump and disappear between the last two cars. Then the headlight was opposite him and Longarm took two giant steps and made his leap.

Chapter 15

Longarm's foot hit the step of the locomotive's cab, his left hand caught the grab-bar, and his right hand swept his pistol out of its holster in a split-second series of coordinated movements.

His unexpected entry into the cab and the sight of the Colt's muzzle swiveling to cover the engineer and firemen proved so distracting to them that they did not notice the slight forward lurch the train gave as Conyers pulled the coupling pin to cut off the last car from the string.

Longarm had already memorized the phrase that he intended to use on the engineer and fireman. *"Arriba los manos!"* he called, raising his voice so they would be sure to hear him over the noise of the train.

For a moment the two crewmen stared unbelievingly at the apparition that had appeared from the blackness of the night, the tall, masked *gringo* who clung with one hand to the grab-rail and threatened them with a revolver in the other. They they decided to believe in the reality of the Colt's blued-steel muzzle and raised their hands.

Longarm had also composed in advance a few other useful phrases from his limited vocabulary of seldom-used Spanish. His first had been so successful that he decided to try another. Swinging the Colt to threaten the engineer, he commanded, *"No solpe el pito!"*

"Bueno, hombre!" the engineer said quickly. *"No tiramos! Hacemos algún que se dice!"*

Longarm nodded. *"Si hace que dice, no tiene miedo,"* he said. *"Servise* locomotive *y todo sera bueno."*

"Sí, hombre," the engineer told him. *"Qualquier que quiere."*

"Bueno," Longarm replied.

He watched the trainmen for a moment. Their eyes were fixed on his Colt, and the looks on their faces told Longarm that he had nothing to worry about from them. He looked ahead along the track, and in the cone of light cast by the engine's headlight he got a glimpse of Boone waiting to jump aboard. The train was starting up the next long grade by now. It began to slow down, straining on the uphill pull, and the engineer reached for the throttle bar. Longarm stepped up into the cab and shoved the Colt's muzzle into the man's ribs.

"No hacele!" Longarm said harshly. The engineer dropped his hand and sat motionless.

Suddenly there was a jar and the engine began picking up speed. The engineer instinctively started to raise his hand, but Longarm jabbed his ribs with the revolver's muzzle and the man brought the hand down at once.

Shots sounded over the clanking of the locomotive. Longarm risked leaving the engineer and fireman unobserved for the moment it took him to move back to the step and glance toward the rear. There was only the single passenger coach behind the tender now, and orange flashes of muzzle blasts were cutting the night from its windows.

Longarm looked ahead. At the edge of the headlight's glare he thought he could make out the figures of the *peon* and the horses. He held his place while the train ground on up the long grade, slowly losing speed.

A brilliant burst of flame spurted far down the tracks, and for an instant the scene was brightly lighted as Pete's dynamite charges blew up the trestle. Before the light died, the rumble of an explosion sounded—a dull, rolling thud that, for a second or two, overrode the mechanical clanking of the straining locomotive.

A moment or two slipped by. The rifle fire from the coach had stopped now. Longarm glimpsed the waiting horses as the engine chugged laboriously past them. He holstered his revolver and was on the verge of letting go when he caught a glimpse of movement at the back of the tender.

Clinging to the grab-bar, Longarm let off two fast shots at the shadowy form he could now see mounting the top of the tender. The man dropped.

Longarm wasn't sure whether his snapshooting had been accurate or whether the man trying to reach the engine had just flattened himself out when he saw the Colt's muzzle flash, but he knew it was time for him to get off the train. He slid the revolver back in its holster and leaped.

While he was still in midair, Longarm got a flashing glimpse of the passenger coach as it went past him. He saw a confusion of men in the tan uniforms of the Mexican army milling around in the coach, then it was gone and his feet were hitting the hard ground.

Longarm went down, rolling to lessen the impact. He was twenty or thirty feet from the tracks when he stopped and stood up, testing his arms and legs to make sure everything was still working. The train had continued chugging up the long slope, but it slowed to a stop while he was looking at it. Silhouetted against the bright cone of light from the headlamp he saw men dropping off the coach and milling around, and heard faintly the shouts of the officers trying to assemble the soldiers.

Hooves clattered in the darkness. Longarm called, *"Aquí, hombre!"* The hoofbeats drew closer and he could make out the dim forms of the horses with the *peon* astride one, leading Longarm's mount. The man saw Longarm and reined in; Longarm swung into the saddle and the two men started back to join the others.

By the time they reached the spur leading to the abandoned mine, the rest of the group had already arrived. Recco had produced torches from his saddlebags, lengths of sticks with oily rags twisted around one end. He was lighting the torches between shouts to his men to work faster. The *mozos* handling the horses had already worked the silver car through the rusty switch that shunted it to the mine spur, and were now switching the horses to the opposite end of the boxcar, to pull the car into the canyon that led to the mine.

Tom Boone rode up and reined in beside Longarm. Keeping his voice low, he said, "Damn it, we're better outlaws than we are lawmen, Longarm. Everything went as smooth as the skin on a baby's butt. You think we've been in the wrong line of work?"

"I wouldn't exactly say that," Longarm replied. "All I can

think about right now is how I'm going to explain this deal to Billy Vail when I get back to Denver."

"You won't have to worry about that for a long time," Boone replied. "Our real job hasn't even started yet. Now we've got to figure out how we're going to get away from Recco's gang with Curley Parker, and after that, how we're going to persuade him to tell us about his gold cache."

"Just eat the apple one bite at a time," Longarm advised. "That's what I been doing. It might not get me no further no faster, but it sure saves a lot of fretting."

"I never had much taste for apples," Boone said. "But I'd sure give a pretty penny for a shot of good U.S. bourbon right this minute, even if Recco did tell us there'd be no drinking in the hideout or on the job."

"I wouldn't say no to a drink, myself. Even bourbon would taste good, if I had me a cigar to go with it."

Amid shouts from Recco and his gang as they urged the horses ahead, the silver-laden boxcar began to move slowly along the spur that led to the mine. It reached the slope into the canyon and gained speed. Recco jumped on the boxcar and climbed atop it to handle the brake and keep the car from overrunning the horses. With a great deal of creaking and the occasional splintering of a decayed tie, the car rolled into the canyon.

Longarm and Boone exchanged glances, and Longarm nodded. He glanced around the right-of-way; Conyers, Pete, and Gotch were hunkered down, talking, paying little attention to the silver car. Nudging their horses ahead, Longarm and Boone followed the creaking boxcar as it rolled slowly along the rusted rails.

Helped by the downslope of the canyon floor, the silver car made fast progress over the half-mile or so of track that lay between the switch and the entrance to the mine. The tunnel that led to the abandoned shaft slanted off the canyon wall, and the tracks entered it on a slight curve. Longarm and Boone dismounted and followed the car on foot, the light from the smoking torches giving the scene a spooky, unreal atmosphere.

Thirty or forty feet along the tunnel, the old shafts began to open from the walls. They were just high enough to allow a man to stand erect in them, and Longarm could have spanned their width with his outstretched arms. He glanced idly into the first two, saw nothing but trodden earth and pick-scarred walls, and was about to go by the third when a half-dozen bulging burlap bags caught his eye.

"Wait a minute," he told Boone.

Stepping into the shaft, Longarm lifted the mouth of one of the bags and peered inside. Only the dimmest light trickled into the opening from the torches ahead, but he saw that the sack contained nothing more than a dozen or so sticks of dynamite. At one side of the bags lay a large coil of fuse.

"Did you find anything interesting?" Boone asked, stepping into the shaft.

"Nothing but some old dynamite they must've left behind when they quit working," he replied. "Let's get on back outside where the air's fresher. Recco can handle what's left of this job without any help from us."

At the mouth of the canyon, Longarm and Boone found that the other escapees had been caught up in the reaction of lethargy that follows a period of intense and dangerous action. Conyers, Gotch, and Pete were lying on the hard ground beside the right-of-way, half asleep. Longarm and Boone joined them, and dozed fitfully until Recco and his crew returned.

Daylight was an hour old and the sun was bathing the western wall of the box canyon when they got back to camp. The uplift that had followed the successful diversion of the silver had evaporated during the long ride, and all the men were tired and edgy. Maruja did not greet Longarm openly when the hungry group hurried up to the cooking fire, but she looked at him with knowing eyes and gave him the secret ghost of a smile, then turned her head to gaze in the direction of the brook.

Curley Parker, looking more and more like a skeleton than the husky man he had obviously once been, joined the group when they settled down around the fire for breakfast. While they ate, Boone gave the old outlaw an often-interrupted account of their night's work; Parker could not resist breaking in occasionally with a word of approval, or to recall an incident from some job he and one of the gangs he'd led or ridden with had pulled off in the past.

Longarm was silent; he devoted himself to the refried beans and fried eggs and tortillas that had been the unvarying breakfast menu since their arrival. Equally silent were the three men from the gang of *mozos* who'd handled the horses and who had joined the group without a word being said when Recco had given the word to saddle up and ride. As soon as the last egg had been eaten and the final tortilla had been taken from the stack that had stood eight inches high on the edge of the griddle, the men around the fire fell silent.

Conyers broke the hush. He asked Recco, "When's Mentutes going to be here to pay us off?"

"Tonight, maybe. Maybe not until tomorrow. Why? You ain't got anyplace special you want to go, have you, Conyers?"

"No. I just like to get what's coming to me when I've done a job, that's all."

"You don't have to worry about Mentutes," Recco said. "He just wants to make sure the silver's safe before he pays, that's all. He'll be here, so rest easy."

"Oh, I aim to do that," Conyers replied. He scooped up the last bit of egg yolk from his plate with what was left of his *tortilla* and popped it in his mouth. After he'd chewed and swallowed, he stood up and stretched. "Somebody wake me up when Mentutes gets here, if I don't rouse up when I smell that wad of cash he'll be carrying."

Conyers walked off, whistling. Pete and Gotch followed soon after, and when Parker tottered to his feet to start back to his bedroll, Boone went with the old man to help him. Longarm was left sitting with Recco and his men around the fire. The women had gone back to the *jacales* as soon as they finished cooking.

"You got something on your mind, Long?" Recco asked.

"No more'n usual. Why're you asking?"

"Oh, I just thought because you stayed behind—" Recco let his words die away, and shrugged.

"I reckon I'm just about like Conyers and the others, waiting for Mentutes to get here with the payoff money. Like these fellows here that come back with us. Ain't that what they're waiting for too?"

"These are Mentutes's men," Recco said quickly. "They wasn't with the other ones that handled the horses: they're supposed to wait here and go back with Mentutes. The others took the horses back, they ain't in on the payoff."

"You mean these three are?"

"Hell, Long, I don't know!" Recco replied edgily. "They said they was supposed to stick with us, so I guess Mentutes is going to meet 'em here. Why're you so interested?"

"No reason. Just wondering. Your friend Mentutes keeps a real close mouth, don't he?"

"Like everybody else in our line," Recco pointed out.

"Oh, sure." Longarm fell silent.

After a moment Recco said, "You know, I've got half an idea you'd like to pull out when you get your share of this job."

"I hadn't thought about it, one way or the other."

"Don't forget we've got a deal to go after the gold the old man's got cached away."

"That's been on my mind, Recco. As I see it, the trouble's going to be getting him to tell us where he hid it. Parker don't seem inclined to talk to anybody much but Thomas."

"I notice you been doing a lot of talking to Thomas lately. I thought you and him wasn't on any kind of good terms."

"We ain't. That don't mean we're still fighting mad at each other, the way we was when we got to the prison. Hell, we're grown-up men, Recco. Ain't no reason for us to be hard-assed and maybe mess up a job."

"I guess that follows," Recco said thoughtfully. "Tell you the truth, I ain't got much use for Thomas myself."

"Seems like I remember you saying something like that about me, not too long ago."

Recco sat silently for a moment, then said, "That was before we put in together. Things is sorta different now."

"Sure. Things begun to change between me and Thomas when I seen him working on Curley Parker. Hell, soon as I found out who Parker was, I seen what Thomas was after! He was hoping the old man would tell him where that army gold's stashed."

"You think Parker's told him?"

"Now that's hard to say." Longarm frowned. "Parker's been real close-mouthed with me. Maybe he's talked to Thomas. Wasn't any way for me to tell, that's why I dragged 'em along when you busted out."

"But you don't have no more use for Thomas now than you did when he turned you in for taking his bribe?"

"How'd you feel if you'd been me?" Longarm asked.

"I'd still be ready to shoot the son of a bitch," Recco said curtly.

"Well, then." Longarm shrugged. Deciding that the conversation was taking a turn he didn't want to pursue, he stood up. "Seeing as there ain't nothing better to do, I guess I'll catch forty winks myself."

Longarm stood by his bedroll for a moment, staring down at the tousled blankets. Then he started toward the brook. He looked for Maruja as he walked down to the little stream and turned along its bank until he reached the crossing. A rustling in the brush behind him sent him spinning around. He drew as he turned, and was ready to fire the instant he learned whether or not he had a target. Seeing Maruja coming toward him along the stream, he holstered his Colt somewhat sheepishly.

Maruja had stopped when Longarm whirled. She stood staring at him, her eyes wide with a mixture of astonishment and fear. She said, "You are scare me, Brazolargo. I am theenk you weel shoot me."

"Now, you know I wouldn't do that, Maruja." Longarm went back along the brook to where she'd stopped. "There's been times when somebody's come up in back of me with a gun, though, so I figure to be ready when I turn around. You understand that, don't you?"

Maruja nodded slowly. *"Sí."* Then she asked, "You are *pistolero*, like other ones Blás ees breeng here, no?"

"I guess you'd have to call me that now. Why?"

"Ees because you are not to act like them. You—you are not bad man, Brazolargo, thees in *mi corazón* I am know."

"Maybe I'm worse than you think."

She shook her head. "No. I am to see the *pistoleros* Blás is breeng before. They are not like you. Thees ees why I have sadness when I find out you are to go."

Longarm frowned. "Maybe you know something I ain't heard about. Who told you I was going to leave?"

"Nobody ees tell me. I am hear Catalina talk weeth Recco so soon after you are feenish *la comida*."

"Catalina's one of the women that cooks, one you help?"

Maruja nodded.

"You're the only woman I said two words to since I got here," Longarm told her. "What give her the idea I was going to leave?"

"Was not you only, Brazolargo," Maruja explained. "I am hear Catalina tell Recco she is have only the food to feex for so many men as here at *el desayuno* tomorrow morning. She say ees nothing to cook for *la comida* and *la cena*."

"And what'd Recco say?"

"He ees tell Catalina she ees not to worry. He say she ees not to have beeg meals to feex *mañana, sobre el desayuno*."

"But he didn't call my name, or anything like that?"

Maruja shook her head. "No. But eef all others go, you are go weeth them, no?"

"I ain't real sure that's what Recco's got in mind, Maruja. I aim to go and do a little finding out, though."

"You are go to do thees theeng now, Brazolargo?" Maruja's face grew sad. "I am theenk we are to go—"

"Up on the ledge there, to the cave," Longarm said. "That was what I come out here for too. What I got to do can't wait, Maruja. You understand why?"

"Eef you say eet ees, I am onderstand. We are wait for tonight, no?"

"We are wait for tonight, yes." Longarm smiled. He grew very serious as he went on, "You ain't talked to nobody else about this, have you?"

"No. I am come to find you first."

"That's good. Now do something for me, Maruja. Don't say a word about what you heard Catalina tell Recco, or what he said to her. Will you promise me that?"

"*Seguro*, Brazolargo. I am promise."

"Good. Now there's something else I want you to do. After supper tonight, as soon as you can slip away, you go up to that cave up there. Take along a blanket or something, because I want you to sleep up there tonight."

"And you weel come to be weeth me?" she asked.

"If I can, Maruja. And if I can't, it won't be because I ain't tried. You stay here a little while. I don't want anybody to see us going back to camp together."

Longarm was thoughtful as he walked back to the camp. What Maruja had just told him, coupled with his earlier conversation with Recco, had raised in his mind some disturbing thoughts.

Old son, he told himself as he made his way slowly along the bank of the little brook, *it might be you're just seeing ghosts under the bed again, or would be if you had a bed. If Mentutes does show up here before the day's out with the payoff money, then everything's on the up and up.*

But it's sort of fishy, him telling that woman so certain that she wasn't going to have to worry about meals for us after tomorrow. Now, you might be wrong about what you're thinking, but you go on thinking what you are until you see the color of Mentutes's money. Because the only sure way Recco'd have of knowing we wasn't going to be here to eat any meals after breakfast tomorrow is if we was all the kind of men that don't eat meals at all. And that's dead men, old son.

Chapter 16

Recco was nowhere in sight when Longarm got back to the hideout, nor was his horse in the rope corral. None of the women or the men who were the hideout's regular occupants were visible. The three pistoleros Recco had brought back from the mine were very much in sight, though. Still wearing the crossed bandoliers and wide gunbelts that were the symbols of their trade, they sat on the ground in the scanty shade provided by one of the *jacales*.

Their rifles leaned against the wall of the shack, and though it was the hour after noon, when all of Mexico traditionally retired for siesta, they were peeling the cornhusks off tamales which they took from a large pot on the ground in front of them. As fast as one of the little meat-filled cornmeal rolls was peeled, it disappeared into a gaping, mustache-fringed mouth.

Longarm watched them covertly for a few moments, standing at the edge of the hideout, then walked unhurriedly to the first shack in the line of three that stood between the cooking firepit and the corral. He lifted the spout-fitted can that he'd seen one of the women carrying back there after she'd started the noonday cooking fire the previous day.

A sniff at the spout confirmed his suspicion that the can held kerosene. He took out the bandanna he'd used as a mask the night before and doused it with the fluid, then walked back to where his blankets were spread. Drawing his pistol, he unloaded it and removed the cylinder, then methodically started to clean it.

While he worked, the hideout began to awaken from the hushed sleepiness into which it had fallen after the men had eaten their belated breakfast. Gotch was the first to stir. He sat up from the tangle of his blankets, stared around blankly, then hurried in the direction of the latrine near the rope corral at the back of the canyon.

Boone roused himself next. Since the group had arrived, he and Curley Parker had slept at the opposite side of the firepit from the others, just as Longarm had chosen to spread his blanket a little apart from the spaces occupied by Conyers, Gotch, and Pete.

Boone came over to Longarm, and stood for a moment watching him try to remove an especially stubborn spot of rust on the Colt's cylinder. He shook his head.

"You're never going to get that gun in good shape," he said. "The one I got hold of is a lot worse, so after I'd looked at it twice, I decided not to bother even trying to clean it."

"Well, I got to admit it's sort of a losing battle," Longarm told him. He wiped the excess kerosene off the cylinder and frame assembly, slipped the cylinder back into position, locked it, and tried the trigger-pull two or three times before he reloaded the weapon. He added, "It hurts me just the same to see a good gun go to pot this way. Especially when it's me that's depending on it."

Boone nodded abstractedly. He was looking at the trio of pistoleros. He asked Longarm, "What in hell are those fellows eating, and where'd they get it?"

"I keep forgetting you ain't been down this way before," Longarm said. "Those are tamales they're putting away, a little dab of meat and red pepper plastered over with cornmeal and wrapped up in a shuck before they're cooked."

"Where'd they get 'em?" Boone repeated.

"I guess the women fixed 'em up."

"Why in hell didn't they fix us some? I kept waiting for the women to come out and fix something, but it sure doesn't look like they're going to. I looked around for Recco to ask him why we haven't been fed, but he's gone off somewhere."

"I noticed that too. I guess the women are all having their siesta, and maybe they just figured we was going to sleep through till suppertime."

"Well, I'm hungry enough," Boone said. "It's Parker I'm worrying about, though. We've got to keep him alive, dammit, and he's not strong enough to miss and meals. That's why I came to see if I could find some grub."

"I got to admit my bellybutton's scraping against my backbone," Longarm said. "And for all I know, the women might've fixed us a pot of them tamales. Why don't we just mosey over and find out?"

While Longarm and Boone were talking, Conyers and Pete had emerged from their blankets and were standing, looking around the hideout area.

Conyers called, "It's about time we hung on the feedbag, ain't it? You had anything to eat yet?"

"Not a bite," Longarm replied. "We're just going over to see if we can't rustle up some grub."

"We'll go along with you, then," Conyers said. He started over to join them, followed by Pete.

Longarm tapped on the sagging door of the nearest shanty. A woman's voice called, *"Quién es?"*

"We're looking for some food, ma'am," Longarm said.

"Cómo?" she asked.

"Grub," he replied. "Eats."

"Ah. Es que quieres comer?" she asked.

"Sí," he called in reply. *"Comida."*

"Pues, hay tamales sobre el tarro! Comelos ahorita, y poco tiempo cocemos la cena," she said impatiently. *"No encomodarme al vez de la siesta!"*

"What'd she say?" Conyers asked.

"Near as I can make out, she says that pot of tamales them men of Recco's are dipping into is all we're going to have until suppertime."

"We better go get our share of 'em while the getting's good, then," Pete said. "I seen them fellows chomping away, and the way they was going, that pot might be clear empty by now."

Marching around the *jacal*, the four men found the pistoleros still eating, though their pace was more deliberate than it had been when Longarm first noticed them. The pistoleros watched the approaching men, but did not stop eating.

Longarm looked at the ground at the pistoleros' feet, covered with pink-tinged cornhusks, then peered into the pot. It was almost half full. He pointed to husks on the ground.

"Seems to me you've ate your share of them tamales," he said quietly. "It's our turn now."

Two of the pistoleros looked at the third, their eyebrows

drawn together questioningly. One of the two asked, *"Qúe dice el gringo?"*

"Quiere comer."

"Pues, dejales," the man said. *"No olvide que dice Recco."*

"Y tu, Barrera?" the middleman asked of the third.

"Lo que seas," the third man shrugged. *"Soy completado."*

With the needle-pointed toe of his lavishly stitched boot, the pistolero pushed the pot toward Longarm. *"Tomelo, gringo,"* he said arrogantly. *"Come bueno en nuestros sobrantes."*

Longarm got the gist of the pistolero's words, though even if he hadn't, the man's tone would have been enough. His jaw tightened, but he knew this was not the time to begin swapping insults. He picked up the pot and started for the firepit, the others following him.

"You know," Boone said judicially, when they were out of earshot of the pistoleros, "I don't think they've got much use for us."

"Yeah," Conyers agreed. "They need a good lesson."

"If we stick with Recco, maybe we'll have a chance to give 'em one," Gotch suggested.

Longarm stopped at the firepit and put down the pot. "Well, dig in. It don't look like much, but I reckon it's all we're going to get till supper."

"I'm going to take a few over to Curley," Boone said. "He didn't feel too good when he woke up a while ago, maybe a bite of food will help him."

After Boone had left, Conyers frowned at Longarm. "How come you're getting along so good with Thomas?" he asked. "After all the trouble he's got you in, seems like you'd still be mad."

"Oh, I am," Longarm replied. "I just made up my mind not to let it show until we finish up this job."

"If we ever do," Pete put in sourly. "I ain't so sure I wanta stick with Recco, once we get paid off for what we done. Hell, this ain't no kinda place for a man to be. I like a town, where a man can have a drink and find a woman when he feels like he wants one." He grinned lopsidedly and added, "Which is right now, as far as I'm concerned."

"Yeah. We sure didn't get nothing like that where we been," Gotch said. "And this place here ain't much better."

Longarm, hunkered down beside the pot, eating tamales,

began debating as to when he should confide his suspicions to his companions. He decided he'd keep quiet until he saw what developed when Recco returned, and kept on eating.

Recco did not get back until late afternoon. By that time the mood of Conyers, Gotch, and Pete had gone from mild dissatisfaction to sullen anger. They started toward Recco as he swung out of the saddle and tossed the horse's reins to the *peon* who'd run up from the *jacales* to meet him. Recco lifted the saddlebags off his horse and slung them over his shoulder before turning to face them. Longarm sensed an argument and joined the trio waiting for Recco.

Recco read the message in the faces he saw. "I been doing my best to find Mentutes and get him here to pay you off," he said. "But you don't have to worry. Blás will be here tomorrow for sure with the money."

"You told us yesterday he was going to be here today," Conyers said. "What's holding him up?"

Recco shrugged. "Damned if I know, Conyers. I waited at the old mine for him to show up and check the silver, but he never did show up. It was too late to go looking for him after I decided he wasn't going to get there. I thought I'd better come on back so you men wouldn't start worrying."

"We ain't worrying," Pete told Recco. "We're goddamned mad. We done our jobs when you told us to. Now why ain't your friend Mentutes here to pay us like he said he would?"

"I know how you feel, Pete," Recco said. "All I can tell you is, this ain't like Blás. But let it go by tonight, will you? Remember, he's the outside man that made our breakout work. He come through then, he'll do the same this time."

"He damn well better," Conyers said.

"Listen, I brought you something to make you feel better," Recco said quickly. He laid his bulging saddlebags down and unbuckled them, then upended them carefully. Bottles of liquor rolled out onto the ground. He said, "I already told you, Blás don't allow drinking here, but you're due a good blowout. Come on, drink up! There's plenty for everybody."

Gotch and Pete wasted no time. Conyers moved a little more slowly in going over to the bottles, but he was not too far behind the other two. Longarm took his time getting up. He waited for the other three men to pick up a bottle in each hand and move away from the saddlebags before he went up. He looked at the labels on the bottles and found they were all the same; native *aguardiente,* a raw but potent sugar-cane brandy. He turned away without picking up a bottle, but Recco called to him.

"What's the matter, Long? Liquor not good enough for you?"

"It ain't that, Recco. Maybe I got funny tastes, but about the only liquor I really enjoy is a good Maryland rye."

"Now where in hell would I get fancy whiskey in a place like this?"

"I don't guess you can." Privately, Longarm was wondering where Recco had gotten the eight or ten bottles he'd brought back. "But that don't hurt my feelings none. Anyhow, I don't relish a drink of anything unless I got a cigar to go with it."

Recco picked up one of the bottles and thumped it on the bottom with the heel of his hand to spring the cork, then worked the cork out. He held the bottle out to Longarm.

"Come on, Long!" he urged. "Have just one drink with me, to celebrate the job we pulled off last night!"

Longarm made a quick decision. He didn't want to quarrel with Recco, but he didn't trust him, either. Recco's apologies and explanations of Mentutes's failure to show up had struck a false note; they'd brought more than one question to Longarm's mind. So had the liquor he'd produced, in defiance of the ban on drinking in the hideout, which he'd attributed to Mentutes.

"A swallow or two won't do me no harm," he said. Recco's black eyes were fixed on him; Longarm tried to find some expression in them, but there was none. "Go ahead, Recco. After you."

His face expressionless, Recco tilted the bottle and took a long, gurgling swallow. He extended the bottle to Longarm, who took it and put down a gulp that he thought would satisfy Recco. The *aguardiente* was about what he'd thought it would be, too sweet for his taste and harsh with the bite of raw alcohol. Out of the corner of one eye he saw Tom Boone walk up while he was drinking, but when he took the bottle from his lips he did not look at Boone. Instead he held the bottle out to Recco, who pushed it back.

"Keep it, Long. You might change your mind about wanting another drink."

"Well now, I might at that," Longarm said, realizing instantly that the bottle he carried away would be that much less liquor for Conyers and Pete and Gotch to consume. "It ain't half bad, for *aguardiente*." He looked at Boone for the first time, and nodded curtly. "Thomas. How's your friend Parker doing by now?"

"What's the matter, Thomas?" Recco asked instantly. "The old man ain't sick, is he?"

"Not sick," Boone replied. "Just puny."

"You might give him a slug of Recco's liquor," Longarm suggested. "Maybe a little shot would do Parker good." He stressed Parker's name, hoping Boone would get his message.

"It might, at that," Boone agreed.

"I'd give you this bottle, but it's been drunk from," Longarm went on. "Recco's got plenty more, though, enough for you and Parker to have a bottle apiece, if you're as thirsty as Conyers and Pete and Gotch look to be."

Boone's eyes flicked quickly over to the blankets where the three escapees were sitting, tilting up their bottles, then he said, "I guess I'll take Long's advice, then, and get Parker and me each a bottle."

"Sure, there's plenty for everybody," Recco said. He indicated the bottles that still lay beside his deflated saddlebags. "Help yourself."

Boone picked up two of the bottles of *aguardiente*, and Longarm knew that his message had gotten through to the Secret Service man. Boone started back to where Parker was propped up in his blankets, watching. Longarm saw him sit down and begin talking to the old outlaw.

Tucking under his arm the bottle Recco had opened, Longarm said, "Guess I'll go over and stretch out awhile before supper." Looking innocently at Recco, he asked, "It'll be about the usual time, won't it?"

"Sure." He gestured to the pistoleros. "I've got to get them started on another job Blás wants them to do."

"Thought you hadn't seen Mentutes," Longarm said.

"I haven't. Mentutes has got more than one job going, Long. He sent them here so I could start them out at the right time."

Longarm nodded. "I see."

Going back to his blankets, Longarm stretched out and put the bottle on the ground beside his blankets, thinking that later on he'd find a way to tip it over and let it drain. The conversation between Recco and the cook, which Maruja had repeated to him earlier, was still in the forefront of his thoughts.

There were a few other matters that bothered him: the location of Mentutes's headquarters or home or whatever base he might work from; the real reason why the chief organizer of the breakout and the theft of the silver-car hadn't shown up as Recco had promised he would; the source of the liquor that Recco had brought to the hideout, and the reason he'd brought it.

Longarm looked distastefully at the bottle of *aguardiente*. For a moment he wished it were Tom Moore and that he had a cigar to smoke while he had a swallow. He leaned back and closed his eyes, and the next thing he knew, the noise of Catalina preparing supper awakened him. He looked around. Boone and Parker were sitting up, but Conyers and Gotch and Pete hadn't been roused by the noise.

Recco had not returned and the pistoleros were nowhere in sight. The bottle of *aguardiente* still stood beside his bedroll. He tossed the bottle as far as he could throw it. The tinkle of glass it made as it hit the rocky ground made him feel better; it also roused the three men who'd been sleeping. They sat up, staring around groggily. Then, as though the idea had occurred to all of them at the same time, they groped around for their bottles and started toward the supper fire.

If Recco's idea had been to get his dissatisfied gang members drunk so they would forget their anger, the *aguardiente* didn't do its work very well. Supper was a sullen affair, with Conyers, Gotch, and Pete drunk enough to be quarrelsome but not enough to be happy.

They ate in morose silence at the beginning of the meal, gathering around the big pot of *albondigas,* fishing the little balls of chopped meat from the chili sauce in which they'd been cooked, and chewing them morosely, washing them down with gulps of liquor from the freshly opened bottles they brought to the cooking fire. Then one unhappy remark about Mentutes's failure to show up was dropped, followed by another, then still others, until at last Conyers made the first overt threat.

"You know what we're going to do if that damned Mentutes don't show up here tomorrow?" Conyers demanded, staring at Longarm. "We're going after him!"

"How you think you're going to find him, Conyers?" Longarm asked. "Recco never has told any of us where Mentutes lives."

Conyers stared blankly at Longarm for a moment, then his face twisted and he exploded, "What the hell are you getting at, Long? It ain't Recco we're mad at, it's Mentutes! Recco's our kind, he wouldn't sell us out." He looked at Longarm scornfully and added, "But I guess a turncoat lawman wouldn't understand about that, now would you?"

"You been drinking a mite too heavy, Conyers," Longarm said mildly. "I won't hold what you said against you. And don't forget, we was all in that train job together. I got as much of a stake in it as you have."

There was an uncomfortable silence, then Conyers jerked his thumb in the direction of their bedrolls. He said, "Come on, let's go get comfortable. We'll wait till Recco gets back and see what he says about Mentutes."

Gotch and Pete nodded owlishly. Longarm started to caution them to sober up, but when Conyers tilted his bottle to his lips again, he decided he'd be wasting words.

Instead he said, "If I was you men, I'd sleep with one eye open till we get squared away with Recco and Mentutes. The more I look at them two, the less I like 'em."

"Don't worry about us, Long!" Pete said. "We can look out for ourselves, we don't need no nursing."

Longarm opened his mouth to reply angrily, but closed it before the words in his mind came out. For the first time he realized that the feelings of the others had not changed, that they were accepting his company only because they had no other choice, just as had been the case in prison.

Pete drained the bottle he was holding and looked around. "There's some more of this stuff someplace." Getting to his feet, he weaved over to the place where Recco had emptied his saddlebags and came back carrying the two remaining bottles of *aguardiente*. "Guess we drunk all but these," he announced. "Well, come on, Conyers, Gotch. Let's go over where we can be comfortable and have us a little nightcap."

Longarm was left standing beside the firepit, trying to think of a way to warn the three men without giving them the idea that he was trying to wet-nurse them. He'd been unable to come up with any ideas when Boone came over.

"You and our friends have different ideas about some things, it seems," he said. "I was afraid, for a minute there, that you were going to give us away."

"They're too damn drunk to listen to reason, Tom. But I'll

give you the same tip I gave them. Sleep light."

"You going on anything but a hunch?"

"No. But there's something ass-backward about this deal we got into. It don't smell right to me. Never has, I guess."

"Hell, we're all nervous, Long," Boone said. "Chances are Mentutes had to scrabble to get his hands on as much cash as it's going to take to make the payoff. But there must be fifty or sixty tons of silver in that boxcar. He'd be a fool not to come through with what he's promised them."

"Mentutes don't strike me as being a fool," Longarm replied. "That's one of the things that bothers me. Just remember, look out for yourself and Parker if things begin to shake loose."

Boone nodded. "I sleep with one eye open whenever I'm in enemy territory. Now I'd better get back to Curley. He's not in real good shape yet."

Longarm went to his bedroll and lay down. The ammunition in his pants pockets gouged into him; he emptied the pockets, laying the cartridges where he could grab them at once if he needed them. He started to pull the blanket up over him, but thought better of it. He looked around. The nearest cover was twenty yards away, in the thin stand of cacti and low-lying desert juniper that extended a dozen yards from the little brook.

Placing his hat at the end of the blankets where his head usually rested, he pulled and tugged at the blankets until they took and retained a shallow hump that, in pitch darkness, might be mistaken for the form of a sleeping man. Then, taking the Spencer carbine he'd gotten from the man killed in the breakout, he made his way into the brush and stretched out on the bare ground.

When he woke with a start, Longarm's first thought was that he'd been awakened by the one of the drinkers. He'd lost track of the length of time he lay awake before dropping off to sleep, but after he'd lain quietly for a few seconds he remembered that the hideout had grown quiet even before he dozed. When he'd fallen asleep, the loud buzz of talk from the blankets where Conyers and Pete and Gotch sat drinking had finally given way to drunken snoring. The *jacales* had been dark and quiet since soon after Catalina left the cooking fire. From the blankets where Boone and Parker lay, there was no sound.

Almost total darkness engulfed the canyon, for the quarter moon had not yet risen. All that Longarm had to go by was sound, and the air was completely still. He was about to try to go back to sleep again when he heard a faint grating of feet on hard ground. The noise brought him up to his knees instantly, and he strained his eyes once more, trying to penetrate the darkness.

He heard nothing for a long moment. Then the silence and the darkness were broken at the same time. A thin, piercing trill of someone whistling preceded by a split second the bright streaks of muzzle blast from four guns, their reports coming so close together that Longarm would have taken them for a single report had it not been for the red-orange flashes.

Although the muzzle blasts lasted for only a tiny fraction of a second, they impressed on Longarm's eyes the sight of three dark figures standing over the blankets where Conyers and Gotch and Pete lay snoring, and a fourth silhouette of a man standing beside his own empty bedroll.

Chapter 17

Longarm's revolver was in his hand almost before the red glow that silhouetted the images of the four men had faded from the retinas of his eyes. He drew with the instant reflex that had become an instinct, his muscles responding to years of having reacted spontaneously to danger. But then reason took over from instinct and kept him from tightening his trigger finger.

Darkness had already hidden Longarm's targets. The high, steep walls of the canyon cut off all but a narrow strip of the sky, and the blackness shrouding the canyon floor was so deep that even with his eyes adjusted to the dark, Longarm could see only five or six feet ahead. Reason dictated that if he could not see anyone, no one could see him, but that a shot fired now would give away his hiding place.

There was no doubt in Longarm's mind that Recco and his three pistoleros had fired the shots he was sure had killed Conyers, Pete, and Gotch, and had been intended to kill him. He got proof when a match flared in the darkness, revealing Recco's face. Now Longarm had a target. He fired, guessing at the location and angle of Recco's body by the glow of the match. He knew the gamble he was taking by firing at a target he could not see, and a split second after he'd triggered the shot, Longarm knew he'd lost his gamble, for instead of crumpling to the ground, Recco flicked the match away.

"*Esta Long!*" Recco shouted to his pistoleros. "*Enterarte y matele!*"

A scraping of boots moving over hard earth broke the hush

as the pistoleros started to obey Recco's command. Longarm picked up his Spencer carbine and used the noises made by the gunmen to cover the lesser sounds he made as he moved. He picked his way by memory around the edge of the area where the escapees had been sleeping, trying to reach the spot where Boone and Curley Parker had been bedded down.

He found them by groping through the darkness to the spot where they'd put their bedrolls. They were together, standing indecisively, Boone supporting Parker.

"Let's move!" Longarm urged them in a whisper.

"What the hell's going on?" Boone asked, matching Longarm's low whisper.

"Mentutes is making his payoff. Or Recco's making it for him," Longarm replied.

"How many of 'em agin us?" Parker asked. His voice was weak and reedy.

"Four," Longarm said. "If we move fast, we can slip past 'em in the dark."

"Slip past, hell!" Parker snorted. "Gimme a gun! If there ain't but four, the three of us can take 'em!"

"Maybe so, if we could see 'em, but we're better off if we move out," Longarm told him. "Now keep quiet and come along!"

Ahead of them, the noises of the pistoleros' feet were grating as they searched the area where they'd seen the muzzle flash of Longarm's shot. Using the noises the pistoleros made to mask their own movements, Longarm guided Boone and Parker toward the brook.

He'd thought at once of Maruja's ledge as being the only defensible spot within their ability to reach. Setting his course by watching the high wall of the canyon where it cut off the stars, he led Boone and Parker in an arc that avoided the area where Recco and his men were searching. He heard the soft whisper of the little stream and headed for its sound. They were almost there when a figure loomed in the darkness a half dozen feet ahead.

Longarm got in the first shot, but the pistolero's dying reflex triggered his revolver. The slug whistled past Longarm, but behind him he heard Boone grunt. The Mexican gunman had fallen. Behind them, voices were raised and the scraping of boot soles turned into thuds as Recco and his two remaining gunmen ran toward them.

"You hit, Tom?" Longarm asked.

"I got one, but it's all right," Boone gasped. "I can keep going, if it's not too far."

Longarm stepped up closer to Boone and Parker. The Secret Service man was sagging, and now it was Parker who supported Boone. Longarm helped them cross the brook, wading it, not wasting time looking for the regular crossing. He stayed behind them as they started up the canyon wall, feeling for the trail with their feet, slipping now and then when they made a misstep. Longarm remembered most of the trail's windings and helped his companions up the canyon wall. They mounted as fast as they could, ignoring the noise their scrabbling footsteps made.

From below, Recco called, *"Son trepando de la cañon! Vente 'ca pronto! No dejarse evitan!"*

"Can you make it with Parker the rest of the way?" Longarm asked Boone. "It ain't far. They likely won't find their way up here till daylight, but I'll hang back of you in case they do."

"Sure we will," Boone gasped. "But we'd better get moving, because I'm not getting any stronger."

"We'll make it between us," Parker said. His voice sounded stronger, but Longarm knew it was only because the excitement had brought out the old man's last reserves of vitality.

Below them Longarm heard a buzz of low, angry voices, as Recco and the remaining gunmen found the body of the man he'd shot. He handed the carbine to Parker.

"Here. Don't use it unless you got to. We'll need it if we get caught up there," he told the old outlaw.

Longarm helped the pair get started up the trail again. He listened as the noise of their progress faded; there was nothing but silence from the canyon floor. Making the best of the lull, Longarm followed Boone and Parker. He moved slowly, setting his feet down with care, trying to avoid any noises that would give away their movements. He didn't know how familiar Recco was with the canyon, but he assumed that the place had been used for quite a while by Mentutes. In any event, the Mexican pistoleros would know its layout, since they were Mentutes's men.

When Longarm got to the ledge, Parker and Boone were both stretched out on the ground, and to Longarm's surprise, Maruja was bending over them. She looked up when she heard Longarm.

"Maruja!" he exclaimed. "I didn't look for you to be up here. How'd you—"

"I am come up so soon as Catalina feeneesh to cook," she said. She shook her head. "Was *tanto mas borrachera, estorbadamente*."

"It's a good thing you did," he nodded.

"*Si*, Brazolargo," she replied. "I am not like eet when ees like so." She motioned to Boone and Parker. "I am hear shooting. These are your friends, no?"

Longarm nodded. "Yes. How are they?"

She shook her head. "*El viejo*, he ees *muy debilitado*, but ees worsely the other one."

Longarm bent over the two supine forms. Parker opened his eyes. "Don't bother about me," he said. "I'm a tough old rooster, I'm gonna be around awhile yet. I ain't so sure Thomas is gonna make it, though."

Turning his attention to Boone, Longarm could tell that the old outlaw's fears were justified. The Secret Service man was unconscious and his breathing was ragged, a barely audible rasping in the silent darkness. He felt Boone's torso, found his shirt wet with blood, the wound low in his chest still seeping a thin trickle. He heard cloth tearing, and then Maruja was pressing strips of thin cotton into his hand.

"Ees for *vendajes*," she said. "I am see he ees need them before you get here."

Longarm put a wad of cloth over the seeping bullet hole and bandaged the wound as best he could. Boone did not regain consciousness while Longarm was attending to him. When he stood up, Longarm shook his head.

"He's in bad shape. Needs a doctor, but there ain't much way to get him to one."

"What ees happen?" Maruja asked. "I am hear theengs, and I am theenk you are een much trouble, but I am not to know."

Longarm explained what had happened. When he'd finished, Maruja said thoughtfully, "We are stay here, then? Until you are keel Recco and hees pistoleros?"

"That's about the size of it," Longarm nodded. "We got the edge on 'em as long as we stay here where we are. They can't see us or get at us if we're careful, and there's only Recco and two of them gunhands left. Give us a little luck, Maruja, and we'll come out of this all right. All we got to do is set tight

184

and wait for daylight. I just hope Bo—" He caught himself in time and amended, "Thomas lasts that long."

Boone did not last, though. He died just as the first faint gray light of dawn was stealing over the edge of the cliff that towered above the ledge. Longarm had sent Maruja into the cave, telling her to lie down and rest. He was stretched out on his stomach, peering over the rim, trying to see through the dimness that still obscured the canyon floor, when Parker called him.

"Long," the old outlaw wheezed, "I'm afeared Thomas just cashed in his chips."

Longarm crawled back to look. Maruja came out of the cave to join them. Boone's eyes stared up at the brightening sky, but his chest was still, his face waxen. Longarm nodded to Parker and pulled Boone's shirt up to cover his face. Parker watched silently, then looked at Longarm.

"You and him wasn't on the kinda bad terms you let on to be, was you?" he asked.

Longarm frowned at the old man, startled. "What gave you that idea?"

"Hell, son, I been around men a lot longer'n you have." Being addressed as "son" gave Longarm a start. Parker went on, "I could tell, after I watched you awhile. You two was planted in that prison to see if you couldn't weasel outa me where I stashed that gold me and my gang stole, wasn't you?"

Longarm decided it was time to lay all the cards faceup. "Something like that. How long did it take you to tumble to it?"

"About the time it took me to size you up. I knowed your name—hell, there ain't anybody on the wrong side of the law that don't know about Longarm. But till I seen you, I wasn't real sure, then I could tell right off that you ain't the kind of man that'd do what you was supposed to've. And there wasn't no reason I could see for Thomas"—he stopped and looked questioningly at Longarm—"that wasn't his real name, I guess?"

"No. His name was Tom Boone. He was with the Secret Service. They still ain't give up on finding that gold, you know."

Parker chuckled. "I know. Didn't figure they would."

"Well, that ain't neither here nor there," Longarm said.

185

"Right now we got more important things to worry about. You take it easy, Curley. I'll see what I can do about Recco and them two gunmen he's got left."

Maruja followed Longarm back to the ledge and stretched out beside him. "Hadn't you better go back and rest some more?" he asked her.

She shook her head. "No, Brazolargo. Ees no way to rest. Eef you are to watch, I weel watch too."

"All right," he agreed. "But there's going to be shooting, and when it starts, I want you to scoot back into that cave where you'll be safe."

"Eef you say I must, I must," she agreed. "But for now I stay weeth you. I wan' to help you to stop *mi primo danoso*. He ees make much the trouble for *mi familia* too."

"How, Maruja? You told me they was in trouble, but you didn't say what kind."

"Ees een no more trouble, Brazolargo."

"Well, that's good."

"Son muerte. Mi esposo, mi madre, mi padre."

"Dead?"

Maruja nodded, her face expressionless. *"Si. Le escuadra descarga."*

"Shot? A firing squad?" Again she nodded. Longarm said, "I'm sorry. I didn't understand that when you told me at first."

"Not to be sorry. Was over a long time—two years now."

"And it was Mentutes got 'em into trouble?"

"Sí."

"How?"

"I am not to know all of how, Brazolargo. Blás, he ees do theengs for *Gobernador* Duran, then *el gobernador* ees get in trouble weeth *federalistas*, and then *federalistas* are come get *mi familia*. And then *federalistas* shoot them. I ask why, after trouble ees over for *Gobernador* Duran, and he ees again beeg man, but Blás he ees say notheeng, ees say, 'You do not onderstan' thees theeng, Maruja, you are woman.' So Blás ees bring me here, and steel I do not onderstan. Ah, sí, Blás ees *mi primo*, but he ees make me to hate heem."

So much had been crowded into the past few days that Longarm had almost forgotten Maruja's relationship with Mentutes. He asked her, "How much do you know about your cousin, Maruja?"

"Tan cosa de ninguna." She shrugged. "I am see heem only

one time before ees trouble my family have. Then *mi madre* she ees tell me, go weeth Blás. He ees bring me here. Ees all."

"You know where he lives?" Longarm asked.

"Not to be sure." She frowned. "Ees *hacienda* close to canyon, but I am not know wheech way we go when Blás ees bring me to here. Ees in *coche*, you onderstan', weeth curtains at weendows. I am not see outside."

"How long did you ride in that carriage?"

"Two maybe three hours. Ees not far, I am guess."

"Well, I got an idea how we can find him, if it's as close as all that. Now, just to make me happy, Maruja, go back to the cave. It's getting light now, there'll be trouble pretty quick."

Gazing over the rim of the ledge again, Longarm resumed his watch. The dawn light had brightened enough by now to give him a fairly clear view of the canyon floor. A rooster somewhere behind the crude shacks crowed to greet the day as Longarm looked; he jumped when the raucous crowing cut through the still air, shook his head in disgust at the tautness of his nerves, and went on scanning the floor of the canyon.

Wherever Longarm turned his eyes, from the corral at the back of the canyon to the slit of its narrow mouth, he saw no sign of movement. The bodies of Conyers and Gotch and Pete lay sprawled on their blankets where Recco's gunmen had murdered them. The *jacales* were dark and quiet, and only an occasional movement of the horses in the rope corral showed that anything alive was left in the canyon.

Longarm was about to turn his head and give his eyes a rest, when the horses in the corral began to mill and whinny. He swiveled his head quickly.

At some time, either before daylight or while he'd been back with Parker, the ropes that served as a gate had been dropped. Three horses were emerging through the gap. Longarm had to look twice in the still uncertain light to see the legs of the riders looped across the backs of the animals. It was an Indian tactic Recco had adopted, which turned the bodies of the horses into shields for the men who were using them.

Longarm drew his pistol, but after a second look at the horses he laid it on the ground beside him, where he could pick it up quickly. He wasn't sure the .41 Colt he now carried would be effective at that range. He picked up the Spencer carbine and reached into his pocket for shells to slip into the magazine, to replace the three he'd fired. His hand came away empty, and he remembered belatedly that he'd emptied his pockets of spare ammunition while trying to get comfortable when he'd first gone to bed.

Feet scraping behind him on the stony ground of the ledge brought Longarm's head around quickly, ready to scold Maruja and tell her again to go back where she'd be safe. It was not Maruja coming to join him, though, it was Parker. The old outlaw was dragging himself along slowly and was obviously hurting. He stopped beside Longarm and peered over the rim of the ledge. He snorted.

"Hmph. Comanche trick. I seen 'em use it a lot of times."

"Yes," Longarm replied noncommittally. "I'll have to wait till they raise up to aim and pick 'em off one at a time."

"You short of shells?"

"Four in the Spencer, four in the Colt."

"Man needs a full cylinder when he's going into a fight."

"Not if it costs him half of his leg. Colts are fine guns, but they got that bad habit of going off when you leave a shell under the hammer."

"Oh, I know that. But when I was going out on a fracas, I took the risk."

"We do things different, I guess," Longarm said flatly.

"No need to git riled." Parker's remonstrance was delivered in a mild tone. "I always put a handful of shells loose in my pocket too. Guess we're different about that, ain't we?"

His pride stung, Longarm retorted, "I had my pockets full when I laid down. They gouged into me, so I took 'em out and put 'em on my blankets. They're laying there right now."

"Don't do you much good down there, do they, son?"

Abashed and aware that Parker was right, Longarm said in a quiet voice, "Not right now, they don't."

"You got any ideas?" the old man asked.

"I told you what I aim to do," Longarm replied, his voice sharp. "They can't shoot without raising up above their horses' backs. Soon as they do that and give me a target, I'll take 'em one at a time."

"That'd work, I guess. From what I heard about Longarm, you're supposed to be a pretty fair shot." Parker was silent for a moment, then added, "But my way's faster!"

Before Longarm could move to stop him, the old man grabbed up the Colt and leaped to his feet. He fired at the horses and one of them bucked, dislodging its rider. Longarm stopped trying to pull Parker down and swung the Spencer around. He dropped the exposed pistolero with the shot he let off.

"Now, dammit, get down before you're hit!" he called to Parker, who'd moved a few feet away from him, out of reach.

"Let's do it my way, son!" Parker shouted, his thin old voice gleeful. "I'll sting the critters, you drop the men!" He let off another round from the Colt. It missed, and he took more careful aim before firing again.

Longarm saw that there was no reasoning with Parker. He aimed at the uncovered gunman on the canyon floor, and brought him down.

Return fire was coming from Recco and the remaining pistolero by now, and lead was singing across the ledge.

Longarm saw Parker's body jerk as a slug went home, but the old outlaw was now aiming at the two men who'd exposed themselves. Longarm joined in with the Spencer. He wasn't sure how effective Parker's shots would be, but was certain of his own. He drew a bead on Recco, and he and Parker fired at the same time. Recco dropped. The remaining pistolero dropped his rifle and crumpled to the ground as Longarm got him in the carbine's sights and put a .50-caliber bullet in his chest.

In the sudden silence that followed, Parker let out a wild victory shout, a whoop that set the canyon walls to ringing and returning the cry in echoes. Then the old man sagged. The Colt dropped from his hand and he folded into a small heap on the ground.

Longarm and Maruja reached him at the same time. They stretched him out, straightening his arms and legs. Blood from two bullet wounds in his chest was spreading over his shirt. For a long minute or two Parker lay motionless, and Longarm thought the old outlaw was dead. Then he stirred and opened his eyes.

"We give 'em hell, didn't we, son?" he gasped.

"We did that, Curley," Longarm agreed.

"Never thought I'd cash in my chips helping a goddamn federal marshal get hisself outa a scrape," Parker smiled. "I was always one of the fellows on t'other side."

"Hush up, Curley," Longarm said. His voice was low, almost gentle. "Talking's just going to make you weaker."

Maruja came up, strips of cloth in her hand. Parker saw her

and shook his head. "Little lady, ain't no use in trying to bandage me up. I know when I'm a goner. But I thank you for thinking about me, just the same."

"*Señor*—" Maruja began.

Longarm said, "He's right, Maruja. If he don't want you to do nothing for him, don't press."

Parker said, "Thanks, Long." His voice grew stronger as he drew on the last surge of vitality that Longarm knew often came to me just before death. Parker went on, "Dammit, I'm too old to go back in a cell. But you knowed that, didn't you, Long? You knowed right off that I wasn't aiming to let you take me back to no prison. You knowed that what I had in my mind wasn't just helping you out."

"I keep telling you, you ain't going to die," Longarm felt compelled to say.

"Hell, I'm gittin' too tired to argufy with you," the old man sighed. He lay silent for a moment, then spoke urgently, "Long. I know it was in yours and Thomas's—Boone's—minds to weasel outa me where that army gold's hid. But I owe you for treating me like a man after we got out."

"Don't give me and Tom too much credit, Curley," Longarm said. "We done what we felt like we had to."

"Sure. A man does," Parker agreed. "You'll find that gold buried in Cold Creek Canyon, Long. Up north of Fort Mohave about sixty miles. We burned the wagon, but likely some of the iron fittings is still there."

"Thanks, Curley. If it's still there, I'll find it."

Parker smiled weakly. "Being the man you are, I bet you damn well will," he said. The smile was still on the old outlaw's face when he died.

Chapter 18

"Are we go now to find Mentutes, Brazolargo?" Maruja asked as she watched Longarm tying behind his saddle the small sack of provisions she'd scraped together from the deserted *jacales*.

"Best thing I can think of is to ride for the border. I got to get you where you'll be safe, and where I can get to a telegraph office," he replied. "As far's Mexico's concerned, right this minute all I am is a jailbird that busted out of prison. If I get crossways of the law, they'll likely send me back."

Maruja made no reply, but mounted the horse Longarm had chosen for her and waited for him to swing into the saddle. They rode out of the canyon mouth, leaving behind the shallow graves that Longarm had spent most of the morning digging. They were both silent. Longarm turned the horses in the direction he remembered that Recco had led them when they set out to steal the silver car. He knew that sooner or later they'd come to the tracks of the spur that ran north, and after that it would only be necessary to follow the railroad line to the U.S. border.

Maruja waited until they'd ridden several miles before she broke the silence. "Brazolargo," she said, frowning. "when you are again *policía federal* of your country, you weel come back and arrest Blás Mentutes, no?"

"My boss ain't likely to send me back," Longarm told her. "I ain't finished my own case yet, which is uncovering that gold Curley Parker stole all them years ago. That's my duty, Maruja, and I'm sworn to do it."

"Duty!" Maruja said angrily. "Ees all you can say to me?"

"It's all I can say right now. But I'll wire my boss about Mentutes, and he'll wire his boss in Washington, and his boss will wire the *federalistas* in Mexico City. They'll arrest Mentutes. You'll be safe across the border by then, and after they arrest him, your police will see that nobody bothers you when you come back to testify at Mentutes's trial."

"Our *policía* weel not arrest Blás Mentutes," Maruja said bitterly, shaking her head. "He ees man of *el gobernador de Sonora*. Do you not see thees, Brazolargo?"

"Seeing something and proving it's two different things, Maruja," Longarm reminded her. "Anyhow, your federal police don't want us *gringos* meddling into their business."

"Then Mentutes ees get off free," Maruja said. "What he ees do to *mi familia*, the silver he have Recco steal, the men who are keel here in canyon, ees all like never was."

"Don't be too sure about that, Maruja," Longarm told her. "That silver Mentutes had Recco steal belongs to the Mexican government. They ain't going to let Mentutes off light."

Maruja spat. "Hah! Mentutes ees geeve beeg *mordida* to *el gobernador*, and he is geeve part to the *federalistas*, and Blás Mentutes ees never be punish."

Longarm could find no answer to that. He knew the way bribes—*mordidas*—passed from hand to hand until they found their way into the pockets of men powerful enough to order charges against criminals to be dropped. Then he reminded himself again that the duty his oath required of him was clear. His job was not to help the government of Mexico put a criminal into prison, but to get back to Arizona Territory, find the stolen army gold, and finish his case.

Silent again, they rode on over the humps of the hills and into the shallow valleys, seeing nothing but more hills, more valleys, and everywhere the rocks and boulders and cactus that dotted the barren ground. The sun rose to noon and they stopped to eat, chewing in silence on the hard, edge-curled tortillas that were all Maruja had been able to find for food. In the heat of early afternoon they reached the railroad spur, the only straight line in a land of jagged, ridge-topped hills and steep-walled gullies.

After riding parallel with the tracks for almost an hour, they entered territory that Longarm remembered from the attack on the train. They rode up the slope to the rise where he'd boarded the engine, and looked down at the gently sloping sides of the shallow valley where the mine entrance lay. Longarm reined in quickly, as did Maruja. At the Y where the short spur into the abandoned mine branched off the railroad track, a carriage stood, a dozen horses around it.

Maruja said quickly, "Ees Blás Mentutes's *coche*, Brazolargo! I am see eet many times!"

Longarm had seen no sign of a guard posted to watch the carriage and horses. He asked Maruja, "You real sure about that?"

"*Seguro que sí!* I am know the *coche*, I tell you!"

For a moment, while he studied the scene below them, Longarm said nothing. Then he smiled grimly and told Maruja, "It looks like we found Mentutes, whether I wanted to or not."

"You are to arrest heem, then?"

"I'll have to see. From the looks of that horse herd, he'd be pretty hard to nail down, if there's a man for every horse, and me with just enough ammunition to half fill a pocket. But you lead the horses back downslope, where nobody below there can see 'em, and I'll take a look."

Pulling the knot from the saddle strings that held the Spencer, Longarm took the carbine and checked its magazine. Then he waited until Maruja had led the horses below the brow of the slope, and started for the mine. To his surprise, no guards had been posted along the spur or at the mine's main tunnel, where it slanted in from the canyon in which the rail spur ran.

Longarm entered the dark tunnel without hesitation. He stood for a moment inside the entrance, staring into the darkness and letting his eyes adjust to the gloom while he recalled the layout of the main tunnel and the shafts leading off it. Feeling his way by his boot soles on the decaying ties that supported the rusted tracks, he moved deeper into the tunnel until he saw a glow of light spilling around a curve in the shaft some distance in front of him. He could hear a murmur of voices now, but was unable to make out anything that was being said.

For a moment Longarm halted, then edged cautiously ahead. The light grew brighter as he progressed, and now he could hear movement from beyond the curve. He moved with even greater caution than before, advancing almost inch by inch until he encountered the strewn litter of old railroad ties and mine timbers that littered the shaft.

As the light grew brighter ahead, the voices grew louder— two men in casual conversation. They were speaking Spanish, and Longarm lost part of their talk, for he was forced to struggle with his own scanty knowledge of the language as he tried to translate the conversation.

"Cuánto más hay en el vagón?" one of the men asked in a loud voice, almost a shout.

"Tanto mucho de he ya descargada," the other man answered.

"Dice los obreros darse prisa!" called the man who'd spoken first.

"Sí, Don Blás. Prestamente!" came the reply.

Longarm had now reached a point where he could peer around the curve in the tunnel. Lanterns stood along the wall, and light pouring from the open door of the boxcar that stood ten or twelve yards beyond the curve indicated that there were other lanterns inside.

In the half-light shed by the lanterns, the boxcar itself dominated the tunnel, blocking it almost completely. From its door men emerged in a steady line, each carrying three ingots of silver. Even the three that each man carried made a heavy load, to judge by their arched backs and the slowness of their movements as they carried the silver bars from the boxcar and added the ingots to a pile that was growing between the rails at the end of the car.

Directly in front of Longarm, on a crude bench made by piling railroad ties, sat two men. Their backs were toward Longarm, the growing stack of silver ingots between them and the boxcar.

Longarm recognized Blás Mentutes at once by his bulk. The second man was thinner than Mentutes, and taller; he had on a peaked military cap and some kind of uniform. Since all he could see was the back of the second man, Longarm could not tell whether the uniform was that of the Mexican Army, the *guardía civíl,* or the *federalistas*. The uniforms of all three services were familiar to him, but were so much alike that seeing only the man's back made identification impossible.

Now the uniformed man turned to Mentutes and said, *"Esta sera muy agredable a Don Fernando. Es un tesoro tanto rico."*

"Lo conozco," Mentutes grunted. He took a cigar from his pocket and lighted it. The smoke drifted back along the tunnel, and reminded Longarm how long it had been since he'd enjoyed the flavor of his favorite cheroots. Mentutes went on, *"El porcentaje de Don Fernando sera hacerle su ambición quedarse el presidente."*

Longarm had heard enough. He stepped back as silently as he'd crept up, and made his way back along the tunnel. He walked slowly, picking his way carefully through the debris that lay on the floor. Feeling his way along the wall, Longarm stopped when he reached the shaft where he'd found the dynamite that had been left behind when the mine was closed. Inside the shaft, the darkness was even deeper than in the main tunnel.

Before entering the shaft where the dynamite lay, Longarm felt in his pocket to see how many matches he was carrying. Even though he had no cheroots to light, the habit of carrying matches was too strong to break; on his first day at the hideout he'd picked up a few from the box that Catalina had brought out to light the cooking fire. His fingers tallied the matches. There were only four.

Entering the shaft, Longarm bent over and laid the carbine to one side. He located the dynamite by feel, running his fingers over the floor's packed earth very slowly and cautiously until they encountered the rough fabric of the burlap sacks that held the sticks of explosive. Then he groped around until he located the coil of fuse and the boxes of caps.

He could not tell by feeling of the coil how long the fuse might be, and had long ago forgotten how to interpret the raised sections of the fuse casing that told how many feet the fuse would burn per minute. He shrugged and laid the coil at the mouth of the shaft, then pulled an end with him back to the sacks of dynamite. Still working by feel, he crimped a blasting cap onto the end of the fuse, using his strong teeth, then knelt beside the sacks that contained the explosive.

Now Longarm used one of his scanty supply of matches. Its glow showed him that the sticks of dynamite in the one sack that had been opened were piled like so many jackstraws, deep in the bottom of the burlap bag. He let the match burn down until it scorched his fingers while he tried to memorize the position of the individual sticks and select one that could be extracted without disturbing the others.

In the course of his travels, Longarm had picked up a passing knowledge of dynamite. He'd heard miners talking about the explosive, and lodged in his mind were stories of the effects aging had on it. He knew that old dynamite was unstable and unpredictable, that the touch of a finger or even a breath might cause it to go off. Setting his jaw, he reached into the sack.

Handling the greasy cylinders as though they were eggs that

had been cracked and might break completely at the slightest touch, Longarm freed one stick from the jackstrawed heap in the partly opened sack and held it carefully while he revolved the cylinder until his fingers encountered the seam left when the heavy, waterproof paper tube had been formed.

Using the lightest touch he could manage, he picked at the seam until it gave way. Then, bit by cautious bit, he tore away a strip of paper from the circumference of the cylinder until his fingertip encountered the greasy contents.

Now Longarm drew a deep breath and held it as he worked the capped end of the fuse through the gap in the paper cover until it was firmly embedded in the stick. He did not release his breath until he laid the stick back in the sack.

For a moment he stayed on his knees to let his breathing normalize. Then he found the carbine, went to the open end of the shaft, and picked up the coil of fuse. Unrolling it on the floor as he moved, he started for the mouth of the main tunnel.

Halfway there, he ran out of fuse. Taking one of his three remaining matches from his pocket, he flicked it into life with a thumbnail. He held the match to the end of the fuse, but no stream of sparks shot from the core of the fuse to show that he had ignition. He held the match until it scorched his fingers, then struck another. The first match had apparently warmed the core, for a thin line of sizzling sparks shot from it almost at once. Longarm held the fuse long enough to be sure it would not fizzle out, then dropped it and ran for the mouth of the tunnel.

He got to the end and into the cut and was a few yards down the railroad tracks when the earth shook under his feet. He looked back in time to see the mouth of the tunnel light up with an unearthly glow. The ground was still quivering when the boom of the dynamite reached his ears.

A cloud of dust, mixed with clods of hard soil, rose from the wall of the canyon above the mineshaft. Then, slowly but inexorably, the canyon wall began to slip and crumple in upon itself. The line of its rim changed; a huge, semicircular dent, like the bite of a giant's jaws, appeared where the wall of the canyon had formed an almost straight line. Then the dust settled down in the sudden stillness that followed the explosion. Longarm turned and started toward the mouth of the canyon.

He was a bit more than halfway there when he met Maruja. She was running down the tracks, gasping for breath, her hair disheveled. Her long skirt was dirty and torn, its waistband pulled out from beneath the wide embroidered sash she wore. The skirt was torn across at her knees, and the loose hem dangled around her ankles. She ran to Longarm and threw her arms around him. Longarm got a glimpse of her hands; they were grimy and scratched, and one was bleeding.

"*Ay, gracias a Dios,* Brazolargo!" she exclaimed. "*No 'stas muerte!*"

"Now, you can see real plain I ain't dead!" he replied. "What's happened to you?"

"*Los caballos!*" she said. "They are hear beeg boom, and ees make them to scare! *Son escaparse!*"

"Run away? You couldn't hold 'em?"

"*Sera imposible,* Brazolargo! When they are hear noise, they are *loco con panico!* I try, they are pull reins, I am fall down, they pull out my arms, but they run!" Maruja twisted her head to look up at Longarm. "You are to make the beeg bang, Brazolargo?"

"I guess I did. Mentutes was in the mine with somebody I never seen before, had a bunch of his men unloading the silver. There was some old dynamite laying around, so I touched it off. You don't need to worry about Mentutes anymore, Maruja. When we get across the border, I'll see that word gets sent back where he is. He might still be alive when they dig him out, but I wouldn't take any bets on it."

"*Bueno.*" Maruja smiled. Then the smile faded and she said, "But ees many *kilometros* to the border. How we are to go there now? We do not have horses."

"Well, it ain't your fault, Maruja. You done all you could. But don't worry. You seen all them horses a little ways up the track, and the coach too."

Maruja drew back and looked at Longarm for a moment before she shook her head. "No, Brazolargo. They are all run too."

"You mean *all* of 'em?" When Maruja nodded, he asked, "What about Mentutes's carriage?"

"*Quebrarse.* Ees no wheels on *coche* now."

Longarm looked at the railroad tracks that stretched to the north, rising up the long slope beyond the canyon's mouth. "Well, I guess it's going to be a long, dry walk, so we might as well get started."

They began walking up the long grade, trudging in the center of the railroad tracks. They detoured around the blown-up section where the trestle had stood, and continued to the crest. Longarm stopped short. Less than a quarter of a mile ahead, there stood the locomotive, tender, and lone passenger coach of the train from which Longarm and his companions had stolen the silver car a few nights earlier.

"Maruja," Longarm said, "our luck just changed. Looks like we got us a ride to the border."

"You mean to steal *el ferrocarril?*" she gasped.

"I wouldn't say steal it, Maruja. Maybe borrow it for a while, but I'd give it right back, when we get off at Yuma City. Now, you stay here a minute. I don't want you to get hurt if the train crew happens to make trouble. I'll motion for you when it's time to get aboard."

Staying in the center of the tracks, the blind spot that the men in the locomotive could not see, Longarm walked up to the end of the train. The day coach was deserted. He boarded it and walked through, climbed up to the top of the tender, and stepped quietly to its front end, where he could look down into the locomotive's cab. The engineer and fireman were playing Conquian, the Mexican national game. Absorbed in their cards, they did not hear Longarm's silent approach.

Holding the carbine casually, but covering them with it effectively, Longarm said in a conversational tone, "Both of you lost the game. *Arriba sus manos!*"

If the trainmen had not understood Longarm's first remark, the command in their own tongue brought their heads up, and when they found themselves staring into the Spencer's muzzle, their hands flew up quickly.

"Sangre de Dios!" one of them gasped. *"Es lo mismo bandido dela salteamiento delante!"*

"Sí, Chaco," the other agreed. *"De verdad, lo mismo."*

"Habla inglés?" Longarm asked.

One of the men shook his head, but the other said, "A leetle I speak. *No mucho.*"

"You waiting for somebody?" Longarm asked them.

"Sí, señor," the English-speaking one replied. "Ees come from Hermosilla the men to feex the track. We wait for them."

"When are they due to get here?"

Pulling down the corners of his mouth, the man replied, *"Quién sabe, señor? Hoy, mañana, no se.* We are tell to wait, so we wait."

"If you don't know how long you'll be waiting, it won't

hurt you to accommodate us with a little ride, then, will it?"

"*Cómo?*" asked the crewman, his eyes bulging. "A treep, *señor?* Ees no place, only to Yuma Ceety, we can go."

"Well, it happens that's just the place we want to go," Longarm said. He pointed to the boiler with the muzzle of the Spencer. "You got steam up?"

"*Un poco. No es bastante proponer el locomotura.*"

"You better start shoveling, then," Longarm commanded, pointing to the coal in the front end of the tender. "*Quiero va enmediatamente.*"

"*Hace que dice, Chaco,*" the English-speaking man said sharply. "*El señor quiere ir tan pronto como es possible.*"

When the fireman began shoveling coal into the firebox and the engineer turned his attention to the gauges, Longarm climbed off the tender, walked far enough away for Maruja to see him, and waved for her to come up to the train. He helped her step up into the coach, and followed her inside the decrepit car.

"We'll be riding to Yuma City as soon as the fireman gets up enough steam," he said.

Maruja looked at him, her eyes wide. "You are steal the train, no?"

"No. Like I told you, just borrowing it awhile. But we're real close to being out of trouble, Maruja. Once we're in Yuma City, there ain't nothing much bad can happen to us."

Maruja sighed. "Ees like dream. You are better to kees me, Brazolargo, so I see am I awake."

Longarm's kiss left no doubt in Maruja's mind that she was awake. She clung to him, rubbing her body against his, until he felt himself growing stiff.

"Now this ain't the right time or place—" he began.

"Has not been time or place too long," she whispered. "I am want you to be weeth me, Brazolargo, now we have nothing to stop us. I am want to feel like you are make me feel before. Is not that you want me?"

"It ain't that I don't want you, Maruja," he replied. "Except we ain't out of the woods quite yet. Now, you ride back here. I don't aim to take any chance on you getting hurt, if there's trouble."

"You are not to be weeth me?" she asked.

"I can't. I got to be in the engine, where I can keep an eye on the crew."

"Where are we to go?" Maruja asked.

"There's not but one place we can go, and that's Yuma City. I guess we can talk our way across the border, but I'd sure like to have a little money to tide us over once we get across."

Maruja smiled. "Ees easy. I have money."

Longarm's jaw dropped. "Where'd you get it, if you don't mind me asking?"

"I am not get eet, Brazolargo. I am have it. Ees from time before I am go weeth Blás from home, before *mis padres son arrestando*."

Maruja untied the knot of her wide embroidered sash. She turned it over to probe in a tiny pocket, almost invisible in the stitching on the sash.

While her fingers were busy, she said, "Ees always say, *mi madre*, 'Keep money weeth you,' so I do." She slipped a French *louis d'or* from the slitlike pocket and held it out to Longarm. "Here. Ees more, eef you want them."

"Thanks, but this'll be plenty for now, Maruja."

Longarm bent down to give Maruja a long kiss. Then he went on, "This'll buy us food and a nice place to sleep when we get to Yuma City. I'll send off some telegrams as soon as we get there, and get some money of my own, then I'll pay you back."

She shrugged. *"No es importante*. Eef you need more, ees here."

"Sure." Longarm kissed Maruja again, but when he felt her hand searching for him, he removed it gently. "No, Maruja," he told her softly. "But we won't have to wait too much longer. Just set quiet now, and we'll be together again before the night's over."

"You are sure, Brazolargo?"

"I promise you that. And I ain't a man that breaks his promises."

Chapter 19

Maruja stretched luxuriously on the bed and rubbed her hands along its clean white sheets. She was naked, and her flesh gleamed like rich, fresh cream. Her full breasts stood proudly even when she lay on her back, their rosettes puckered after her bath. When she kneeled to speak to Longarm, the dark curls of her pubic hair glistened in the lamplight.

She said to Longarm, "Ees feel funny, the real bed, Brazolargo. Eet ees too long seence I am een one. But eet ees lonesome, the bed, unless you are een eet weeth me."

Between intervals of soaping and rinsing, Longarm had been watching her enjoy the bed. A cigar clamped between his teeth, he was sitting in the tin bathtub that the room clerk had brought into their room in the U.S. Grant Hotel. He said, "I'll be there in a minute or so, soon as I get off the rest of this desert sand and coal dust."

Crossing the border from the little hamlet of Algodones, on the Mexican side of the Colorado, to Yuma City and the United States, was much easier than Longarm had thought it would be, though their walk had been longer than he'd expected. They'd watched the lights of Yuma anxiously as they approached the river, following the railroad tracks.

From the engineer of the commandeered train, Longarm had learned that the only bridge was the one built by the Southern Pacific Railroad a few years earlier, when the SP construction superintendent had outfoxed the rival Texas & Pacific by spanning the river in defiance of army orders. At the west end of the bridge, the rails it carried split into a double track, one set branching southwest to join the Mexican National Railroad spur leading to Algodones, the other entering California.

Since it was a railroad bridge, no one had yet given thought to closing the span to foot traffic. Longarm and Maruja simply stepped from tie to tie until they could put their feet on United States soil. Yuma City was still some distance away, but now they were sure its lights were not a mirage created by hope.

Skirting the SP yards just south of the town, they'd walked on in, unnoticed and unchallenged. Longarm's only visit to the little border town had been brief, just long enough for him and Boone to step out of the stage that had brought them and their escorting deputy marshal from Prescott and into the accommodation wagon that carried them to the Territorial Prison.

Longarm had kept their walk to a slow pace as they entered the first streets. When he saw a saloon that obviously catered to railroad crews and other working men, he told Maruja, "Now, you wait right here, and if anybody says anything, just forget you can talk English. I won't be but a minute."

"You go to saloon?" Maruja had asked worriedly. She hadn't missed his close inspection of those they'd passed.

"Yes, but I ain't going in to drink. I don't want to go paying for our hotel room with this French gold piece, it'd make the clerk remember us too easy. I'll buy a bottle to get the gold piece changed, but that's all."

While Maruja waited outside, Longarm went into the saloon. Scanning the backbar, he saw no Tom Moore, but did spot a bottle of Daugherty's.

Tossing the *louis d'or* on the bar, he said, "I'll take a bottle of that Daugherty's, if you got a full one."

After he'd taken a good look at the coin and at Longarm, the barkeep stepped to the backbar and dropped the *louis d'or* on a small marble slab that lay on the bar above the till. The coin rang with a purity of tone that attested to its authenticity. The barkeep passed the bottle of Daugherty's over to Longarm and returned an eagle, a half eagle, and three silver dollars in change. After a short and silent debate with himself, Longarm invested a quarter in a half-dozen cigars. They weren't his favorite cheroots, but after having been without a puff for such a long time, he had no doubt that he'd enjoy them.

Evidently the hotel clerk was accustomed to seeing patrons who were so travel-stained as to look almost disreputable. He hadn't blinked at the appearance Longarm and Maruja presented, and in reply to Longarm's question about a restaurant, he recommended one just across the street.

"And have us a bathtub full of hot water in our room when we come back," Longarm had said, pocketing the two dollars he'd gotten in change from the half eagle.

Longarm finished rinsing off the soap and stood up, small beads of water glinting in his full brown beard and in the mat of brown curls on his chest. He tossed the butt of the cigar into the spittoon that stood beside the dresser. Watching Maruja cavorting nude on the bed while he was in the still-warm water of the tub had made him slightly tumescent. Maruja smiled when she saw him, and jumped off the bed.

"So, now I am to make you dry," she said, picking up the huckaback towel that was draped over the back of the room's only chair and stepping up to the tub.

She stood on tiptoe and reached high to dry Longarm's thick brown hair, laughing delightedly when it resisted her efforts to smooth it flat. She toweled his beard, her fingertips caressing his lips, then rubbed the towel briskly over his back and chest and down his waist to his hips and buttocks. By now the warm, fresh aroma of woman-flesh fresh from a hot bath, and the occasional brushing of Maruja's warm skin against his while she wielded the towel, had brought Longarm almost fully erect.

Maruja moved around in front of Longarm and began toweling his crotch. A dreamy smile of anticipation formed on her face when she felt him throbbing and growing through the fabric of the towel.

"Now you mus' go seet in chair while I am to dry the feet," she said. "I am not like to bend so far as to floor."

Longarm moved to the chair. Maruja lifted one of his legs and dried his thigh, then turned her back and straddled the thigh, clamping it between her own while she bent to run the towel along his calf. The sight of Maruja's plump buttocks quivering as she moved was too great a temptation for Longarm to ignore. Grasping Maruja by the hips, he lifted her small body into the air and brought her down on his jutting erection.

Maruja groaned joyfully as Longarm entered her. She let the towel fall to the floor and placed her hands on Longarm's knees. Leaning forward, supported by her hands, she arched her back with catlike sensuousness, her hips squirming, helping him to go deeper. As she swayed from side to side, her breasts swung in the air like small, ripe melons. Longarm grasped them and began to rub their protruding tips, and Maruja's groans of joy broke into throaty whimpers as her body began to tremble.

"*Ay di mi!*" she sighed. "*Que embeleso dame su verga, Brazolargo!*"

"I feel pretty good myself," Longarm said. "But maybe we better go get on the bed so we can move a little freer."

"*Sí. Hacemos.*"

Longarm stood up, lifting Maruja with him. He carried her across the room, still deeply inside her, and when he reached the bed and moved to lift her so that she could lie down, she stopped him by grasping his wrists.

"*Portiempo no frente a frente*, Brazolargo. *A detrás, como animal.*" Maruja brought up her knees and planted them on the edge of the bed. She leaned forward, raising her buttocks high. "*Ah!*" she sighed. "*Dámelo hasta aquí! Quiero todo que tienes!*"

Longarm lunged into her before she had finished speaking, and her words ended in a throaty cry, which she repeated as he pulled away and thrust again and again.

After a long period of quietude, Maruja stirred. They lay without speaking for several minutes, then suddenly Longarm felt Maruja begin to shake. He turned to look at her, and saw tears streaming from her tightly closed eyes.

"What's wrong, Maruja?" he asked.

"*Es nada*," she said, not opening her eyes.

Longarm took her chin and gently turned her face to his. "If you're crying, there's got to be something wrong."

"I am not cry for now, Brazolargo," she said. "I am cry for tomorrow."

"Now that don't make sense."

"Not for tomorrow, maybe. But for time when you weel go from me, or I must go from you."

Longarm could find no quick answer; he knew as well as she did that they would not be together much longer. He stood up and went to the dresser, uncorked the Daugherty's, and took a good swallow before lighting a cigar.

Through the cloud of smoke that hung around him, he said, "Nothing lasts forever, Maruja. Sure, I got my duty to do, so I can't stay here any longer'n it's going to take to get all the loose ends pulled together. Maybe two or three days. But what bothers me is, where are you going to go?"

"Thees I am to ask myself all the time while I am seet in *el ferrocarril* when we come here," she said, frowning, her tears gone as quickly as they'd come. "Ees in your country *familia de mi madre,* her seester is marry to beeg *ranchero* and ees leeve in California."

"Well, that's just a hop, skip, and a jump from here," Longarm said thoughtfully. "You know where they live? California's a pretty good-sized chunk of land."

"I know address. Maybe you send to her the *telegrama,* say I am like to come there?"

"First thing in the morning," Longarm promised. "I got a few other wires I got to send, anyhow. And I'll stay right here with you till we hear from your folks."

"Ees good," Maruja sighed. Then she smiled invitingly. "We are have leetle more time together, Brazolargo. Ees best we do not waste any of eet, no?"

Chapter 20

Longarm swung off the stagecoach in Prescott just as dusk was settling in. Jim Glass was waiting to meet him. Glass looked past Longarm as the other passengers alighted, but asked no questions about Tom Boone. When Longarm suggested they go to Glass's office where they could talk undisturbed, his only reply was a nod. They walked slowly along the brick-paved street in the direction of the square, and after they'd covered half the distance to their destination, Glass finally broke his silence.

"From the reports I've had out of the south," he said, "you and Tom Boone really turned the territorial prison inside out."

"We had more good luck than we was entitled to," Longarm said, and then added, "till it turned bad. Boone ain't coming back, you know. I buried him and Curley Parker someplace down in Mexico."

"I had a hunch something like that had happened, when Boone didn't get off the stage." Glass paused and said, "I suppose you know I didn't intend for things to turn out the way they did."

"We never figured you did, Jim. Nobody's to blame for how it all come out. Main thing is, we know now where Curley Parker hid that army gold."

"Yes. And I hope you feel up to starting out tomorrow to dig it up. There's a Secret Service man who got here this morning on the overnight stage from Needles, and he's ready and raring to go. I had a hard time keeping him from starting off by himself."

"How'd the Secret Service find out so fast?"

"Why, since you and Tom Boone dropped out of sight after the prison break, they've been after us damned near every day. Telegrams from Washington, and lately from this fellow named Wood, in San Francisco. He's the one who got into town this morning."

"And couldn't wait to go looking? Even if he didn't know where? That don't sound like he's right smart."

"Oh, he's smart, Long. He's head of the whole western division of the Secret Service, but he told me he's retiring as soon as he closes this case." Glass opened the door of his office, and he and Longarm went inside. Closing and locking the door behind them, Glass continued, "Wood had the idea from the wire Billy Vail sent him that you'd mentioned in your telegram where the gold's hidden. If you'd told Billy where the cache is, I wouldn't have been able to hold Wood back."

"Now it wouldn't have been real smart of me to put that in a wire, Jim. Every telegraph operator along the line can listen to anything being sent, unless it's one of those special private government lines like you and Billy have got."

"Yes," Glass said thoughtfully. "There'd be a possibility of a leak. And with you still a fugitive, I can see why you'd be careful. But you're the only man alive now who knows where that stolen gold's buried."

"Well, just so there'll be somebody besides me that knows where Curley Parker's cache is at, it's in Cold Creek Canyon, wherever Cold Creek is."

"Cold Creek?" Glass smiled. "It runs into the Colorado about twenty miles south of the Needles crossing. If Wood only knew it, he was a lot closer to that gold when he crossed the river than he is right now."

Reluctance in his voice, Longarm said, "If he's in such an all-fired hurry, we can start out in the morning. I don't know right where the cache is, but old Curley told me just before he died that there'll be the iron from a burned-up wagon close by."

"You shouldn't have any trouble finding it, then. Cold Creek's not much of a stream, and the canyon's not a big one."

"Then all I'll have to trouble you with is digging out my gear and introducing me to this fellow Wood in the morning. I'll go over to the Hassayampa House and get me a room for the night, someplace where I can get out of these stinking rags and have me a bath before I get into my own duds tomorrow."

Dressed in his own clothes, his familar .44 Colt in its well-worn cross-draw holster on his belt, his derringer in the vest pocket opposite his watch, Longarm felt better when he got up from the breakfast table at the Silver Bell Café. As he walked around the corner of the square to Glass's office, even his feet felt relieved to be back into his stovepipe cavalry boots and out of the needle-nosed pair of toe-pinchers he'd gotten at the outlaw hideout.

Both Glass and Eben Wood were waiting for him when he got to Glass's office. After the introductions had been completed, Longarm sat down next to Wood, opposite Glass. Wood and Glass had been talking when Longarm came in and while they finished their interrupted conversation, Longarm sized up the Secret Service man.

Eben Wood was far from looking as old as he must be if he was getting ready to retire, Longarm thought, studying the other man through the smoke of his after-breakfast cheroot. Wood was a stocky man, broad in the chest, lean in the hips, with a head that, in spite of his wide shoulders, looked a trifle too big for his body.

There was something vaguely familiar about his face—the pinched nostrils, the set of his jutting jaw, the manner in which he moved his head when he talked—that kept reminding Longarm of someone he'd known, but he was at a loss to remember who it was. Wood also had an abrupt way of speaking, the habit of a man accustomed to making quick decisions and giving orders—he expected to be obeyed without questions being asked. He and Glass finished their conversation, and Wood turned to face Longarm.

"I suppose you're ready to leave, Long?" he asked.

"All I got to do is pick up my saddlebags and rifle from the hotel, and we can be on our way, Mr. Wood."

"Good. And what's more to the point, do you know where we're going and the quickest way to get there?"

"Well, we ain't got a lot of choice," Longarm said thoughtfully. "We can take the stage to Needles and pick up an army accommodation wagon and a couple of horses from the remount station at Fort Mohave. Or we can get some horses here and ride the whole way, but we'll still have to get a wagon at the fort to haul the gold out in."

"You didn't answer my questions, dammit!" Wood barked. "I asked if you knew where to go and which is the quickest way for us to travel."

Longarm hid his surprise and irritation at the Secret Service man's manner. He said levelly, "No, I don't know to a mile or so where we're heading for, but Jim's got a map here that'll show me where Cold Creek Canyon is. And horseback from here's the quickest way, provided you can stay on a horse from daybreak to dark over some pretty sorry trails for two or three days in a row."

"Don't worry about me staying on a horse," Wood said. His snappishness had abated somewhat. "I ride over the dunes twice a week in San Francisco. I can hold my own. Now, about that wagon. Why not pack out the gold on horses?"

"It ain't a way I'd pick out, if I was doing the choosing, but I guess you're the boss in this show—"

"I am," Wood broke in. "Secret Service jurisdiction covers the U.S. Treasury and the military."

"I ain't arguing about you being in charge, Mr. Wood," Longarm explained carefully. "It's just a way of saying that if it was me by myself, I'd pick out a wagon."

"Why?" Wood asked. "I need reasons, not opinions!"

"I got a couple of reasons," Longarm replied mildly. "In the first place, it's likely that the gold'll be in several boxes, if it was being shipped the way the army usually does it. It's going to weigh considerable, and we'd need maybe three packhorses besides our own mounts, to carry the gold and all our shovels and such. That many horses is bound to attract some attention. And don't forget we're going into damn dry country, and there's going to be the little matter of toting enough water and feed for ourselves and whatever critters we take along. A wagon with two horses to pull it would be a hell of a lot easier and safer."

Wood seemed to relent a bit. "All right," he said, "we'll take a wagon, then. But not an army wagon. I imagine we can find one in a livery in Needles."

"I imagine so," Longarm agreed. "And we'll be able to pick up some Mexicans or Indians there to do the digging, too."

"No," Wood said quickly. "We'll do that ourselves."

Longarm sat silently for a long minute, looking at Wood. The Secret Service man stared back at him with equal intensity. Finally, Longarm asked, "Tell me something, Mr. Wood. When you go out for your rides over the dunes twice a week, do you carry a shovel and do some digging too?"

"That's not only an idiotic question," Wood said sharply. "It's impertinent as well! I'll answer it, though. Naturally I don't do any digging when I go out to ride! I dig in my garden almost every day, though, if you're afraid I don't know one end of a shovel from the other."

"Well, I did have that in mind too," Longarm told him. "But what I was really thinking about was the weather." Wood opened his mouth to say something, but Longarm spoke first. "Now if I recall, San Francisco's a nice, cool place, ain't it?" Wood nodded, a frown growing on his face. Longarm went on, "In them canyons along the Colorado at this time of year, it gets to be better'n a hundred degrees in the shade, only there ain't any shade around, so it'll be closer to a hundred and ten. A man that ain't used to that kind of work is apt to keel over after he's lifted a dozen shovelfuls."

This time, Wood was silent for a longer period than before. When he finally did speak, he said, "I see I've underestimated you, Long. After the mess you and Boone made of this job, I'll confess I didn't have a high opinion of either of you. But you have a valid point. I'll hire native laborers, as you suggest."

Longarm nodded soberly. He said, "That's a good idea, Mr. Wood. You won't have any trouble finding the help you need, when you get to Needles."

"What do you mean, *I* won't?" Wood asked. "The way you said that gave me the impression that you don't plan to go."

"I don't," Longarm replied. "A man like me hasn't got any place on a job with a man like you. Just now you said that Boone and me messed this job, but I notice you're glad enough to get the information Tom Boone gave up his life to get. Since you wouldn't want a man that messes up jobs going out with a man as good as you think you are, Mr. Wood, I'm heading back to Denver."

Longarm strode away and had almost reached the door when Wood called, "Wait a minute, Long!"

Longarm stopped, looked back, and said, "I can be just as impatient as you are, Mr. Wood, and my patience is getting real thin about now. Unless you got something mighty important to say, you better just let me go right on out that door."

"Deputy Long," Wood began, then he stopped and swallowed hard.

Longarm knew he was looking at a man who was having a hard time trying to swallow his words. He waited.

Wood began again, "I think I've just made a fool of myself, Long. I've worked in cities for so many years that I forget how different things are out here on the frontier. This is your territory, and I should listen to your advice. We'll do things the way you think best."

"No, sir," Longarm said. "I wasn't trying to run things or take over from you. Now I figure you know your job, because you're a mighty big muckety-muck in the Secret Service—a hell of a lot bigger one than I could ever get to be, even if I wanted to, which I don't. I want to get back that gold as bad as you do, because I know what it cost to find out where it was hid. But the way you been talking about doing things, you ain't even going to find it, much less get it back."

Wood nodded. "I'm beginning to see that. I've made my apology, and I hope you'll accept it."

"That I do, Mr. Wood. And if we understand each other, I guess we better get busy and go after that army gold."

Though the distance from Needles to Cold Creek Canyon was just over twenty miles, the heat and terrain had turned it into a two-day trip. At Needles they'd hired the livery wagon and two draft horses, as well as a pair of Papagos. At a miners' supply store they'd picked up picks and shovels, and Wood had bought a pair of denim jeans, which, although they looked incongruous with his starched collar and necktie, were undoubtedly far more comfortable than the heavy wool suit he'd been wearing. After the first day on the trail, however, the collar and tie had joined the suit inside a duffel in the bed of the wagon.

Since they'd left Prescott, there'd been no arguments. Wood had accepted Longarm's choice of the two Papago Indians who now sat on the tailgate, dangling their sandled feet inches above the desert floor. Wood had been courteous, even though his manner remained distant.

They finally reached the canyon in the middle of the second

day, but it took them almost until sunset to find a narrow strip of ocher soil that slanted at a passably gentle incline down to the canyon's floor.

Cold Creek Canyon had no creek running through it, though there was a sandy strip down its center that indicated where a stream had flowed along the floor at some earlier day. There were also watermarks on the coarse reddish soil of the floor, which gave evidence that the canyon flooded from time to time. Except for these signs, the canyon was a barren place. Neither the walls nor the floor had any outstanding features that might have been used to mark a spot where a cache had been made.

"How long do you think it's going to take us to find the place where the gold is buried?" Wood asked, after they'd ridden in a zigzag course over the yielding soil for almost an hour. "We won't have enough light in a little while to do much more looking today."

"Well, that's hard to say." Longarm thought for a moment. "If Parker and his gang come in from the Colorado, they'd most likely have buried the gold before they got this far. If they come in the same path we did, it'd most likely be over on the far side of the canyon."

"How did you arrive at those conclusions?" Wood frowned.

"Well, that slope we come down looks like about the only place a team can get down between here and the mouth," Longarm explained. "So if Parker's gang used it, they'd want to go over to the other side, which don't seem to have a real trail down it. And if they come up from the river, they'd likely have come just far enough this way to get out of the sand that piles up at the mouths of canyons like this one."

Wood nodded his satisfaction at the answer. "Very shrewd," he said. "As nice a piece of deduction as I could've made myself."

They rode along the canyon wall until the light failed, and made camp for the night. There was no firewood, as Longarm had foreseen, so dinner was jerky and parched corn, washed down with scanty draughts of water from the keg lashed to the side of the wagon bed. As they had done the previous night, Wood slept in the wagon, Longarm on a blanket spread below the vehicle, and the two Papagos shifted for themselves.

Longarm was up at the first trace of dawn. The air was cool and clean, the sky just fading from blue to gray over the eastern wall of the narrow canyon.

"Let's try the other side this morning, while it's in the shade," Longarm suggested as they chewed on their breakfast jerky. "If we don't hit paydirt by the time we get down close to where the sand starts at the mouth, we'll come back on this side and see what we find down below the place where we come in."

"You talk as though you've been here before, Long," Wood observed, a trace of suspicion showing in his voice. "Are you sure this is your first time here?"

"I'm sure, Mr. Wood. Thing is, when you seen one canyon like this, why, you've seen 'em all. Oh, there's little things that are different here and there, but mostly country like this runs pretty much to a pattern."

Finding the gold cache was so simple that it was a bit of an anticlimax.

Longarm was driving the wagon, following much the same zigzag pattern he'd established the afternoon before, when they'd explored the wall on the side they'd descended. The horses were feisty, fresh with the day and their breakfast of oats, and he was forced to hold them in. Wood was scanning the ground on the near side of the wagon, Longarm on the offside. The Secret Service man was having a hard time keeping his attention on a stretch of bare ground that was exactly like the ground they'd been over the previous day.

"Now that's an odd rock formation," he remarked to Longarm. "I always thought there weren't any truly square-edged lines in nature, but that stone looks as though it might've been chiseled by a sculptor."

Longarm looked where Wood was pointing. He reined in and said, "You come closer to calling that one than you know, Mr. Wood. It wasn't chiseled by any sculptor, but it sure wasn't made by nature, neither. That ain't no stone. It's iron."

"Are you sure? It's exactly the same color as a thousand other brownish-red stones we've seen on the way here."

Longarm was wrapping the reins around the whipsocket, getting ready to leave the wagon. He said, "All them other red rocks has got some purple in 'em. That red there is rust."

Wood leaped out of the wagon on one side, Longarm on the other. The Papagos watched without curiosity. Longarm tried to pick up the object Wood had seen, but it was embedded in the soil too deeply for him to budge. He kicked it, first on one side, then on the other, until he could pull it free. He held it out for Wood to see: a rectangle of cast iron, eight inches wide and some fourteen to sixteen inches long, almost an inch thick. A rectangular hole two inches wide by three inches long had been machined in the precise center of the metal plate.

"It's manmade, all right," Wood said. "But what the devil is it?"

"What we got here's the base of a wagon-jack," Longarm told him. "That hole's where the lifting-ratchet fits. You'll find a wagon-jack that'll fit this base in every army wagon that goes out in desert country like this, where wheels sink down in the sand a lot."

Wood was trying hard to maintain his calm. He said, "Let's look around. Maybe we'll find something else."

Within the next few minutes they'd found metal strapping, a broken spring leaf, a wheel hub, and a whipsocket, all within a dozen yards of the spot where Wood had spotted the jack base.

"Well, we know where they burned the wagon," Longarm said. "Now all we got to do is find where they buried the gold."

"What's your idea about that, Long?"

"Hard to say. They might've burned the wagon a pretty far piece from where they put the gold, figuring they never could get rid of the iron in it. Or they might've figured that's what most folks would think they'd do, and buried it right close by."

Wood gazed around the canyon floor, first in one direction, then in another. Seen from above, the floor had seemed narrow and small. Looked at while standing on it, it seemed very large indeed.

"Since we don't have any way of knowing, it seems to me this is as good a place as any to start," he told Longarm.

Longarm nodded. "It is. I'll get the Papagos started digging, and mark out some lines for 'em to follow."

Drawing a starting line with his boot toe and instructing the Indians to dig along it, Longarm scraped lines at right angles to the first and then crossed them with other right-angled lines until he'd marked out a grid a hundred feet on each side. While he was doing the marking, his toe encountered other bits and pieces of the wagon's iron components: some strapping, a few lengths of rod, a section of a wheel rim.

"Parker's gang burned the wagon right here, that's for dead

certain," he told Wood. "Wish there was some way we could tell as easy where they put the gold."

Following Longarm's grid-marks, the Papagos dug narrow trenches, no wider than their spades, back and forth across the area. Noon came and went, and most of the afternoon had gone by, before they found the first box. A spade grated on metal, and one of the Papagos hailed Longarm.

"Me find," he grinned. "This what you look for?"

Longarm looked at the partly uncovered box. The Papago had struck a corner, his spade making a bright scratch through the surface rust. He said, "Sure looks like it. Finish digging it out and we'll find out pretty fast."

When the dirt around it had been removed, it took the combined efforts of both Papagos to lift the box out of its sandy bed. They set it on the ground beside the hole, and all four men stood staring at it.

There was nothing unusual about the box. It was a foot wide, a foot and a half long, and not quite a foot deep. Sturdy metal handles were riveted to each end, and the lid was secured by a heavy padlock fastened through a hasp. The box and lock were rust-coated, though the scrape made by the shovel showed the coating to be a thin one.

"It's an army money box," Longarm said. He looked at Wood and asked, "You want to open it, Mr. Wood?"

"How? That lock looks to me as though it's still solid."

"A pistol slug in the right place ought to do the job," Longarm said. "Just stand to one side and aim for the keyhole."

Wood's first shot missed the padlock. The bullet left a gray streak on the side of the box as it ricocheted off into the sandy soil. The second shot hit the keyhole. The padlock cracked apart. Wood stepped up, took the lock out of the hasp, and tried to lift the lid. It was rusted shut.

Longarm took a shovel from one of the Papagos and worked its edge into the crack where the lid came down over the box. After a bit of prodding and prying, the lid yielded. Its rusty hinges creaked in protest as Wood slowly brought it up.

"Well," he said, gazing into the box. "Well."

Lying in the box were canvas sacks. The rust had not gotten to them, and they looked clean and new. In solid black block letters, each bore the stenciled legend: UNITED STATES TREASURY. SAN FRANCISCO MINT. $1000.00

"I don't guess there's much need to open these bags," Longarm remarked. "It's easy to see they ain't been touched."

Wood had already upended a bag and was untying the strings that closed its mouth. He pulled the bag open. The sun, noon-high, flashed on the spread wings of the bald eagle that appeared in low relief on the faces of the coins inside.

"A thousand dollars to the bag," Longarm figured aloud. "And it looks like there's ten bags in that box. So there's got to be four more of them. Once we figure out what kind of pattern they're buried in, it ought to be a pretty easy job."

"Pattern?" Wood asked.

"Why, sure. Parker was a smart old coot. He put the boxes in the ground in a line or a square or some way so that when one's been dug up, it'll point the way to the rest of 'em."

Midafternoon arrived before the next box was unearthed, though it lay only six feet from the first.

The going was easy after that. The boxes had been buried in a straight line, six feet apart. Once the line had been established, the distance could be paced off almost exactly. By sundown, all five had been unearthed. Each one, as Longarm had predicted, contained ten bags of gold eagles. One of the boxes was short by five hundred dollars.

"That's all the gang took when they split up, I reckon," Longarm said. "New gold pieces like that, Curley Parker was too smart to let his men spread too many around all at once."

"I suppose you're right," Wood agreed. He looked at the boxes, neatly stacked, ready for the Papagos to load them on the wagon the next morning. "Well, we've found what we came for, Long. I suppose we were lucky to have done the job so quickly."

"Luck's a good half of any job," Longarm said. He tossed away the butt of his bedtime cheroot and stretched. "I'm about ready to turn in. We'll get an early start tomorrow, and by this time the next day, you ought to be on your way back to San Francisco, Mr. Wood."

"Yes." Wood stood up too, and slid his arms into the sleeves of his coat. He said, "This is strange country, Long. Hot during the daytime, cold as sin at night. Tonight I'll be prepared."

On nights when a strange sound aroused Longarm and he snapped awake, instantly alert, he could never be sure what had wakened him. He only knew that his unsleeping sixth sense was warning him of some kind of threat. When he awoke under the wagon, the waning moon bathed the canyon floor with a dim greenish light. An alien sound was still registering on Longarm's ears, a gurgling wheeze coming from somewhere near the wagon.

Longarm lay quietly and waited. The gurgling died out in a final, faint rasp of gasping sound. Then boot soles crunched softly on the coarse soil. Longarm looked toward the sound. A ghostly form was coming toward the wagon. At first all that he could see was a silhouette, then he caught a glint of dim moonlight reflected from the bright steel of a knifeblade. He slid his Colt out of its holster and waited. The moving form came closer, and now Longarm could see well enough.

"Stop right where you are, Mr. Wood," he called. "I'd hate to have to shoot you, but I will if you come any closer with that knife you're carrying."

Wood stopped. "I wasn't going to harm you, Long," he said quickly. "All I wanted was to wake you up so we could talk."

"I'm awake," Longarm said tersely. "Talk away."

"That gold," Wood said. "We found it, didn't we?"

"You might put it that way. With a lot of help from the man that stole it, and one of your own men that got him started talking. You know who I mean."

"Boone, of course," Wood said calmly. "I was sorry to hear about Boone. He was a good man."

"You had it on your mind to get this gold all the time, didn't you?" Longarm asked. "That's why the government never did close the case. In the job you got, you could keep it open, I guess. And did."

"Of course. Oh, you're in my way, but I'm sure we can come to terms. We're the only ones who know the gold's been found, Long. I just took care of the Indians, they can't talk anymore. All we have to do is report that we didn't find anything. I can cover up the rest before I retire, mark the case 'closed.'"

"You figure we can come to terms, you said. What kind of terms you got in mind, Mr. Wood?"

"Three-fourths for me, a fourth for you. Damn it, Long, I've earned three-quarters of it, all the years I've put in trying to find out where it is."

"I wouldn't deal on those terms, Mr. Wood," Longarm said

calmly. "I got another proposition in mind."

"Half, I suppose?"

"No. Not a penny—none for me, none for you. That gold belongs to the government. It's all going back where it came from."

"Like hell it is!"

Longarm saw the glint of the knifeblade as Wood let it drop and reached for his gun. Longarm fired before rolling aside. Wood's dying reflex triggered his weapon, and the slug tore into the blankets Longarm had just left.

With a sigh, Longarm got up and walked over to Wood's body. He looked down at the dead man, wondering why and how, then he shrugged.

Longarm stood where he was for a long while. Then he went to the wagon to get a shovel and do what was necessary. Dawn was breaking, another hot day lay ahead, and he had five heavy boxes of gold to load into the wagon before he started on the long trip back to Prescott.

Look for

LONGARM IN BOULDER CANYON

forty-fourth novel in the bold LONGARM series from Jove